P9-DHK-664

Praise for

The Key to Happily Ever After

"*The Key to Happily Ever After* gave me so many emotions: I loved and cheered for all three sisters and wanted to shake each of them in turn, I swooned for all of the romance, and I got choked up about their struggles and their victories. But mostly, I loved the de la Rosa sisters so much, and I can't wait for the whole world to love them."

—Jasmine Guillory, *New York Times* bestselling author of *The Proposal*

"A charming, fun read. I love these sisters! Clear your calendar— once you start, you won't be able to put down this wonderful story."

—Susan Mallery, # 1 *New York Times* bestselling author of *California Girls*

"This sweet family story/romance will appeal to fans of Susan Mallery and RaeAnne Thayne. Especially suitable for public libraries looking for more #ownvoices authors."

—*Library Journal*

"A beautiful story about the bonds of family and the challenges of love—I was cheering for all the de la Rosa sisters!"

—Jennifer Probst, *New York Times* bestselling author of *All or Nothing at All*

"This is the most aptly titled romance. A true gem filled with heart, laughs, and a cast of delightful characters. I read (and adored) *The Key to Happily Ever After* in one sitting!"

—Nina Bocci, *USA Today* bestselling author of *Meet Me on Love Lane*

"Marcelo movingly portrays sisters who love each other to death but also drive each other crazy. Give this to readers who like Susan Mallery's portrayal of complicated sisters or Jasmine Guillory's sweet, food-focused city settings."

—*Booklist*

"The de la Rosa sisters are much like the flower in their name: delicate and poised but also fiercely strong. As the trio takes over the family wedding planning business, they will need all those traits and more to transform their careers for a new generation. As they forge their paths, both together and separately, these three sisters discover that love—like a wedding—is all about timing. Full of wisdom, wit, and, of course, wedding gowns, Tif Marcelo's latest charmer proves that, sometimes, the key to happily ever after comes along when you least expect it. This endearing, deeply poignant trip down the aisle(s) is full of romance, unexpected twists, and the perfect helping of family drama."

—Kristy Woodson Harvey, author of *The Secret to Southern Charm*

"[A] witty and charming saga . . . This fun rom-com celebrates the profound power of sisterhood."

—*Woman's World*

"Devoted sisters, swoony new loves, and wedding drama—what more could you ask for in a perfect summer read? *The Key to Happily Ever After* delivers it all with Tif Marcelo's enchanting prose. By the end, you'll want to be a de la Rosa sister, too!"

—Amy E. Reichert, author of *The Coincidence of Coconut Cake*

"Marcelo charms in this feel-good story. . . . The layered plot, which includes a dark period in Mari's past that places [a] roadblock to finding love in the present, and the cast of colorful supporting characters, particularly sassy shop seamstress Amelia, are a treat. Fans of Jill Shalvis and Jane Green will particularly enjoy this."

—*Publishers Weekly*

ALSO BY TIF MARCELO

The Key to Happily Ever After

West Coast Love

East in Paradise

North to You

TIF MARCELO

Once Upon a Sunset

A NOVEL

Gallery Books

New York   London   Toronto   Sydney   New Delhi

G

Gallery Books
An Imprint of Simon & Schuster, Inc.
1230 Avenue of the Americas
New York, NY 10020

This book is a work of fiction. Any references to historical events, real people, or real places are used fictitiously. Other names, characters, places, and events are products of the author's imagination, and any resemblance to actual events or places or persons, living or dead, is entirely coincidental.

Copyright © 2020 by Tiffany Johnson

All rights reserved, including the right to reproduce this book or portions thereof in any form whatsoever. For information, address Gallery Books Subsidiary Rights Department, 1230 Avenue of the Americas, New York, NY 10020.

First Gallery Books trade paperback edition March 2020

GALLERY BOOKS and colophon are registered trademarks of Simon & Schuster, Inc.

For information about special discounts for bulk purchases, please contact Simon & Schuster Special Sales at 1-866-506-1949 or business@simonandschuster.com.

The Simon & Schuster Speakers Bureau can bring authors to your live event. For more information or to book an event, contact the Simon & Schuster Speakers Bureau at 1-866-248-3049 or visit our website at www.simonspeakers.com.

Interior design by Davina Mock-Maniscalco

Manufactured in the United States of America

10   9   8   7   6   5   4   3   2   1

Library of Congress Cataloging-in-Publication Data

Names: Marcelo, Tif, author.
Title: Once upon a sunset / Tif Marcelo.
Description: First Gallery Books trade paperback edition. | New York : Gallery Books, 2020.
Identifiers: LCCN 2019032485 (print) | LCCN 2019032486 (ebook) | ISBN 9781982115937 (trade paperback) | ISBN 9781982115944 (ebook)
Subjects: LCSH: Women physicians—Fiction. | Filipino Americans—Fiction. | Travel—Fiction. | Families—Fiction. | Man-woman relationships—Fiction. | Chick lit. | Washington (D.C.)—Fiction. | Philippines—Fiction.
Classification: LCC PS3613.A73244 O53 2020 (print) | LCC PS3613.A73244 (ebook) | DDC 813/.6—dc23
LC record available at https://lccn.loc.gov/2019032485
LC ebook record available at https://lccn.loc.gov/2019032486

ISBN 978-1-9821-1593-7
ISBN 978-1-9821-1594-4 (ebook)

For my grandfather, Lolo Naldo:
Adventurer, attorney, US Army soldier, father,
grandfather, and my first pen pal

part one

Day

Every day is a journey, and the journey itself is home.

—Matsuo Basho

Chapter One

Once upon a time, there was a doctor who loved to run. Up at her version of dawn, she sought solace on the road before her brain was fully awake. She found rest in the movement of her legs as they kept time to the music in her playlist; she escaped into the beats of the song and away from the minutia of the everyday hum of DC life and traffic.

One could find it odd—that running gave her rest—but Diana Gallagher-Cary couldn't explain it any other way. When her feet hit the pavement, the will to move, the direction to take, the speed at which she accomplished each step was of her own volition. She could choose to stop at Starbucks and order that delicious Frappuccino for comfort whenever things—not running—got her down. She could sprint her entire route or walk it without guilt, because running was, solely, for her.

Running also served Diana well when every step meant the difference between witnessing her job's daily miracles or missing them entirely.

Especially today, Valentine's Day.

The labor and delivery ward at Alexandria Specialty Hospital, a generous size at ten labor beds, was almost at capacity. Eight patients were in active labor; of the eight, two were pushing. Another patient was on her way up from the ER, hoping to usher her baby into the world on this auspicious day, or the hour that's left of it. About ten months ago, a summer storm had knocked out power for almost twenty-four hours to most of the DC area, and tonight was the proof.

Diana's job, as the on-call house OB, was to get babies delivered and mothers recovered in a cost-effective and timely manner.

Correction: That was Diana's mission for all patients except for those VIPs who occupied two very exclusive combined labor, delivery, recovery, and postpartum suites, where neither expense nor effort was spared.

With her hands stuffed in gloves where her sleeves ended, her curly hair in a tight bun, and wearing decorative eyeglasses that did nothing for her except protect her eyeballs, Diana approached the woman in VIP suite #1 with practiced measure and natural confidence despite her exhaustion. The back of her neck was damp. She'd sprinted there from the emergency room a floor down, cutting through the nurses' break room to snag a couple of *lumpia* from the Valentine's potluck the night nurses had planned, changing out of a soiled scrub top, and blowing by the elevator to take the stairs in twos, which would have impressed even an Ironman. Her gaze jumped from the silver cart parked near the infant warmer that held all her sterile supplies and equipment for the delivery to the moaning patient on the bed, then to the nurse and husband standing nearby. In the background, beeping machines and the baby's heart rate amplified through a machine's speakers mimicked the beat of one of the dubstep songs on her running playlist.

"Hello, Senator Preston." Diana halted at the head of the bed, where Senator Madeline Preston of Virginia rocked on her hands and knees. "I'm Dr. Cary, the OB on call. I'm covering for Dr. Bahar until he arrives; he had a bit of car trouble."

Madeline's hair draped over her face, and the back of her neck was exposed, shiny with sweat. Her husband, the graying lead singer of the rock band SMAK, stood to his full height at the opposite side of the bed, though his expression was like a child's, vulnerable and disheveled despite his rugged good looks. In his hand was a cup of ice chips.

Madeline moaned. In between breaths, she said, "I don't . . . want you. I . . . want . . . Dr. Bahar."

I want him, too. Believe me. Dr. Bahar was going to owe her one. Diana plastered on a smile and through gritted teeth said, "I understand your concerns, but I promise I will do my very best to fill his shoes." Diana kept her voice light and reassuring to mask her impatience. She hated covering for these VIP doctors; the hospital staff shouldn't have to, with the daily census they carried on L & D. She should've been out there with the rest of her patients.

"They told me that since this is my first baby, I would be in labor forever. They lied." Madeline growled and lifted her damp face. Her eyes glistened with tears. The next second, a guttural sound emerged from her throat, and her gaze seemed to focus elsewhere—inward. Another contraction.

Her husband sprung to his duties; the palm of his hand made contact with Madeline's lower back. He dug in like a Swedish masseur, and his face contorted with effort. His sleeve tattoos wiggled as his muscles contracted and relaxed.

"Good. Breathe, Mama. And great job, Dad. That's the way," Diana said reflexively. She scanned the amount of fluids in the

IV bag and the pattern of the baby's heartbeat on the monitor. Nice and steady. She surveyed the suite. Unlike the rest of the rooms on the labor and delivery ward, which only accommodated mothers in labor and during their short recovery after birth, these suites were used for the entirety of a mother's stay, from labor, to delivery, to recovery, and then postpartum. The VIP suite was also three times larger. Champagne sat in a chilled bucket on the windowsill. Off to the side was a real bed—not a pullout chair—with 1,200-count Egyptian cotton sheets for Madeline's husband for the two nights they would stay if mom and baby progressed without complications. Currently, untouched room service with fine tableware sat on a cart in front of a love seat across from a fifty-four-inch television, which now piped soothing classical music through its speakers, a specific request outlined on Madeline's birth plan. Through the open door to their private bathroom peeked a Jacuzzi tub and a separate stand-up shower.

Diana considered all of these amenities "wants," but Senator Preston and her husband could afford the reservation fee for one of these astronomically expensive suites where the rich and the privileged could have their birth plans followed to a T. In the lap of luxury and comfort, this was deeply unlike the way the rest of the world's mothers delivered their babies.

Diana tore her eyes away from the room's details, pushing her lower-middle-class values down, and planted them back on the person—the people—who mattered: the patient and the baby she was minutes from bringing into this posh environment. Diana had joined Alexandria Specialty Hospital's staff knowing she would be caring for patients across the spectrum of privilege; that, during call, she might have to admit and care for VIP suite patients before their exclusive, personal

OB doctors arrived. It wasn't her job to judge the excess. Outwardly judge, anyway.

"How's it going, Lettie?" Diana approached the nurse as she readied extra sheets and towels at the corner of the room, away from the senator.

Lettie Vasquez, too, was part of the normal staff of the ward, especially assigned to this patient because of her caring demeanor (which this clientele soaked up like a sponge) and her ability to put privilege in its place (like the time when a president's son had insisted she answer his phone calls while his wife was in labor). She was a veteran on the staff, with two decades of experience and wisdom that had helped Diana in more than one sticky situation.

Great nurses were worth their weight in gold and then some.

"Ms. Preston's contractions are coming about a minute apart now," Lettie said while Madeline groaned in the background. "And pretty regularly. I just checked her, and she's ten centimeters and ready to push. Did you eat?"

"Yes, ma'am. I snuck in some of your lumpia a few minutes ago."

A smile graced Lettie's lips. "Good. You have to take the opportunity when you can. Especially tonight, when the patients are nonstop."

"You don't have to convince me. Your food is really the best," Diana declared.

"*Ay,* I'm sure your mom makes better lumpia than I do." She brought the sheets to the baby warmer and turned on the oxygen and suction machine, just in case.

"She tries." Diana snorted as she pulled a face mask from the wall. "She likes to create 'versions.'" Her mother was a wonderful woman, but she spiced up many of the traditional recipes much like she accessorized her wardrobe: randomly. Diana found that her best Filipino meals were during call, when her favorite nurses got together to share food, sometimes even at her request. And though it was uncommon to do so, she'd sometimes join them in the nurses' break room to soak in a bit of her culture—if but one-quarter of it—even for a few minutes at a time.

"That's what food is: versions. But maybe one day I'll share my recipe with you." She glanced askance at Diana with a sly grin. "Maybe."

"Are you both just going to stand there? This baby is going to fall out!" Madeline demanded.

No, the baby was not falling out, but Diana heard the telltale tones of panic and determination in Madeline's voice.

So Diana settled herself on a rolling stool and affixed a mask to her face as Lettie pushed the cart of instruments and a portable overhead light to within arm's reach. Diana aimed the light *just so*. This was the time when the rubber met the road, Senator Preston's moment of truth. This was the moment when the senator would show strength rivaling that of any world-class athlete, when education, economics, and privilege took a back seat. "All right, then. Let's have a baby."

Diana pulled the mask down as she exited the room, face cooling as the hallway AC hit her warm skin. The sounds of success—a crying baby, Madeline cooing, and her husband chatting gregariously on the phone—muted as the suite door closed behind her. Diana's heart rate, which had been at a sprinter's pace, had begun to ebb from the satisfaction of a job well done. Her body didn't know the difference between a runner's high and a doctor's high, and right now, she was on top of the world.

The hallway was quiet until the double doors opened to the

nurses' station. Four wings jutted out like spokes from this one central area, the hub of activity, despite the hour: almost two in the morning. Nurses milled about with clipboards in their hands; others were on their work-assigned phones discussing patients with their respective providers. Nursing assistants pushed vital signs equipment from one room to the other. Diana passed the wide windows of the soundproof nursery behind its own security doors, where two nurses each fed a baby, while a dozen in their respective bassinets waited their turn.

Hospitals were not meant for sleep.

"Dr. Cary." The night's charge nurse, Millie Grant, approached her. All business despite her dangling teddy bear earrings—the unit's staff was required to wear hospital-provided teal scrubs for additional security, and individuality was expressed in myriad ways. Two hospital Spectralink phones hung precariously on her lanyard. "I need you."

"What's up?" Diana, accustomed to multitasking, sat in front of a computer and logged in. She clicked on Madeline Preston's name, then on the notes section, where she typed her standard delivery note, one ear cocked toward the nurse.

15 February
Normal vaginal birth. Infant female born at 0105, 7 lbs. 14 oz.

"Dr. Mendez called for you in the ER." Millie eyed Diana knowingly.

Apgar score 9/10.
Patient's estimated blood loss within normal limits. Current vitals within normal limits.
Assume standard recovery and postpartum procedures.

Diana grumbled at being summoned downstairs, by her ex no less. "Anything else?"

"Ms. Storm just called, and she's on her way. She feels like she's in labor."

"Feels like labor? Signs and symptoms?"

"She thinks she had a contraction a few minutes ago." Millie shrugged, resigned. "And she wants to come in."

"Have you called her provider?" It was, yes, *the* Winter Storm, pop star and social media maven who'd humbly started on the YouTube scene five years ago as a fresh-faced singer with a guitar and was best known for throwing her exes and frenemies into her love—or hate—songs. The bottom line was, besides being a VIP, Winter Storm was high-maintenance as a human.

"Dr. Thompson is on his way. But there's a bigger problem. That last patient who came up from the ER brought our official census to capacity, which never happens."

Diana nodded. The VIP rooms were not counted as part of room availability, since they were opened only when a VIP was actually going to be admitted, and at that point would be allotted on a first-come, first-served basis. And just as there was the risk for VIPs to be admitted to the general population if both VIP rooms were filled, once opened, the VIP rooms could be occupied by non-VIP patients.

"All right, so we transfer out and redirect patients, and open VIP two for Winter Storm," Diana said. "We do what we have to do per the protocol. After we're done here, let the ER know so they can divert potential labor patients. Oh, and inform our hospital supervisor so he's aware of the closure."

Millie did not move, something else clearly on her mind. Diana sighed. Never once had she closed the labor ward to patients, and her body was feeling the work she'd put in tonight. As soon as she got home from call, she was going to treat herself to a bath and a glass of wine. Even if it was going to be at eight in the morning.

"What is it, Millie?"

"Your mother called. Several times on the ward, since she couldn't reach you on your cell." Millie held out a stack of Post-its with what Diana recognized as the scribbled handwriting of the ward's secretary.

She took the Post-its and flipped through them. *Call mother at home* or a version of it was on each one. Diana groaned.

"That good, huh?" Millie surmised. The look of concern was unmistakable on the nurse's face. Nothing would get past her, not in this environment, where most caregivers had an eagle eye for family drama.

It was sometimes a little too close for comfort. Diana stuffed the Post-its into her front pocket.

"How is Ms. Margo, anyway? And how are you?"

Diana slowed her movements and took care with her next words. Millie had called her mother by her Instagram handle, Ms. Margo. Margaret Gallagher-Cary was a celebrity in her own right, if one called going viral because of her wacky fashion sense and keen photographic eye being a celebrity. But what came along with it was everyone knowing—or presuming to know—everything about Diana's and her mother's life. "She's all right. And I'm fine, too, thank you."

"Today's post, actually showing us her bucket list? It gave me all the feels." Her eyes gleamed. "One day I'm going to do a bucket list, too. You'll have to send her my best wishes. But I bet it will be another change for you, won't it? I know I've said it time and again, but if you need anything, at all . . . change, in all ways, is tough."

"Thank you. I appreciate it, but I'm fine." Diana smiled and kept her mouth shut despite wanting to commiserate. She could have gone on and on about how the changes in the last six months had rendered her unsteady. With her granny Leora passing away, and her mother moving in to make Diana's town house her "home base" as she and her best friends conquered this elusive bucket list, on top of *Dr. Mendez* . . . it all gave her whiplash. And Millie would have probably empathized—she might've given Diana some much needed advice. Night after night of raw emotion, relationship-driven conflict, tragedies, and happily-ever-afters within the context of baby-delivering required nurses to have acute social awareness.

But Diana was the MD on call. Though there wasn't a hierarchy in the ward, the reality was that nurses looked to physicians for patients' orders, and sometimes, for the final say. Diana had learned early to compartmentalize, to shove her personal concerns to the rear when she drove into the parking lot of Alexandria Specialty. Narcissism had no business in health care, where her job was to act outwardly, help others, put people first.

Diana clicked on the "log off" button on Madeline's chart, and it reset her plummeting mood. "I have to head out. I'll be on my phone. Time to see that Dr. Mendez."

Millie nodded in understanding, and a wry smile bloomed on her face. "That's right. And don't forget the fourth pillar of our mission here at Alexandria Specialty. 'To provide kind, reliable, and straightforward customer service.' Even to other doctors."

Here was the thing about labor and delivery: it was either feast or famine. Standard procedures dictated that mothers in labor had two methods of entry to the hospital: through the normal prenatal and preregistration process at the labor and delivery ward for those who were patients of providers of Alexandria Specialty, and the ER for all other cases.

Tonight, the ER had been a revolving door of pregnant ladies, but Diana's current focus was on the man in the white coat at the nurses' station holding a clipboard.

"Carlo." Diana stuffed a hand in her pocket and gripped one of her pens to steel herself. She'd successfully avoided him the last week despite them being on call at the same time.

Dr. Carlo Mendez faced her. He was the epitome of perfect proportions; his smoldering look was out of a *GQ* magazine. When they first met, he was even a model on the side. Not only was his face a true work of art, but his body was, too. At five ten, with a chiseled face, wavy and properly disheveled hair, and a mouth full of perfectly straight white teeth, he had been a sight to behold. He still was, until she remembered that he was a cheating rat.

"Hey." He used his flirtatious voice, closed the chart, and gestured her to his office. "I passed by the house before work. I was hoping you were going to be there."

"Nope. I'm here, as you can see. What did you need?"

"I tried to pick up a couple more of my boxes, but Margo wouldn't let me in."

Go, Mom. Pride swelled in her chest. Her mother may be flighty, but she had a backbone still.

"You should have called me before showing up. You know my rules."

He stepped in closer. "Forget the rules, Diana. It's been six months. Can we end this . . . cold shoulder? I want to come home. Hasn't it been tough on you, at all? Haven't you missed me?"

She clicked the pen in her pocket, hard, just enough to take the edge off. It had gotten better for her, actually. The hurt had transformed itself to something she could work with—realization, with some anger—but she was ready to move on.

"You should have thought of that before sleeping with another woman and keeping me in the dark for a good year about it."

His face softened. "Diana, please. I made a mistake. At some point you have to forgive me. I've forgiven you. Look, it's not too late. I mean, construction's going on at our house, for renovations we *both* drew up, for God's sake. We can fix this."

Diana seethed under her breath, though she focused on pasting a saccharine smile on her face. Before they'd broken up—or, before she threw him out of the home they'd purchased together—they'd taken out a home equity line of credit to build a balcony and to renovate the master bath. It wasn't a wedding ring, but it seemed a commitment enough, coming from him. Or so she thought.

"This is about you removing your items unless you want them trashed or donated to the Salvation Army. This is not about me. This wasn't my fault."

"Okay, fine." He shrugged. "You had no hand in our breakup at all. Even if you pushed me away every step of our relationship. I mean, after five years, it got tiring having to extract any kind of emotion from you."

"I'm done." She bolstered her spine straight while attempting to unravel his pretzel of words. He was good at this . . . this talking. The combination of his radio-worthy voice and his disarming cadence always threw her off her game.

"What do you want from me?" She eyed him. "I can tell there's more. Out with it; I've got a ward full of patients waiting for me."

"I miss Flossy."

"Oh, no, no, no." Forget being civil. Diana's voice raised an octave higher. "Don't bring her into this." Flossy was their Havanese, their one baby, and sadly the collateral damage.

"I want visitation."

"That's ridiculous." She raised an eyebrow, wary of this new turn in the conversation. Their breakup had brought out a different side of Carlo. What had been endearing and loving now presented itself as manipulative and passive-aggressive, like the distance had removed the filter she'd placed on him for all these years.

"I received approval from my landlord, and, I mean, she *is* mine."

The hairs on the back of her neck stood. "She is not."

"I bought her with my credit card, if I remember correctly. I left her with you because I thought it would be easier for transition's sake, but I miss her. Hell, you didn't even want her. You wanted to send her back to the breeder."

"You can't have her," Diana said firmly. True, she hadn't been thrilled when he walked in the door three years ago with Flossy, then named Starla by the Sea. She had been firmly against breeders, but Flossy fit in her hands and had this thing with toilet paper—she'd gone bananas over it, tearing rolls to shreds. Diana had become a mother overnight. The dog filled her heart as she and Carlo's relationship grew. Being a fur mama had become a part of her.

But before Carlo opened his mouth for what she knew would be a rebuttal, the ER's double doors opened to admit a woman being pushed in a wheelchair, belly round and high, hands cradling her head. A man, harried, and with a wild look on his face, followed, arms overloaded with jackets and insurance papers from the front desk. A nurse ushered the group into a bay, and the flurry of getting the patient into the bed and taking her vital signs began.

Cecily, the assigned ER nurse, nodded at Diana as she approached. "Francesca Smith. Thirty-six weeks and six days, complaining of a headache, abdominal and back pain for most of the day. No provider listed. Last seen four weeks ago at the Old Town Women's Center."

With an eye toward the bay, where they hadn't drawn the curtains, Diana breathed a momentary sigh of relief. The center was familiar to her—her best friend ran the low-cost clinic and was a lifesaver to so many mothers in the community. No doubt the patient was here because of the education the center provided.

Diana's initial impressions from the hospital monitors were that Francesca's heart rate and respirations were normal, but her blood pressure was high. Too high. Diana suspected hypertension, possibly preeclampsia. The next second, she mentally worked through the algorithm of her diagnosis and the hospital's status, which was at capacity. "We'll have to see what we can do for her here. We might need a transfer because the ward is full."

"I can start transfer paperwork, just in case," Cecily answered.

Per professional courtesy, Diana waited for the nurses to do an initial assessment, and she followed up with her own, which included an ultrasound.

At the session's end, she congregated with Cecily at the nurses' station.

"She's going to need an overnight for evaluation. I'm not loving the borderline low amniotic fluid. Let's do the standard preeclampsia protocol, monitoring, labs, fluids, mag sulfate," Diana said. "We've no beds in L and D. Do you have a spare down here?"

The nurse shook her head as she picked up the phone. "We don't have any beds available for long-term monitoring, and that waiting room is filling up, too. The ICU is packed to the brim as well."

"Damn." Diana's mind went straight to the logistics: the risk of transferring Francesca even ten miles down to the next hospital; then to her ward with its one last serene bed in a coveted, just-opened VIP suite; then to the incoming celebrity patient who had reserved that room.

The patient's husband caught her eye. The coats were on the floor, the papers forgotten on his seat. He was gripping his wife's hand. And as he spoke to the nurse at the bedside, the rest of the ER faded, and Diana heard only his voice. "She never gets headaches. Doesn't get sick, ever," he said. "Please tell me we're staying."

The decision weighed like a balance, tipping left and right. On the left, policy and money; the right, principle and health. In the middle was her conscience, her judgment, her ideals. The spirit of her grandmother hovering above her. Leora Gallagher, the woman Diana had looked up to, the woman she lost just months ago but, just as she had in life, seemed to find a way to insert herself into Diana's everyday thoughts.

Leora had risked it all once in her life, and for one tiny baby, too.

"What would Leora do?" Diana said to no one in particular.

"Who's Leora?" Cecily asked.

Diana shook her head, and the action rattled the balance so the factors jostled in her brain. She said the first thing that came to mind. "Forget it. No need to transfer the patient. We do have a bed upstairs: one of the VIP suites. I'll admit her to that service."

Cecily's eyebrows shot up. "You're sure?"

Diana took a deep breath. Right or wrong, she had to commit. "Yes."

Technically, this patient arrived before Winter Storm, and technically, per their policy, those rooms were accessible to everyone, as dictated by census, once they were opened. And Diana knew well that not only was it either feast or famine in L & D, but in this business, it was all good and fun until it went to hell in a hand basket. She was making the right decision.

So why did it feel like, in avoiding the heat of this hell, she had jumped right off a cliff?

Chapter Two

Diana's instincts had been right. While transferring up to the VIP unit for observation, Francesca's water broke. After over an hour of active labor, the baby went into distress, prompting an emergency delivery by C-section that—while it brought chaos to the ward—ended well. Mom was fine, though still hooked up to an IV medication to bring down her blood pressure; the baby was stable, admitted to the NICU for overnight observation.

Now, Diana perched on Francesca's hospital bed. The woman was tucked under the covers in a fresh hospital gown with an IV in each arm, eyes hooded from exhaustion, the sedative effect of pain medicine, and the remnants of anesthesia.

"Do you have any questions about your care?" Diana asked both the patient and her husband, Mike, who stood behind his wife.

"I just want to see the baby." Francesca's voice was a squeak. In her expression was a trace of fear. For her, the night had gone much too quickly.

"Of course you do. I'll make sure I check in with the NICU

so they can come down and give you an update. And, Dad, you can always go up there, at any time, as long as you have your security band." She nodded at the bar-coded wristband that matched their baby's, smiled, and squeezed Francesca's hand. She wasn't much of a hugger, but times like this even she needed to be comforted. She had succeeded in admitting Francesca to this VIP room, with Winter Storm conceding the space until a room on the postpartum ward cleared in the morning into which Francesca would move, but the worst wasn't over. Her boss had yet to wake up and hear the news. "I'll go now, in fact, and give them a call. Until then, you should rest, okay?"

"Okay. We need to think of a name still." Francesca's eyes blinked in slow motion, as if Diana's permission was a trigger for sleep.

"That's right, you do. If you're taking suggestions, Diana is always a winner." Diana winked, and with a last squeeze of Francesca's hand, stood and walked to the suite's entrance with the patient's husband behind her. As she stepped out, Mike said, "I want to thank you, Dr. Cary." His skin had gone ashen, face crumpled into the start of belated panic. "I didn't know what to do."

"You did the absolutely right thing by bringing her to the ER. You might have saved her life, and your baby's. Her blood pressure was very high, and your baby needed a little help coming out."

"This room, though. We can't afford it. Heck, we couldn't even afford the regular room. And I heard people in the ER talking. Did we take this room from someone else?"

"No, no, you didn't." Diana bit her cheek, stuck on the explanation of who the VIP room sought to serve and whether this was the appropriate time to explain it. "It's about priorities, and who medically needs the room. Right now, that person is Francesca. In the morning, she will have to transfer rooms because someone else will need this one. But not to worry about that—the nursing staff will keep you updated. And as for insurance purposes, I'll be sure to let whoever I need to know that it was my decision to put you in this room rather than transfer out, okay? After all, it was medically indicated." She raised her eyes over his shoulder, to his sleeping wife. Beyond her, the city's lights twinkled through plate glass. "But for now, you must rest, too. Your baby is going to need you."

"Okay." Mike heaved a breath, and a smile shone through. That smile tugged at Diana, a small reward for the decision she had to make. This would be a mess to sort out in a couple of hours, but currently she had a stable patient on her side.

You're always right, Granny.

But as she stepped through the hallway's double doors to the nurses' station—which was now crawling with day nurses congregating with night nurses during the change of shift—her eyes lifted to the only person not wearing the unit-required scrubs. Suddenly, it was as if her foot had been caught in a pothole in the middle of a fast downhill sprint, and the only thing that came to her mind were three words. Granny's words, too.

Here we go.

Diana followed her boss, Dr. Aziza Sarris, two floors up, to her sparse office, where Aziza tossed her keys, wallet, and phone on the desk. She had said nothing to Diana on the walk, which was a slight relief. Diana wasn't one for small talk, and she needed a moment to review her night, for what was likely to be an inquisition.

Aziza gestured to one of her chairs. As Diana sat, Aziza

perched on her desk. Behind her was the open expanse of Alexandria, the tops of buildings, and the pink glow of sunrise. Yet, despite the peaceful scene depicted behind her, her pinched expression told a different story.

At sixty, Aziza had not cared for patients in more than a decade, but she still exuded a maternal, yet professional, nature. She wore her hair in a low, loose bun, always with a strand out of place. Despite the late—or early—hour, she wore her standard cardigan with a colorful lanyard around her neck adorned with bling: pins of her years in medical service, her service organizations, and a select few Disney characters.

Diana spotted a framed picture on the wall of the current hospital staff OBs: herself, Aziza, Dr. Clay Pritchard, and Dr. Justina Folds. She released a breath, remembering that they were a team, and a special one at that. It had been easy for Diana to join the hospital staff because of Aziza, and frankly because of Clay and Justina, too. They were professionals, respectful, ethical. And they actually liked one another.

Moreover, they each truly cared for patients' well-being, appreciated new theories in medicine, and were unafraid of testing the waters. But each was equally careful. Pathophysiology was sometimes ruthless, and stories of careless doctors abounded. Much like a wild child in a group of siblings, there seemed to be a reckless doctor in every department, but not in Alexandria Specialty's OB staff. Four out of four were, hands down, rule followers. For the most part.

"Thanks for staying after a long night, but I feel like we need to get together to discuss some next steps." Aziza clasped her hands in front of her, shoulders rounding. Like a mother readying her child for her punishment, her voice was steady, firm. Her dark eyes were steadfast and penetrating.

Diana sat up a little straighter in her chair, and her heart beat a steady drum of dread. "Next steps?"

"Yes, Diana. Because what the hell were you thinking?" Aziza's expression hardened. The wrinkles between her eyebrows deepened.

Diana inhaled through her nose and bolstered herself. Then she recounted the night to Aziza's unflinching expression.

"I'd do it again," she told Aziza. "I don't have any regrets."

"That's easy for you to say, Diana, but you postponed a delivery tonight."

"Winter Storm wasn't sure she was even in labor, Aziza. Francesca Smith's case was emergent."

Aziza leaned back, face softening. "I'm not questioning your priorities, Diana. It's about you following the policies and procedures. The facilities and the equipment . . ."

"Were used for a patient I determined wasn't stable enough to be transferred out. I mean, the room was technically open." But at her mentor's frown, she acquiesced. "I'm sorry, I am. But it's fixable. I mean, it's already fixed. In a couple of hours, more patients will deliver. Even more will get discharged. Space will open up on the postpartum floor. At most, Winter Storm will have been put off by eighteen hours. I spoke to her myself last night. I also spoke to her physician, who confirmed that she is *still* not in labor, Aziza."

"She might have *said* she understood." As if relenting, Aziza sat down in a chair across from Diana.

Now at eye level, Diana saw that the displeasure in her mentor's eyes was actually disappointment.

"What do you mean?"

"It means that she made a call that quickly climbed up the chain, to the CEO of the hospital. Additionally, we have a nonpayer in our books occupying the most expensive room in this building."

A burn started in Diana's chest. She hated the subject of money; financial considerations were the reality, yes, but they always settled in her belly like a brick. Having grown up poor and now with a best friend who served a disadvantaged population, Diana had a perspective that at times collided with the current state of insurance laws. Times like right now.

"There's more." Aziza took her phone out of her pocket, thumbed it on. She handed it to Diana. The screen was on Facebook, to a Rachel Lam's profile, which had been set to public. A picture had been uploaded, of her holding a baby. The pair looked serene, with the newborn in a onesie and knit cap. The mom wore a faded blue gown with pink and blue stripes: Alexandria Specialty's. Rachel held the baby against her chest, her nose on the top of the baby's head.

But the caption above the photo was long, protracted. Diana squinted at the screen to read it.

Whose life is more important than yours?
Does money make you better than the other person?
When did our society get so out of hand that we've now segregated, from birth, the haves and the have-nots?

"The Lam family is still here," Aziza said. "Apparently, despite the staff's best efforts, news spread quickly on the ward that the newest transfer was going to a VIP room. Mr. and Mrs. Lam didn't realize we had one, and it seems the rest of their friends, and their friends' friends didn't know, either. Her post went viral."

Diana scrolled down to the users who'd commented on the

post. They were a mix of supporters and naysayers. Of those who understood the necessity to separate high-profile patients for their own privacy, and those who questioned the state of the country's health-care crisis.

"I agree this doesn't look good, but I didn't do this." Diana started, then held her tongue to keep from saying she agreed, that transparency in health care had a long way to go. This wasn't the time.

"In a roundabout way, you did. Your break with policy did this."

"It's social media. It'll blow over. As if people don't know that more private services exist. Beyoncé, Kim Kardashian, Meghan Markle—they can't go just anywhere to have babies, or else they'd be mobbed by paparazzi." Diana all but rolled her eyes. The shift ended in a good outcome, and it was ridiculous that social media had a part in this conversation. Sleep tugged from inside her, and she wanted to go home, now more than ever. "What happens now?"

"We have yet to see how this plays out. You were not negligent, but the fact of the matter is that we have been named, Diana. The hospital, the VIP ward. You made a sound medical decision. Frankly, you probably saved that baby's life, but by doing the right thing, you might have exposed something none of us wants to be associated with—even if we do it—and that's serving the rich," Aziza said. "Now people are going to be curious. Not only curious, but the question will be asked—who has the right to special treatment?"

Everyone, was Diana's first thought. But this wasn't a philosophical debate.

"What does this mean for me? The bottom line." There was a reason why she was here, alone, with Aziza. Something was up.

Silence had descended like a thick waterfall around them. In the pause, the words of the HR documents she'd read regarding actions against breaking policy materialized in her head.

"Am I fired?"

"No. But I think you should take some time off. Just a short break, until this all dies down. The hospital is sure to get some press. Winter Storm requested a change in facility for her birth—there's a possibility more will follow suit."

"That . . . that's unbelievable."

"Being a provider means garnering a patient's trust. As of tonight, we lost that on several fronts."

The feeling of dispensability ran through her like hot lava, and rejection singed her insides. She shook her head and willed herself to shut down the emotion. This was about money, that was all.

Aziza continued. "We still have to figure this out. Honestly, in the last ten years, this has never happened. I'm . . . I'm not sure what to do, or what the CEO will want."

"So a short break?"

"Just until the end of the month. Unfortunately, because it would be an extended time off for administrative purposes, some of that might be unpaid, depending on your contract and your vacation days."

About a couple of weeks without work. Diana hadn't taken off work for that long since college. A spark of panic flared and fizzed just as quickly as she thought of her savings, her bank account—yes, she could still afford the worst-case scenario.

Diana was startled by Aziza's hand, which now rested on her forearm. "Look, I was going to bring you in soon to chat, off the record. I've noticed that you've been different recently. That you've been unhappy. Though there's no need to explain—life is a series of peaks and valleys, and I get that sometimes there are rough spots." She smiled. "Use this as a time to recharge. This is more for your protection, really. Apparently, our Facebook page has received some trolls. That's the thing with having an active social media account—it's great when the conversation is positive, but when there's something up, it gets hairy. Anyway, this will be a good time to catch up and breathe a little, focus on yourself and what you need."

"Okay, I'll do what I need to do." Diana nodded, though she knew she really didn't have a choice. One thing: she would certainly not be recharging. Vacations had never been her thing.

Chapter Three

W hat *would* Leora do?" muttered Margaret Gallagher-Cary. She was seated on one of Diana's low, European-style couches with a box open in front of her—a pile to throw away on the right side, and the pile to keep on the left. In her hand was a fan of photos, and somehow, she was supposed to decide where they belonged.

Then it came to her. Her mother, the practical Leora Gallagher, a minimalist and Margo's complete opposite, would have gotten rid of pictures she had no connection to. An old-school Marie Kondo method. It wouldn't have taken her mother a long time to decide, either. Even in the last days of her life, in the ebb and flow of forgetfulness and lucidity, Leora made decisions quickly and without regret.

Except her mother wasn't here, was she? She was dead and therefore wasn't in this conundrum of moving in with Diana and trying to find a way to somehow fit two—no, three homes into her daughter's town house.

Margo tossed the photos in the keep pile. On principle, photographs shouldn't be decluttered—they were memories! Besides, her emotions were in a jumble much like her boxes, haphazardly packed before they sold Leora's home. Perhaps Margo should go through another box. Somewhere there had to be one filled with books that would surely be easier to get through.

But when she tried to get up, she couldn't. So on a silent count to three, Margo heaved herself onto her feet, toes catching on the hem of her bell-bottom jeans (fashion history was cyclical). But her legs stiffened beneath her, joints groaning under her weight.

"Oh, hell, Ma, this box it is," she mumbled, falling back onto the cushion. She scooped photos out of the box once again.

"Ma."

Margo turned to the voice. Diana was at the threshold of the back door—right, Margo had left it open to the storm door so Flossy could get a glimpse of the outside world—with her arms crossed and a grin on her face. "Did I just catch you talking to yourself?"

"I wasn't talking to myself. I was talking to your granny. And, no, she doesn't answer back, so you don't need to rush me to another specialist. Wanna sit and help me go through these photos?"

"No, thanks, I'm cross-eyed and on the verge of collapse." Diana hung her coat on the hallway tree and kicked off her shoes. She disappeared into the laundry room behind her and closed the door. The sounds of what Margo had learned was her daughter's routine commenced: the washing machine door being opened, the melodic buttons of the washer being pressed, the whoosh of the water as it filled the tub, and finally, the squeak of the faucet for that final handwashing before the door opened. Now dressed in a plaid robe, her daughter was all set to take a quick shower before bed.

Diana was so much like her granny that Margo's heart tore a fraction of a millimeter, in the spot where she wished her mother were still alive. Leora had been tickled that someone had inherited her type A traits.

A hand was in front of her. "Need help?" Diana asked.

Margo nodded, taking it, allowing her daughter to bear her weight. Her feet prickled with pins and needles as blood rushed downward, and she took a moment to wiggle her toes to get the feeling back. "How was your night?"

"Long, and long story."

"Did you see the picture I posted last night?" Pride, mixed with trepidation, filled her chest. For Margo, once a professional photographer of actual pictures she developed herself—in a darkroom, no less—social media had become an escape while caring for her mother. Her small window to the outside world, when, for almost a year, Margo felt isolated from the living. She'd filled her lonely moments by taking pictures of the quirky things she found in her mother's home, like Leora's precious sewing kit and her favorite costume necklace, made with misshapen pearls. The mix-and-match pieces of her beloved wardrobe. Or the sky right before a derecho slammed through Northern Virginia. Under the title of Ms. Margo, her alter ego, Margo thrived at a time when everything around her seemed to crumble.

Quickly, Ms. Margo had caught fire, and now, with thousands of followers, Margo still had a purpose despite losing one of the most important people in her life.

But Diana never showed any interest in her Ms. Margo project.

"Ah, I actually didn't get a chance to look," Diana said now.

"I see." Margo's shoulders threatened to slump forward, but she kept a smile on her face. "It's fine."

Diana looked away for a beat. "Last night was chaotic, hence my not calling back, either."

Glad for the change in subject, Margo jumped into it head-long. "I wanted to warn you that Carlo came over. I was in the middle of unpacking my bedroom. I wanted to get all this stuff out of your living room this weekend and packed out of sight." She gestured at the topsy-turvy space in front of them, half-filled with open moving boxes, gifts from clients, and several stacks of photographs and portfolios, so unlike her daughter's usual way of life that it brought a pang to Margo's heart. She'd moved in only a month ago, after the sale of Leora's house was finalized, but one would've never known that she'd spent every day trying to put things away. "He asked a lot of questions as soon as I opened the front door, too many for my comfort and some about Flossy, so I asked him to leave."

"Thank you for trying to warn me. He found me at work." She rolled her eyes. "I don't know where his sudden need to be involved is coming from, but he says he wants visitation."

"Of the dog?"

"Yes. He first said he wanted her—"

Margo's hand flew to her chest. "No way. No how. He brought Flossy home for you." And truthfully, that dog had somehow wormed her way into Margo's heart, too. Margo had never owned pets and had convinced herself she and dogs didn't mix, until Flossy climbed on her lap and settled in. Now she carried Flossy like a baby, sometimes even for her walks.

"I know. He's not going to win this, though. If I have to get a lawyer, I will."

Margo heard the exasperation in her daughter's tone and noticed the dark circles under her eyes. Last night had been her third night of call. "Anyone deliver in the VIP suites?" she teased, to lighten the mood. "Did someone deliver in a champagne bath?"

It earned her a snort, which was a win in her column.

"We had a couple of admissions to the suites. But, I'm going to bed. Can we talk later?"

Cut-and-dry—that was her daughter's style.

"Yeah, sure." Margo looked away and pretended to sift through one of the cooking magazines that had come in yesterday's mail. With Diana, one couldn't just force their way in. Diana revealed her emotions in spurts, and only patience was rewarded, especially these days, when an unshakable cloud seemed to have descended around her. Margo just wished that it would be sooner than later, since she was days away from getting on a plane.

Which was another sore spot between them.

"Might as well try to sleep, since the contractors are a little late. Don't forget, they start the master bath today." Diana looked at her watch and opened her mouth to say more, but her phone rang. She kissed Margo swiftly on the cheek. "But don't worry about your boxes, okay? I'll help you when I get up. Or I can unpack them when you go on your trip."

"All right, sweetheart" was all Margo could say, because there was no sense arguing with her daughter at this time of the morning. She watched the back of Diana's robe disappear up the staircase, and wondered how the hell this was all going to work.

When Margo's friends had complained that their grown children had boomeranged home, Margo celebrated in silent reverie that her dearest Diana had flown the nest without once looking back. Diana had been born on her own trajectory, with an infant sleep schedule that allowed Margo to continue her work without great difficulty. Margo barely had to convince Diana, as a child, to do her homework, to clean her room. In junior high, while Diana's friends had gone through that god-awful stage of not brushing their teeth, there Diana was every night over the sink, brushing and flossing and washing her face. Margo hadn't once worried about the college and career process because her girl had made her own plans and knew exactly what she wanted from her life.

No one told Margo that it was her mother that she should have been worried about. Leora, who had been a titan in every respect, who lived to ninety-nine, transformed in the last year of her life from fairly independent and lucid to a woman Margo didn't recognize and had to care for full-time. And no one had told Margo that in the autumn of her life, she would find herself living under her daughter's roof. Talk about a convoluted circle.

Margo entered the garage and flipped the light on. Not all town houses in Old Town had garages, and while they were lucky to have one, it didn't function well for its intended use. These buildings were built tall and narrow, and despite attempts at modernizing the space, the garage could barely fit a sedan without risking damage to its sides. But it made for good storage, which most homes in Alexandria lacked.

Storage totes lined the back of the garage, from the concrete floors up nearly to the ceiling. Each plastic bin was labeled with its contents in her daughter's neat block letters, so unlike the stereotypical doctor's scrawl.

Margo's boxes, on the other hand, had taken up the middle of the garage, along with the materials for the renovation that

Diana and Carlo had planned before Diana properly and rightfully shoved him out the door.

The placement of Margo's boxes was the perfect representation of her intrusion into her daughter's life.

The construction aside, Margo had to admit: she was messy. Her stuff was everywhere. It jumped out, mismatched from her daughter's things. So, despite agreeing to rest, Margo couldn't. The least she could do was empty a box or two. Maybe three.

She spotted a small box behind the rest of her stash. The cardboard was discolored to a light brown, a sign that it was one of her mother's. Opposite her own penchant to keep things, Leora had been much like Diana—a minimalist. And Margo did not remember if she'd gone through it. She jostled the box; it shook easily. This she might be able to tackle.

The door into the home opened. "Ma." Diana's voice pierced through the quiet garage.

Margo jumped. "Goodness. You keep doing that."

She laughed. "Paying you back for the years you listened to my phone calls on the landline."

"I didn't do that!" Margo gasped, but her feigned ignorance was short-lived. "Okay, so I did. You knew?"

"Yes," she said pointedly. "Anyway, that was Sam who called. I'm going to meet her at the center and go for a quick run."

Margo frowned. It was freezing, and Diana hadn't slept well in days. Then again, on tough days, Diana needed a friend, and Sam was her bestie. But the circles under her eyes begged for Margo to ask anyway. "Are you sure? You were headed straight to bed."

"Yeah. And since I know you're not going to stop unpacking, I'll bring a couple of boxes in for you. Just two, okay?"

"Okay." Margo relented, though Diana's words left a bitter

taste in her mouth. It wasn't what she said but the way she said it—as if Margo herself needing managing. She was seventy-five, not dead. And when Diana kissed her on the forehead like a toddler who needed a mother's encouragement before a difficult task, Margo's insides stirred with unease.

The tables, in fact, had turned significantly.

Chapter Four

Diana tucked her chin into her quarter-zip when she stepped out her door, and the shock of cold sent shivers up her spine. It had snowed the previous week, and a fuzz of white coated the tops of bushes and tree branches. The temperature had stayed at a balmy thirty-nine degrees during the day, cold enough that even at a sprint she didn't break into a sweat but warm enough so a windbreaker wasn't necessary. She shook her arms and legs out to wake them. Exhaustion had permeated every part of her being, but after a night like she'd had, a run would do her good, and Sam had given her the perfect reason to head back out into the sunshine.

She took off at a jog, choosing the sidewalk through a block, then hopping off onto the street, minding the cobblestones and potholes. At 9:00 a.m., Old Town was just starting to wake, with deliveries to local businesses underway and parents walking their kids to school. After a quarter mile, she got into a rhythm, and slowly, her night faded away.

A half mile later, Diana arrived at the Georgian town house

business front and jogged in place, waiting for the door's swing. Sam was notoriously on time, so when five, six minutes passed, Diana entered the Old Town Women's Center to retrieve her running partner.

Unlike the bright, glitzy, sleek hospital building, the center was a long-ago renovated home. Crown moldings trimmed the ceiling and doorways, but the hardwood original floors squeaked with every step. A staircase with formidable banisters led to a second floor of rooms that stored equipment and files, and the staff break room.

"Good morning, Diana!" Sherry Escalante, a nurse educator, bounded down the steps. Black hair in a French braid and wearing Tweety Bird scrubs, she had a life-sized infant doll in her arms, though she held it like a real baby. Like she were breast-feeding.

Diana eyed the position of the doll. Sherry looked down, snorted out a laugh. "I'm prepping the room for an infant-care class. Volunteering today?" She reached around Diana to grab a basket of blankets.

"Not today. I'm here to see the boss." She shied at the answer, guilt riding up her back. It had been months since she'd volunteered, due in part to work and in part to wanting to be buried by work.

"Hopefully we'll see you here soon." With a nod goodbye, Sherry hustled down the hallway to the farthermost room, a classroom.

Diana grabbed a mint from the reception desk, suffering a slap of the hand from the secretary, Paula. She stuck the candy into her mouth and scooted into the office a door down.

It wasn't much of an office but more of a catchall room. To the side were stacked supplies their supply room couldn't fit. In the middle, a large desk burgeoned with papers and books. The desk was shared by everyone on the staff, and each had commandeered a small area as theirs. On the wall behind the desk hung pictures of the babies for whom they'd provided prenatal and infant care throughout the years. Some were now toddlers, some school-aged, and some even in their late teen years. Over a decade's proof of care in a clinic that had somehow weathered the rise and fall of politicians, lack of money, and support.

Currently, Sam Rodale, one of the center's doctors and its founder, was hunched over a chart wearing a multicolored fabric headband that covered her ears. Her black hair was pulled back into a ponytail.

"Give me one second, else I'm going to forget all of this." With a flourish, she scribbled onto the paper, stabbed a period at the end of a sentence, and slapped the chart closed. Unlike the hospital, with its top-of-the line medical records system, the center did most of their work the old-fashioned way: pen and paper. She pushed herself back from the table. Then, as if remembering the time, looked at her watch. "You got here quick!" Sam peered at Diana with dark, all-knowing eyes. She was a decade older than Diana but had the energy of a twenty-year-old, with stamina that had gotten her through three marathons in the last eighteen months.

"I had to get out of the house."

"What's going on?"

"Ugh, not all great, so I'd rather not talk about it." Diana hedged on her answer. Sam was an idealist, the perfect kind of personality to head up a community center. The thoughtful sort, empathetic, and open-minded from serving underserved populations. While she'd never said anything scathing about Diana's current job, her opinion had been written all over her face when

Diana made the announcement that she would be working for Alexandria Specialty and not for her, evident in the thin line she'd created with her lips. "It's just the same old, same old. Moms. Babies."

As predicted, Sam kept a poker face. "Saw the news that Preston was in labor."

"I can neither confirm nor deny. HIPAA, you know." She sipped in a breath, tamping down the bubbles that had begun to overflow from her belly. "Ready to go? Or did something else come up?"

"Ugh. Just got a call in literally the short time since we texted." Sam leaned back in her chair, as if it took all her effort, the air escaping from her lips. "About . . . what else?"

"Money?"

She nodded. "Money. Our classes are overflowing. We need another educator. We also need an outreach coordinator for communities who don't know about us so we can serve more people. All of it requiring money. Perhaps we should have a fund-raiser? Network for more donors? Speaking of, any new connections on your end?"

Twelve hours ago, Diana would have been all for the idea, but now . . . "You know I'm the first to put this place's business card in everyone's hand. But after last night . . . ?"

"What happened last night?"

Diana cracked the door of her worry after a short pause. "I broke policy. I put a noninsured patient in one of the VIP suites."

Sam gasped. "Oh no."

"But I had a good reason. L and D was packed, and we were starting to divert patients. A VIP was on the way, but an emergent case walked in first." Diana lowered her voice. "I made a call. A right one, but I'm officially—and I quote—'on vacation.'"

"How's the patient?"

"Fine. Delivered, Baby in the NICU, Mom still hypertensive, but better. As soon as someone is discharged on the ward, she'll be moved."

"So you absolutely did the right thing."

Diana nodded and leaned back. "That's the only thought that's given me some peace. If we'd transferred . . ." She didn't even want to think about it, that the stress of the transfer might have put either the mom or baby in distress.

Relief spilled out of her with her admission. She'd returned home from the shift overwhelmed with thoughts about the repercussions of her actions but unable to convey it to her mother. She had never been the type to hold back what happened at work, but seeing Margo there, on the couch talking to Granny, wearing plaid bell-bottoms and a denim shirt with its tails tied together like she was straight out of *Saturday Night Fever*, and with her stuff everywhere and then bringing up Ms. Margo?

What was that phrase? *The days were long, but the years were short?* It not only applied to children but to parents, too. Diana could recount the afternoons spent with her mother, the long talks with her about boys and life. She was an only child, and Margo, laissez-faire in her parenting, creative and whimsical, was more of a friend to Diana rather than a mom.

Diana hadn't expected her mother to get old. Hadn't expected her skin to wrinkle, her hands to shake. It wasn't as if Diana was in awe of this change in her mother's physical being, but sometimes it would happen overnight. Like this morning, when she realized that potentially, she might become her mother's caregiver one day, much like Margo had been for Granny.

The inevitability of responsibility—it was too much. Diana's plate was perpetually full. She expected a lot of herself, and she just wished she could have a break from all of it.

Just not in the form of a forced vacation.

Diana shook her head, feeling selfish now. Here she was harboring hard feelings for her mother, who had been a saint to Granny. "Anyway, I'm not in the networking mood."

Sam's lips screwed into a grin. "Should we skip the run and take you out for breakfast instead? Will bacon therapy help your morning?"

"As tempting as that sounds, no. I want to forget my night. Let's brainstorm fund-raising ideas while we run."

"Great." Sam stood and donned her gloves.

Meanwhile, Diana looked out the window, at Old Town. The clinic was off Burg Street by a couple of blocks, away from tourist traffic. Here, businesses were on the first floors of newly converted condos and dotted with families who had lived in the area for generations. It was still the kind of neighborhood where there were equal parts tourists and generational residents, where people still biked to the local farmers market and jogged in general safety.

Diana had admittedly rolled an ankle more than once on its cobblestone streets.

"How about a race?" Diana said out loud, her brain catching up a second later. "A 5K through Old Town?"

Sam laughed, raised a hand up. "Only the hardest thing to plan. And I don't know when you'd get a chance to do all of that with your work schedule." A grin appeared on her lips.

"Wait a minute, I thought I was just brainstorming ideas, not spearheading the project."

"C'mon, I can't do everything. And you're an official center volunteer. Besides, hanging out here these next couple of weeks might do you some good. Serving—"

"Serving is healing," Diana finished the sentence, already feeling better at the idea of it. Her best friend was right. A thread of an idea began. "Okay, so the race could have a low buy-in—twenty dollars a participant. We can involve one of the running stores. Get corporate sponsorships, like Rings and Roses, the wedding shop down the street. I'll think about a race proposal." She started to jog in place; she craved the rush of endorphins. "But c'mon, let's head out before your first patient arrives."

Sam half laughed and shook her head. They both knew it was a matter of time before Diana planned something for the center. When her mind was set on something, nothing would deter it.

If anything, the project would at least distract her from everything she didn't want to deal with.

Chapter Five

*a*s a photographer in her twenties, Margo had managed to coordinate a roomful of indignant theater actors who hated each other and refused to stand within two feet of one another. Later on, she'd taken on the challenge of photographing ten babies lined up in peapod costumes for the rededication of Alexandria Specialty's labor and delivery ward. And in one of her workshops, she'd camped out in a deer stand in the mountains of Shenandoah National Park for hours to snap the perfect shot of a bald eagle. She was a patient woman.

But Margo's patience now was as thin as the tape of the box in front of her, which she popped easily with one of Diana's fancy butter knives. Everything was taking so long. So far, she'd unpacked only one box, though she couldn't get herself to throw anything away. Each item she encountered had a specific event or occasion tied to it, and with every attempt at decluttering, Margo felt a part of herself torn away.

She really didn't want to be a burden to Diana; she'd wanted to surprise her daughter by showing her how much she could accomplish this morning. But unpacking was proving to be painful.

When Margo lifted the box flaps, the scent of *old* wafted from the box. Yes, Margo was old herself—how could she deny it—and she had the right to call a spade a spade. Her friends and her mother had carried those scents, in their cars, their homes, their clothing and sheets. It was the sum total of nose-numbing floral perfume, creams to ease the joints, and lotions to ease dry, papery skin. Margo, to this day, was insistent on updating her perfumes to whatever her Ulta ad had advertised, and avoided baby-powder-scented anything because of these smells.

Not that she wasn't proud of the dozens of candles on her cake every year. The stigma of age and the feeling of erasure, on the other hand? That was another thing.

The box was labeled *Leora's closet* in a stranger's left-leaning penmanship. Margo had paid for two movers to pack up her mother's things and seal up boxes, then splurged on a cleaning team to wash away the years of her mother's memories from their home before the Realtor put it up for sale.

Guilt ran up her spine. Margo, in her eagerness for some freedom from caregiving—it was as if she had walked out into the sun after a year of being underground—had rushed the movers. She didn't take the time to go through her mother's things after she died, and Margo had no idea what she would encounter in this box. Would it make her laugh? Or bring her to tears?

She tossed the rumpled packing paper to the side. Inside was a folded stack of threadbare linens: a yellowed cotton tablecloth with four napkins, a handkerchief edged in blue thread with a delicately embroidered letter *A* in one corner.

She gulped in a breath. *A*, for Antonio Cruz—her father. All at once, a memory flashed in her head of sitting at her mother's round kitchen table, lit dimly from above. They had just finished a breakfast of oatmeal with raisins. Her mother, wearing her standard maid's uniform, stood at their narrow countertop making Margo's school lunch. It would be the last time Margo would see her for the day. Later on, after school, she would let herself into the apartment, park herself in front of the television, and do her homework until her mother returned, late in the evening.

It had always been the two of them, for as long as she could remember. Margo had had a series of aunties—all passed on now—who took up her mother's free time with bridge and bingo. Leora never married, her heart tied to Antonio until the day she died.

But this—Margo had never seen this handkerchief.

She pulled her phone from her pocket and clicked the Instagram app. She squared the handkerchief in the screen's view, tilting it slightly for an artistic effect, and pressed the button to capture it. She typed out a post: *The things you find when you move . . .* and uploaded it to her feed. Almost immediately, a notification window dropped down from the top of the screen: someone "hearted" it. And then another, and another . . .

Her cheeks warmed and she reveled in the moment. She couldn't explain it to her daughter, but those tiny beeps sometimes reassured her. They reminded her that she was still alive, still seen. Even during a short hiatus after her mother's death, which she'd shared with her followers, she had received private messages from absolute strangers. It would have been a lonely time otherwise. The social media experience had been so fulfilling that she even brought her best friends, Roberta and Cameron, into the fray, and they, too created second careers for themselves.

Deep into her thoughts, Margo pulled out another set of linens, wool this time, and unwrapped it to find a picture frame, flipped upside down. When she turned the frame over and saw the picture, she leaned into the kitchen counter for support.

It was a picture she didn't recognize, but the woman was undoubtedly Leora, with her strawberry-blond hair—part pinned upward in a roll—grazing the tops of her shoulders, and Antonio, dark-skinned, slim but formidable, wearing a soldier's brown uniform.

Her father.

Margo touched the hesitant smiles on her parents' faces. Noticed her mother's faraway look, not quite at the camera. Margo knew about the time when this was taken—that part of the story she'd been privy to—the 1940s, when Antonio joined the United States Army to serve with the First Filipino Infantry Regiment in World War II. His story was a hero's, one that she had heard time and again, though it was as threadbare as the embroidered handkerchief, with just enough information that Margo had been satisfied with the story until adulthood.

"God, you were just babies," she said aloud. "Babies and brave."

Leora had repeated this same statement in the past, when Margo had questions about their romance, about her father. It was the kind of statement that cast magic in her imagination but also invariably ended the conversation. What child didn't want their parents to be brave, to be superheroes in their own right, to have some kind of a happily-ever-after?

Margo propped up the picture so her parents looked back at her. There was more in the box, tucked under a large wad of crumpled packing paper. A bit of digging recovered a wooden box with a latch, which she fiddled with and popped open.

Inside was a stack of envelopes, yellowed with age, marked

by a red border, and stamped with the distinct emblem of V-mail.

Victory mail.

She fanned the envelopes in front of her. The first, which stood out from the rest, was a plain white envelope from someone named Flora Reyes. But the rest were from Antonio, with the last addressed from the Philippines in 1945.

Which wasn't possible. Her mother had said her father had died in New Guinea in 1944.

Margo fell into a spiral of memory and history. She couldn't stop reading, couldn't stop rereading. In chronological order, from the first letter to the last from Flora Reyes—a scathing note that left her with more questions than answers, a letter that would forever haunt her—Margo scanned each of her father's words for clues. She checked them against her mind's cupboards, which were filled with snippets of conversations with her mother, like the one on her thirteenth birthday, when she'd said she wanted to know more about being half-Filipino. At eighteen, when she'd saved enough money for a flight overseas, a solo trip to the Philippines, but chose to go to her first photography course instead. Moments where she'd insisted on more information from her mother, just to be placated by Leora's declaration that she had known no other family history than what she'd told Margo: Antonio had been an orphan. He was an only child. He and Leora weren't married; therefore, she received the barest of news when he died.

Margo was petting Flossy in her lap when the side door opened.

"Hello?" Diana called in.

The dog bounced from the couch to greet Diana.

"Sorry I took a little longer. We decided to take the scenic route this time. But Lenny called. His crew's running late at their other job—" Her voice caught. "Hey. What's up?"

"What's up, indeed?" Margo said, eyes on the letters on the glass coffee table.

The couch cushion sank next to her. "Ma?"

Where would Margo even start; where would she begin?

Then, realizing that she hadn't answered Diana's question, she simply plucked one letter from the table. It was only then that Margo looked at her daughter, whose face was aglow from the cold air. Tired as Diana had been before she left, she looked awake now, her spirit lighter than before. Her beautiful daughter, who had her late father's button nose and full lips, but also Margo's and Leora's pointed chin and hazel eyes. But her curly, and sometimes frizzy hair, and her strong, solid build that came with her lean frame—were those from her grandfather? Were they Cruz traits?

These letters affected her, too. They were her legacy.

Margo gestured at the envelopes.

"What's this?" Diana sifted through them. "Letters from Grandpa?"

"Your *lolo*, Diana."

"Wait. But how could that be?" Diana peered at the ink on one envelope. "The date of this postmark. Granny said—"

Then the tears that had refused to come an hour before bubbled up. *Granny said.* Granny—Leora—the epitome of honesty, who believed in truth over kindness, whose words were her bond. The woman who had no filter. Who could be as cutting as an arrow but could love like no other.

"Your granny, my mother. I don't know what to think, but I think she lied."

Manila, Philippines
March 28, 1945

Ms. Gallagher,
*   You don't know me, but I'm asking you to stop*
writing to Antonio Cruz. He is no longer yours, Ms.
Gallagher. He is choosing not to return. He will soon be
my husband. Please, do not keep writing. Do not expect
correspondence in return.

Flora Reyes

Chapter Six

The legend went like this:

    Antonio Cruz crossed the ocean to find work in America in 1933. At fifteen, he was old enough to accompany his father to what the American priests and teachers in his small barrio in Ilocos Norte depicted as a country full of wealth and possibility. His mother had died the year before, his father was bereft with grief, and America was greener pastures. His father sold their land, leaving their modest life for the United States.

    This idea proved the opposite upon arriving. Antonio didn't attend school and instead worked the land next to his father as a migrant farmworker in California, among other men and boys. They put food on the table for Americans, but they lived in poverty. They lived in squalor, in shared spaces. Water was scarce among the workers despite the abundance of clean water in the country. For while Americans wanted their work, they shunned and segregated Filipinos and other minority farmworkers.

    Antonio and his father moved to the town of Marysville,

where Antonio's father found regular work in a local restaurant as a cook. Antonio was bright and amiable, and the restaurant owner often used him, too, for errands and deliveries. During one of these deliveries to a seamstress, Leora used to say with a twinkle in her eye, was where he met Leora. Leora Gallagher was one of the town's seamstress's girls, hired to do piecework and mending.

Antonio and Leora became friends. She was a year younger than he. They made conversation in passing, during short walks. She found out that he loved to read. Then began their secret meetings in one of the orchards at sunset, where she would sneak him a book from the home of Mrs. Lawley, the seamstress. They had been aware that what they were doing was forbidden. Leora had an unforgiving father and friends who were vocal in their disdain for the Filipinos who had immigrated to California. But by 1943, they both harbored a secret—they had fallen in love.

Leora had written the first note. A secret one she left in the notch under "their tree" at the orchard, sometimes tucked in the pages of a book when Antonio exchanged one book for another. It would be the beginning of a back-and-forth, and in this anonymity of pen and paper, they shared all their hopes and dreams. Their notes could contain one or ten sentences, but no matter the length, they were later burned. Seasons turned into years, and the short notes became promises of love and commitment.

But life was not a plateau; life was a series of mountains and valleys, and World War II began.

Antonio wanted to go to war, of course, as did all the young men. While their blood and sweat was spread over American land, their hearts were in the Philippines. Leora knew he wanted to go; it was evident in the excitement in his voice. So despite the resentment that she could not help harboring—not at him, but at the injustice of the world—she did not hold him back. She promised to wait, promised to write.

Antonio was naturalized as an American in a mass ceremony during training, and unbeknownst to Leora, she was pregnant with Margo after a rendezvous before he boarded the silver carrier to New Guinea with the First Filipino Infantry Regiment, with a final destination of the Philippines.

Antonio died a war hero, in New Guinea, within days of arrival.

Except—after seven decades, Margo had just discovered—he really hadn't.

Diana filled her tight lungs with air after she read the last letter of the bunch. Everything that had bothered her in the last twenty-four hours had faded into oblivion. Her issues with Carlo, her patients, her job—all had taken a back seat to the letters that had appeared out of the rubble in her garage: a volcano of information that destroyed everything true about her family history.

And behind the lava? Anger.

"What the fuck?"

"Diana!" her mother admonished, crunching into another saltine cracker. She had taken a sleeve from the pantry sometime between the sixth and seventh letter, and was down to less than half a sleeve. "Language."

"Mother. Language is the least thing you should worry about." She flapped the letters in the air. "I mean. What the hell is this? Is this a prank?"

Of course it wasn't a prank, though Diana had to ask. Every envelope's postmark seemed authentic, the peeling stamps real.

Her mother shook her head, her fingers lightly touching her lips. "And your granny isn't here to say otherwise."

"Well, then we have to find out. There has got to be more— there must be clues."

And Diana was off and running, in her head at least. This was what made her a good doctor—it wasn't her ability to work without sleep, and it wasn't her photographic memory. Nor was it her empathy, which was quickly waning these days. It was her zeal for the answer, the diagnosis, the algorithm through which a coordinated series of questions turned a choose-your-own-adventure puzzle into a solution.

Diana stomped to the garage before she heard her mother answer. She flipped the lights on. Junk greeted her—three generations' and an ex-boyfriend's worth. Her eyes darted away reflexively to stifle her increasing claustrophobia, and she sidestepped to where her grandmother's things were stacked.

But when she came upon them, the tops of their boxes were unsealed.

"I've already gone through them," her mother said from behind her. "Before you came home."

Diana opened the boxes anyway and looked inside. She found framed pictures, books, Christmas ornaments. Little snippets of her grandmother, though the boxes were free of anything truly telling. Diana and Leora were similar in this respect. Everything in her granny's house had had a function. When Diana was growing up, it'd been a relief to trounce through Granny's home in comparison to her own mother's, who had walls of photographs staring back at her, papers littered about, her workspace spreading out into the entire house.

Margo had a paper trail that could have pinned her down at a diner in West Virginia in 1996 for a photography assignment. Leora, on the other hand, was a mystery.

But now Diana wished Leora had been a pack rat.

"Sweetheart."

She looked up then, at her mother leaning against the doorframe. "I've already looked. There are no other clues."

"That's it? You're not gonna do anything else?"

"Like what? I'm seventy-five years old. We have no other blood family. Whatever those letters show—well, too much time has passed."

"The truth is still the truth." A notification beeped from inside the house, interrupting Diana's launch into her philosophy that the truth was best, no matter how much it hurt. Out of instinct, she patted the pocket of her long-sleeve fleece, only to find it empty.

Realization dawned. Facebook. Twitter. Instagram. Ancestry sites. Plain old Google. The internet kept the stalest of information alive and relevant. "I think you're wrong, I think the truth might just be easy to find."

part two

Sunset

The first stab of love is like a sunset, a blaze of color . . .
—Anna Godbersen

USS General John Pope
April 6, 1944

My dearest Leora,

    As promised, I wrote as soon as the ship left port. The mood is somber, and in my cramped rack, no one is saying a word. It seems everyone has taken to paper, probably writing their sweethearts like I am.

    Be proud of me, my heart. I can't remove your sad expression from my memory. It has only been two days, but I can still feel you with me, your bare arm against mine, my fingers in your hair. I can still see your look of regret. I, too, am sad. I wish I didn't have to go, but I could not have turned my back when called to duty. Our world is under attack, both yours and mine.

    I can't ignore my country's needs. I know this was not what we discussed. But sometimes our world dictates our actions. Sometimes the world tests us, but I believe it rewards us, too. By doing this, I honor my father so he can be proud of me. I will also earn the right to go before your father proudly. I know you think I'm too optimistic, but I'm hopeful.

    Write to me? I may not receive your first note until we get to New Guinea, but your letters will be my lifeline. Tell me all about home. Tell me everything about my father, the town, and what kind of fun you're having with your friends. Do you remember my friend Onofre, from the barbershop? He has promised to send you my letters as soon as he receives them, and he can mail your letters to me. We can trust him.

Until then, I will think of you every moment of the day. At sunset especially, when I imagine you are in the orchard, under our tree, thinking of me at the same time.

Iniibig kita.

As ever, yours,
Antonio

Chapter Seven

lora Reyes Philippines
  Flora Reyes Cruz Manila
Flora Cruz Manila Philippines

Diana faced page upon page of internet search results for what had to be two of the most common Filipino last names and the biggest metropolitan city in the Philippines. She methodically clicked on each news and image link, each address and profile—ranging from a Flora Reyes in the United States who had previous addresses in the Philippines to the hundreds of women of the same name in the Philippines—even adding the name Cruz in case the two had truly married. But the Flora she was looking for had to be at least in her nineties. Maybe a hundred years old. And maybe she was dead.

Which would make this entire search pointless.

The sun peered through the blinds in front of Diana's desk, and she blinked at the glare. It woke her from her trance after her nights on call and staring at the half-dozen tabs open on her computer, at the notes she had jotted down on the notepad next to her.

She'd spent the last day and night researching without a tangible lead.

How hard was it to find a person in the internet age? Still hard, apparently. Despite technology, digital footprints, and degrees of separation, the world's population had increased at the same feverish pace. And what if Flora Reyes wasn't even on the internet?

Diana's phone dinged a text notification, from Sam.

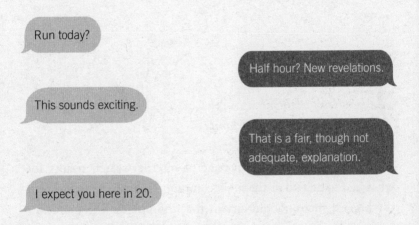

Run today?

Half hour? New revelations.

This sounds exciting.

That is a fair, though not adequate, explanation.

I expect you here in 20.

A second notification, an email this time. Diana bent over the laptop, changed tabs to her email. And upon seeing the sender, she scooped the laptop into her arms, energy renewed, and flipped the lights on as she made her way to her mother's bedroom.

She rushed to her mother's bedroom door. With a customary knock that was more of a wallop than a rap, she entered, not bothering to mask her steps on the hardwood floors. She approached Margo, who was asleep, with her eyes covered with a leopard-print eye mask, and clothed in pajamas with caricatures of Mona Lisa in varying expressions. Diana touched her mother's wrist. "Ma?"

Her mother's lips twitched, and the wrinkles around her

mouth bunched like reeds of hay. She took a deep breath and let out a long exhale, as if falling into deeper sleep.

Diana could've waited to speak to the woman until it was a more appropriate time. She should've. The last couple of days had left them both in this strange suspended state. After their initial discussion about the letters, they'd both retreated to their corners. Diana had begun her research, and her mother . . . well, she couldn't assume to know what her mother was doing, except that she had been busy on her iPad.

Diana touched Margo's fingers, tugged a little. "Ma."

Finally, Margo came to. Her hand groped for the mask and peeled it off, pushing back her dyed light brown hair—if there was one thing she was intent on, it was keeping those grays away—eyelids fluttering open to reveal her brown eyes. A smile fanned across her face. "Hi, honey."

"Hey."

Her eyes narrowed in suspicion, reading Diana's expression immediately. She inched up in the bed. "What is it?"

"I stayed up most of last night to do research on Flora Reyes, but it was tough. Those genealogy sites were a maze, and Reyes is about as common as Smith and Johnson." Diana bit her lip.

Her mother side-eyed the laptop. "And?"

"What if I told you that I asked for help?" She reached for her mother's cat-eye-shaped reading glasses by the table and set the computer on her lap.

Margo peered at the email through spectacles, face tilted up slightly. Her mouth moved as she read the words, face placid at first. Then her jaw dropped ever so slightly and her eyes cut to Diana's face. "A private investigator?" She took off her glasses. "Could you hand me some water?"

Diana picked up the glass of water from the bedside table, most likely tepid after sitting out most of the night.

Her mother sipped, silence settling around them like a sheer blanket. "How did you find him?"

"Google—he had great reviews." At her mother's questioning stare, she rolled her eyes. "I couldn't sleep. Anyway, I gave this person all the information we had, and voilà, he emailed back with an offer to work with me. Us. He has a contact in the Philippines. Read the email."

Diana pointed to the screen and read the email anyway. "'I feel that this would be a very simple fact-finding mission.'"

"Di," Margo said warily.

"There could be nothing to find out, or there could be an entire story we don't know about, but it's worth some research, isn't it?"

"That's the thing, Diana. It was so long ago," Margo said, glancing away for a beat. "And even if there's something to find, do we want to know?"

"I mean, why wouldn't we?"

"I've told you that life was tough for your granny when I was born."

"I know. She was on her own after she got pregnant with you."

"Me, who ended up looking so different from her." Her mother nodded, her smile wan.

"Oh, Ma." Diana knew this story by heart, too, of both Margo and Granny being shunned the rest of her life by Diana's great-grandfather. Leora had been sent across the country, just shy of giving birth to Margo, and settled in what would become Old Town Alexandria. Leora had worked as a caregiver and then a domestic helper, passing Margo around to newfound friends in their small but tight-knit Filipino community for care until she was school-aged.

"What I'm trying to say is that despite Granny's rough start, *I* had a good life. And now I have a daughter who has grown up to be a successful doctor, with her entire future ahead of her. What more do we need to know?"

Diana shook her head. This would not be pushed aside, stacked in piles like the papers that used to litter her mother's house. This wasn't like finding an extra dollar bill in a pants pocket. "I disagree. We aren't the same people with this news. I'm not . . ." She hesitated as a surge of shame and disappointment ran through her. She pushed it back down, unable to trace it, except that it mimicked the sinking feeling she'd battled for months now. Even given her penchant to assume fault, she wasn't responsible for this recent news. But the fact remained, she wasn't going to let these letters go without further investigation.

"I can't just pretend these letters don't exist," Diana said.

"Honey, we're not even sure if these letters are authentic."

Diana sat back, surprised at the turn in conversation. "You think they're fake?"

"No, you're putting words in my mouth. I'm just saying we don't really know the context." She put up a hand. "You weren't the only one who stayed up half the night thinking about all this. I admit, I was shocked by the letters, but they simply are what they are. So what if he died in the Philippines and not in New Guinea? So what if he lived a little longer than Granny said? If my father were alive today, he would be over a hundred years old, which means he's passed, most likely. It's too late." Her eyes fell to her lap. "And, if my mother lied on purpose, it must have been for a reason. Those were different times, and she was a survivor. I have to trust that she knew what was best."

"What if I need more?" Diana asked, after a beat.

"What if I don't?" Margo's eyes flashed back to her. "Since your granny died, I've been feeling like an orphan. Besides you, I have no family. Despite having my best friends still around, it's frightening to realize that my generation is the oldest, that there's no one for me to look up to, to look at and compare myself to."

Diana nodded; she understood. That was why she had asked her mother to move in with her after Granny died. Her decision had been automatic; she didn't even discuss it with Carlo. Diana, too, loved her granny—she missed her dearly, every day. Having her mother around, she thought, would ease both their losses.

And blood came first. Carlo, on the other hand, couldn't comprehend the scarcity of Diana's family, not with his five siblings and dozens of relatives scattered in Puerto Rico and on the East Coast. He was able to trace his lineage several generations, while Diana, on the other hand? Nothing beyond her Granny and Antonio. Unfortunately, Diana's father had died of a heart condition when she was five; and much like her mother, he was a flighty man, in more ways than one, with no family of his own.

"And now, I consider this time my second chance," Margo continued, bringing Diana back to earth. "Taking care of your granny, though I would never trade those hard days for anything, opened my eyes. Life is short, Diana. Life is to be celebrated and experienced, and I want that for you, too. Without Carlo. You deserve this second chance, also." She closed down the laptop. "*I don't need to know more, my love.*"

The sound of the laptop shutting sparked a white-hot frustration. Of course her mother was at peace—she had done exactly what she wanted to do in her life, and she said so herself. But Diana wasn't looking for a second chance. She was still on her first chance. Her first, and she was alone, with her job in jeopardy.

"I need to go on my run," Diana now said simply, and stood, gently taking the laptop from her mother. She didn't have the headspace for an argument. "What are your plans today?"

"I've got coffee with Roberta and Cameron, to go over our trip." Margo looked at her clock with a faint smile. "We meet in an hour."

And with the reminder that her mother cared more about coordinating her bucket-list trip than their own family tree, Diana headed to the bedroom door, eager for space between them. "All right. I'll see you then, this afternoon."

But before she stepped out, her mother said, "Diana? I know you'll do the right thing."

She spoke over her shoulder. "That's all I want to do, Ma."

"Earth to Diana."

Diana blinked at the chalkboard menu behind the counter, and then to Sam, in front of her in line. They'd taken a detour after their run, to Old Town Coffee & Tea for Sam's extra-large Americano and some pastries for the center's monthly staff meeting.

"Are you sure you don't want anything? On me?" Sam asked.

"Nah, I need my stomach to settle after that sprint you took me on."

"You know you loved it."

"Yeah, I did." Diana smiled as she took one of the two bags

of pastries handed to them. The buttery smell of croissants wafted through the brown bag, and she sniffed it, the act pushing her last conversation with her mother to the periphery. Her mouth watered. "Mmm, maybe I *will* have one."

Sam leaned back against the café front door to open it, and a bell rang to signal their departure. The temperature dropped as they crossed over the threshold, and a chill made its way into Diana's bones. "So . . . care to finally catch me up on what's going on? You were pretty quiet on our run," Sam said.

Diana told her about the letters as they walked down Burg Street, chins tucked into their long-sleeve fleece shirts. After she mentioned the private investigator, Sam halted in the middle of the sidewalk.

"Holy shit. What a difference a couple of days make. How are you not parked somewhere either taking shots or scarfing a whole lot of chocolate?" Her breaths came out in puffs of white.

"I don't know. I think I'm still in shock." They'd stopped in front of Rings & Roses, one of two wedding shops in Old Town, and Diana caught herself examining the A-line silhouette of the wedding dress that fit the width of the darkened front bay window.

She had had an A-line dress on order once upon a time, when she was ninety-nine percent sure Carlo would propose on their third Valentine's Day together. The store had had a sale going on, and in anticipation of the wedding she was going to have, she'd nabbed her princess dress at 50 percent off.

Diana was much better now, but six months ago had been a different story, when the bottom of what she thought was a well-reinforced box gave out. She and Carlo had adored each other, but soon she'd found that there was a limit to this adoration. That limit was when her attention veered when Granny died, when she no longer treated Carlo as if he were the only light in her world. Then her mother spent more time with them; shortly after, she'd moved into their town house.

Over time, Carlo became jealous. He hated being the third wheel in an otherwise healthy relationship between mother and child. He hadn't liked being upstaged, and soon, what they had built split apart seam by seam.

It didn't help that he'd already found a fourth wheel. Now, Diana realized that the *other woman* had been an excuse. And while she had been strong enough to throw him out after she'd discovered his infidelity, still, Diana fell apart.

Except, it didn't look that way at first. She'd simply thrown herself into her work; she hardly slept, volunteering for call at every opportunity. She buried herself in anything but emotion, anything to keep her from coming home, where, slowly, pieces of Carlo were disappearing. Because living with someone for five years had meant letting that person seep into every seam of one's life—crumbs had nestled in deep despite the various attempts to vacuum them out—just when Diana thought that the last of him was gone, she'd find a magnet from a tourist spot they'd once visited. Or a bookmark tucked into one of their shared books. A men's sock in the wash.

Work became her solace, where she ignored time, exhaustion, and common sense, until it took an intervention, a check-in with her primary care physician—yes, doctors had their own doctors, too—to make her realize that the grief over her breakup, her Granny's death, and her mother moving in had taken a toll.

But no, right now was not like back then, because she was aware of it. Right now, it wasn't grief she was feeling but surprise. Like everything in her box had spilled onto the floor and she had been handed a completely different box to put everything in, with secret compartments.

"I see the way you're looking at me, and no, I'm not thinking about Carlo. I mean, not in the way you think." Diana glanced at her friend briefly. "My brain is all about the what-ifs. Would I be here today if my grandfather had come back? Would I have met Carlo? Would my mother be as infuriating?"

"You know you can't play that game. Like, what if I decided to have a latte instead of an Americano yesterday? Would I have spilled it over the files I was working on, which set me back an hour trying to re-create my documents, only to miss another first date?" She grinned. "Know what I mean? You will drive yourself to madness that way."

"You had a first date yesterday and didn't tell me?"

"Don't change the subject."

"First dates are important."

"See? You and your mother are more alike than you think. You both like to avoid stuff. In your case? Feelings."

Diana looked up at the dress, laughed at the memory of trying hers on with Sam and the proprietor of Rings & Roses behind her. "You want emotion? I should have trashed the dress instead of selling it. That would have been more fun, if less economical. Anyway, we should get out of the cold. Your coffee is going to be frigid."

Diana walked three steps, then stopped and looked back. Sam hadn't moved. "Well?"

"Promise me you will try not to play the what-if game, okay?"

"Yeah, yeah, fine. Let's go," Diana said nonchalantly, avoiding her friend's eyes. And finally, to her relief, Sam picked up her step.

But as they came around the corner to the center, Diana spied a group of people milling at the entrance. In front was the unmistakably recognizable face and big hair of Ursula Woods, field reporter for *Northern Virginia News*.

"What's she doing here?" Sam asked.

Ursula, as if signaled about their arrival, raised her face to them. She smiled, then began a steady march in their direction. She spoke while she was still feet away. "Dr. Cary. If I could have your thoughts on the equity of luxury birth suites?"

"Oh my God," Diana said. "This isn't good."

"Here, give me all of that." But instead of waiting, Sam scooped the bag from Diana's arms. "Just go," she said over the top of her coffee.

"But what are you going to—"

"Are you kidding? This is a good chance for me to do some promo."

"But I didn't get to ask. What should I do? About the PI, about all of it?"

"You do what you always do. Triage, diagnose, treat, Diana. Just remember to share your load. Don't shoulder this entire responsibility. And good luck."

So Diana did what she did best—she ran.

USS General John Pope
April 9, 1944

My dearest Leora,

We have been on this ship for 64 hours and
25 minutes. I know this because my bunkmate
reminds me of the date and time each and
every morning.

We are packed in our sleeping quarters as
tight as tomatoes in a bushel, our bunks stacked
four up from the ground. Like tomatoes, some are
already bruised. Some are already homesick.
Others are frightened of the water; some say
that they have nightmares about drowning. And
there are others, like me, who simply want to get
to our destination so we can return home.

Despite his insistence on marking time, I've
found a friend in my lower bunkmate, and
you would like him, too. His name is Ignacio
Macapagal. He's eighteen years old and so very
innocent. He is cheerful from the moment he rises
until he sleeps, and while he works, he tells stories
about his mother in Tacloban, a small barrio in
the Leyte province. It's been four years since
he's seen her, and she was the reason why he
enlisted.

Sometimes I watch him while we play
dominoes and tidy up our rack, and I wonder if
you and I were as happy as he is when we were

eighteen. If we dreamed as much as he does. He doesn't speak of the possibility that he might not see his family, and part of me is worried that he doesn't understand that the war has been going on, that the Japanese have already invaded.

Although we've only spent three days on this ship, I am already kin to him. I want to protect him.

The Filipinos I have met have come from all over the US, and despite the close training before we left port, where I thought I met everyone, I'm meeting new people every day. By the time we reach New Guinea, maybe we will all be friends.

I bet you want to know details of the ship, so I will share them. It's suitable. Our bunks fit us nicely, and there's enough space to put away our things. While it's dark below deck, up above there is more than enough light and sun and ocean air for all of us. The chow, well . . . chow is chow, but I'm grateful for a full belly at night. There's a strict lights-out policy, which I don't object to, because first call in the morning comes way too quickly.

We train during the day, study things. Preparation is our only focus during this journey. I read my small pocket Bible at night, though some men brought their own books too and I may ask to trade.

But mostly I think of you. I think of our last night together. It will be forever imprinted into my heart. Our last time together was special. So special, Leora. Then I think of your travel home and you pretending you weren't with me, and I want to say I'm sorry for that. It's shameful to lie, to have lied about us all this time, and I regret that we've had to hide who we are.

When I return, it will be different. This war has made it different. I will march to your father and tell him how much I've loved you since we met. I know you doubt him, but I have faith he will accept me, will accept us.

Almost time for lights out. Write to me, my darling.

Iniibig kita.

As always,
Antonio

Chapter Eight

Iniibig kita. I love you.

Margo mulled over Antonio's words—her father's, she reminded herself—as she stuck a spoon in her matcha latte, cutting through the foam flower. *Iniibig kita* was a formal term of endearment that connoted a devotion, a loyalty. It implied an absolute. Forever.

It didn't make any sense. If *iniibig kita* was written in every single letter her parents wrote, how did their love fall apart? Why were these letters kept secret? What really happened? These were words reserved for commitment, and yet her mother had been left to raise her alone.

Despite her declaration to Diana that she didn't need to know more about these letters, Margo still fidgeted with unease. The truth was, she wasn't sure how she felt about them, except that their presence had caused a wider rift between Diana and her. Diana had become obsessed, barely leaving her computer the last two days, stuck in the past, while all Margo wanted was to move on, and to share the excitement of her trip with her.

The chair across from her was pulled out with a squeak. A ceramic saucer clinked softly against the table, waking Margo from her trance. She smiled up at her friend Roberta Probst out of habit. Roberta was one of her two brunch dates this morning, a standing date since Leora passed. It was a weekly kind of thing, filled with tea, baked goods, and business chatter, and when Roberta, a vlogger who did reviews and tutorials for mature skin care and makeup, ran over her notes for her next reviews.

As she sat down, Roberta gazed at Margo in expectation, smiling too sweetly. "Do you notice anything different about me?" She blinked her dark eyes repeatedly.

"Um . . ." Margo scanned her friend's face. The woman was beautiful—with golden-brown skin from her Mexican heritage, perfectly shaped eyebrows, and prominent round cheekbones—but because she was always testing a new product, over time Margo had become numb to the subtle changes unless Roberta walked in with a completely different palette of makeup colors. "This is a trick question."

"Then I was right. This product is a fail." She tucked a strand of hair behind her ear with coffin-shaped fingertips.

"But your manicure, on the other hand, is impressive." Margo grinned.

A smile melted on Roberta's face. "Thanks, and you are, as usual, stunning. I love that peacock fascinator. It matches your bow tie perfectly." She gestured at Margo's hair. "But I'm talking about my fake eyelashes."

"You have lashes on?"

"Exactly." She sighed. "They're supposed to look natural."

"Well, they seem to have certainly achieved their goal." Margo peered closer, then moved back. "Maybe it's my eyes, but . . . yes . . . I guess I see them now."

"There's a fine balance between just enough and too much, especially for our age, and I was hoping this would meet it. It's the first set that hasn't irritated my eyes. What a disappointment. I don't like giving *meh* reviews. I get such hate mail for them—they're boring apparently."

"Haters gonna hate," Margo said, imitating what she'd seen on social media. "You do what you want. We're too old to care."

Roberta took a sip of her coffee. "Tell that to Cameron, who's insisting that I take a stronger view. Apparently the meh reviews don't get quite as much traffic. He wants me to commit to doing some harsher pans if I don't like a product."

Margo sipped her latte as she listened to her friend complain about Cameron Ayers, the third member of their three-pack of lifelong friends, whom Roberta had guilt-tripped to volunteer as her video editor.

"Do you think it would be awkward if I fired him?" Roberta asked.

"You're not going to fire him. Video media was his career, if you've forgotten, and he was, and still is, good at it. And it was *you* who wanted to monetize your channel." She eyed her friend, whose red lips were pressed together in a frown. Margo knew Roberta's facial expressions down to a T, and this one expressed acceptance. She would do what Cameron asked her to.

Speaking of, Cameron entered the café, pulling his sunglasses off his face. He was wearing a polo shirt tucked into his jeans, his standard everyday attire. His mostly-salt-and-very-little-pepper hair was combed neatly backward, and around his chest was a cross-body bag that carried his must-haves: his computer, a leather notebook, and three trusty gel pens.

Margo's insides warmed. Cameron had always been handsome, but these days, he was downright debonair. It was unfair for men to age so gracefully while Roberta was searching for the perfect lashes and Margo was scouring her closet daily for just the right outfit. Cameron had always been Cameron, a little geeky, humble, endearing, and good-looking but clueless to it.

Did she have a crush on him? Maybe? Yes? Whatever this was, the feeling was long-standing but harmless and safe. She kept it close to her heart; it was a secret she hadn't shared with anyone. Her friendship with Cameron and Roberta was uncomplicated and perfect, and she had refused to do anything to ruin it.

She had known them for decades, all of them having grown up in Old Town, which was something special in an area that consisted of more transplants than originals these days. And Cameron and Roberta were home to Margo. They'd witnessed the stages in one another's lives, good and bad.

"Ladies." Cameron unslung his bag and set it on the floor, then sat between them.

Margo could guess what he would say next: *I'm starving.*

"I'm starving." He echoed her thoughts, and raised his hand to their favorite server, a young woman they had seen grow from a gangly child to a beautiful older teen.

Can I have a bagel with light cream cheese and a coffee, please?

"Can I have a bagel with light cream cheese and a coffee, please?" he asked the server.

Margo shook her head in amusement.

He grinned. "What did I miss?"

"I was just saying that you keep nagging me about views." Roberta's lip curled up in a snarl.

"You asked me how to monetize, and I gave you my opinion."

"But I want to tell the truth."

"Truth comes in many forms," he said. "In this case, truth

would be better served with more enthusiasm. Don't you think, Margo?"

"Hmm?" Margo was stuck on his statement about truth, harkening back to her conversation with Diana that morning. What she saw as truth was not how her daughter saw it at all. Diana wanted something tangible that explained things, that would change her life, while Margo saw truth as reality, the result of what had already happened.

"Yeah, I agree." She snapped to, to Roberta's scowl. "I mean, you only have a few minutes to capture an audience, and *meh* won't keep them on."

"Great, take his side."

"Sorry." She shrugged, sheepish. And, with Diana still on her mind, she unleashed her thoughts. "Though if the audience is Diana, then nothing works. She doesn't talk about the bucket-list trip, my . . . our work, and though she follows me on Instagram, she never likes my photos. It drives me crazy, if I'm honest. In the past, I thought she was just a little embarrassed, and with my mother passing and Carlo leaving, I thought she was too busy and preoccupied. But now I'm actually starting to get offended."

Roberta lips turned downward. "Have you spoken to her about it?"

"No—and in the scope of real life, it feels too petty to bring up. We're all trying on this new normal, and I don't want to push her."

"Right, but how awkward has it been?" Cameron asked.

"Very." Margo had a sudden need to give her mom a call, to ask for her advice. Leora had always been able to tap into Diana's psyche better than Margo ever could. Neither Cameron nor Roberta had children; they both considered Diana their own, and it felt wrong for Margo to talk ill of her.

The next second, her stomach gave way. Her mother was no longer around. Not to give advice and not to set the record straight about those letters.

"You okay? Your face just fell." Roberta silenced a text that came in and flipped the volume switch to off. "Tell us."

Margo nodded. "Can I ask you a personal question, Roberta?"

"Margaret." She rolled her eyes. "I have one word: *shapewear.*"

A laugh bubbled through her. About a year ago, Roberta had had her first date in a couple of years and was convinced that she needed shapewear underneath her dress. Margo had agreed to shop with her; it was a welcome break from taking care of her mother, and good thing because Roberta needed two extra hands to shimmy the full body Spanx up her torso. In the end, they'd decided to ignore the patriarchy and ditched the idea altogether.

"All right. That's my cue," Cameron said, standing. "I'm going to see about the status of my coffee."

Roberta rolled her eyes and said to Margo, "You can ask me anything."

Margo took a breath and told her about the letters, about Diana's desire to seek out the truth. "And I was wondering"—she swallowed the knot in her throat—"I wanted to know how . . . since you had mentioned before . . ."

"Ah, you wanted to know about my finding my birth parents." Roberta leaned back. Regret passed across her face, and immediately Margo wished that she hadn't added to her friend's pain. For Roberta, despite finding her birth parents almost three decades ago, it hadn't ended happily.

"I'm sorry, I shouldn't have . . ."

Her face opened in a sincere expression. "No, no. Please." She touched Margo on the arm gently. "I'm okay talking about it—thanks to my therapist." She heaved a breath. "Sometimes, when I'm feeling at my worst, that's when it haunts me. Why did my biological parents not want me? I know we've never talked about it in detail, but my birth parents had lived grand old lives as grandparents. With their older children. I was the youngest born, an unwanted pregnancy they couldn't afford. Now how's that for some crap—knowing that the reason you were given up was because they just couldn't handle one more baby?"

Margo reached for Roberta's hand, then and clutched it.

"But see? Before I sought them out, I thought I was just a cast-out kid. Now, I know the details of it all. Before, I invented the circumstances of my adoption. After, it was my choice to forgive, which I admit took me a long time. Dealing with a truth like that is like facing a loss, especially since my upbringing with my adoptive parents wasn't so pleasant. But do I regret finding out? No." She frowned. "That is some confusing stuff, right?"

"It's really confusing." Margo nodded.

"As long as you know what you're getting yourself into, Margo. That's all I'm saying. Prepare yourself for the worst-case scenario. I don't want us to be sitting here six months from now, or hell, in the middle of our burro ride down the Grand Canyon, with you upset at me for enabling a curiosity that you might regret later on. Diana might press you to make that decision before you're ready, but it's you who has to live with whichever choice you make."

"She's not that bad," Margo said, then added, cackling, "Yes, she is."

"She can be decisive, and we both love her for it." Roberta laughed. "But somehow you have to find the balance between her right to know and your own hesitance."

Margo bit her lip and looked beyond the windows of the cafe, to the street, at the pedestrians passing by, some with her tan skin color, not quite beige or brown. Growing up, she had always been the different one because she was never all the way anything. Not one race or the other. She was taught some of her Filipino culture from the families she met in the Fil-Am community, but by default she associated her own personality and mannerisms with the women who showed her how to live: her mother, faux aunties, her teachers, and her daughter, too. Who Margo was today was because of what she was born into, a hard-scrabble life as a latchkey kid with big dreams.

But were genetics just as important?

"Is it safe to sit down now?" Cameron said, walking up to the table, with a steaming cup and a plate holding a bagel. "I'm armed with my cup of coffee and am ready for anything."

"It's just family drama, as always," Margo said.

"Well, I figured." After setting down his food, he set a piece of caramel candy down next to her tea. "They just poured a bowl out at the counter."

"Where's mine?" Roberta asked.

He raised an eyebrow. "You don't even like caramels. You complain they get stuck in your teeth."

Roberta huffed and speared him with a look. "Fine. You're off the hook."

Margo took a sip of her tea, grinned into her cup, and snuck a look at Cameron. In their younger days, the girls didn't appreciate his sweetness, his steadiness. But as they got into their forties and fifties, his date card had grown to a mile long. By then, people had realized that Cameron was exactly the kind of man a woman wanted in her everyday life. But he never did commit. Despite his deep friendship with Margo and Roberta, he had trust issues.

"Let's change the subject. Our TALWAC plan," Roberta said with a wide grin.

"TALWAC?" Margo asked.

"Our '*Thelma and Louise* without any crimes' plan?"

"Oh!" Margo laughed. "I didn't realize we named it."

"I watched the movie on Netflix last night, and I was inspired. Do you think I'm more Thelma or Louise?"

A year ago, their threesome devised a plan to fulfill their retirement dreams, and to document, and maybe earn money from them along the way. A video-recorded bucket-list adventure: two best friends, but without crimes or drama, though Roberta would've welcomed a young Brad Pitt in a heartbeat. At the time, Margo had simply placated Roberta—discussing it took her out of the weeds of caregiving. But Leora had found out about it and explicitly requested in her will that Margo use the modest sum of money from her life insurance to make the dream come true after she passed.

Their first trip was to New Orleans.

"Wait. Where am I in the initials? TALWAC doesn't have Cameron implied. I mean, there's a *C* there, but that would be 'Thelma and Louise without any Cameron' and that doesn't work."

Margo laughed. Cameron was always so literal.

"You *are* the 'without crimes' part, since I'm sure you will be the one putting us on a curfew and reminding us of our senior-citizen discounts," Margo joked. Both Roberta and Cameron were on fixed incomes, too, but they'd saved money over the years. And their social media revenue helped. That and their senior-citizen and AARP discounts.

"Anyway, we need to discuss activities and scripts for the two days we're in New Orleans." Roberta clicked her phone on. "Let me get my list of ideas up."

The state of Diana's living room came to mind. Three days. They were leaving in three days, and Margo had yet to tackle those boxes. And now, with these letters, a thought rose above the rest. "I don't think Diana cares that I'm leaving."

"Of course she does, Margo. But you've gotten accustomed to feeling needed every moment of the day. And now you're *just* Mom." The expression on Roberta's face was sincere and without malice. It spoke of their shared experiences, of being a caregiver—for Roberta, caretaking of her husband years ago—and of bearing the exquisite pain of loving someone unconditionally at the end of their life.

"Maybe she's just in denial," Cameron added. "Denial is some strong armor."

"You're right," Margo admitted now, a bravado seeping through, blurring the guilt and the claustrophobia she had been feeling since moving in with Diana. She and her daughter were both adults. Diana had had a rough six months, but Margo's last couple of years had been gutting. This trip, with her friends who loved her and saw her through some rough days herself, was important to Margo, and she had to keep moving forward.

After heaving a breath, she said to Roberta, "What videos are you proposing?"

But Roberta's face had scrunched down into a frown. She thumbed through her phone with her mouth in a silent O.

"Roberta?"

"Did"—she thumbed the screen—"did Diana mention anything different about work?"

"No. Why?"

"Anything, you know, about being called out in the newspaper because . . ." Her friend passed her the phone. "This was just linked through Facebook."

The screen was opened to the *Northern Virginia News*: HOW THE 1% HAVE THEIR BABIES: DID YOU KNOW?

"Where have you been young lady? It's past dinnertime." Margo tossed the kitchen towel on the counter, hands still damp and resting on her hips. "I texted. I called. What's the point of you having a phone if you don't return voice mails or messages?"

Her daughter halted in her tracks. "Mother?"

"Don't 'Mother' me. I want you to tell me the truth. Right now. Right this instant."

Diana looked to the left and right exaggeratingly, as if Margo had directed her demand to someone else. It was something Margo wouldn't have dared to do with her own mother, even as an adult. Maybe she had been too nice to Diana, given her too much leeway.

"Diana Gallagher-Cary."

"Margaret Gallagher-Cary," she teased.

And that darned daughter of hers hiked her hands on her hips to imitate Margo. Diana screwed her face into a scowl, contorted like one of their holiday photos where they yelled right before the self-timer fired. "Do a funny face!" Margo would say, and they'd always don the same look: Margo with her tongue sticking out, Leora sucking her cheeks in and crossing her eyes, and Diana with this scowl.

Margo couldn't help it; she busted up. It was that or cry at the memory.

Damn it, there went her initial anger. She had never been a disciplinarian.

"I'm sorry I didn't call or text." Diana walked forward and pushed a manila folder into Margo's hand. "How did you know something was up? I swear you have a sixth sense."

"It's all over the news," Margo said, though intrigued by the folder. She sat back on the kitchen stool, the day's news and her meeting with Roberta and Cameron slipping from her mind as she took out the contents.

"What was all over the news?"

"What is this?" Now completely confused—they obviously were talking about two different things—Margo flipped through photographs and two typewritten documents. Her heart began a steady thump.

She glanced up briefly at her daughter and then back down at a candid black-and-white photograph of a woman wearing a dark sheath dress at a ribbon cutting. She had scissors in her hand, poised against the ribbon, while a man in a traditional Filipino formal shirt, a barong tagalog, held the ribbon straight.

Margo stared at the man's face.

Her daughter took the barstool next to her. "I went to see the private investigator, Ma. I'm sorry, but I did. I wanted to tell you, but you were already gone by the time I got back from my run. His name is John Prescott and he's local, in Frederick, and it didn't take him long. Just today, to find out some real information. It's why I was away all day—I hung around while his contact in the Philippines did whatever they had to do."

"Dear God." Margo wasn't ready for this. She'd just gotten

used to the idea of it all, that something beyond them existed, but actual answers? It was kind of unbelievable.

The lump in her throat divided and grew like a cancerous cell.

Diana took the rest of the papers from her and set them down on kitchen counter, so Margo had a clear view of the documents. Diana pointed at the colored photocopy of a woman in a flowered dress, hands clasped. Behind her were the spiky leaves of a tropical plant and the outline of a two-story home with thatched roofs and balconies. The woman was dark-skinned, stern-faced, pride evident in her eyes. "This is Flora Reyes."

"How do you know this is the right woman?" Margo pulled the photo closer to her and skimmed a finger over it. "You said it's a common name."

"She matches all the criteria. The PI pieced together the possible birth and marriage dates. This woman married an Antonio Cruz in 1946. Her current address is within Metro Manila."

"Current?"

"Yes. She's still alive. And, Ma?" Diana said firmly.

"Yes?"

"I'm planning to see her. And I want you to come with me."

Chapter Nine

Diana watched as indignance and anger washed over her mother's expression. This, she hadn't expected. Her mother was emotional, but she skewed toward sadness and disappointment rather than anger, denial rather than snark. And with her current choice of outfit—a crisp white shirt with a teal iridescent bow tie, black capris, and suspenders—Diana thought her mother would cheer for her newfound discovery.

But her mother wasn't cheering now. "Absolutely not."

"What?" Diana frowned, confounded for a second. Her mother was always down for an adventure, until Granny had gotten housebound. And Margo had never refused her in the past. Then again, Diana had never asked for anything more than her mother could provide; she put herself through most of college with the help of her mother's meager contributions—an artist's wage, after all, was inconsistent and never commensurate to the work she did.

"Wait . . . you're serious."

"As a heart attack. I asked you to do the right thing," Margo said.

"And that's what I did. I don't understand why you don't want to know more. This is your father. My grandfather."

"That's exactly it." She held her hand up. "This is *my* father. Did you stop to think that I needed more time? To process all of this? To think? You just made a big decision. You asked someone to snoop into people's lives, not even thinking about the potential that you might change ours a million percent."

"So you're mad at me?"

"Yes," she said, then sighed. "No. I just wish we could have talked about it beforehand, because this morning's conversation was a chat, not a unanimous decision. But, you do this, you know."

"I do what?" Diana frowned, not liking where this conversation was going.

Margo took a deep breath. "You just *do*. Sometimes without thinking, without consulting. You take responsibility when, maybe, it's not yours to begin with."

Diana bit her cheek. She hadn't told her mother anything about her work, and yet, somehow Margo knew how to poke her where it hurt.

"I'm sorry," Margo said, wiping her hands on her thighs. "I didn't mean it, at least not all the way."

"Does that mean you're going to come with me?"

"No, dear, I'm not." She blinked at her. "Aside from the fact that I'm not convinced it's a good idea, I'm getting on a plane, for New Orleans, remember? For a trip that has been planned to a T."

Diana couldn't help it, she snorted at her mother's gall to just drop off her stuff at Diana's home and run away. Of course Margo had mentioned it, but Diana had thought . . . she'd thought her mother would come to her senses. "Right. Your *bucket-list* trip."

Margo frowned at her. "Hey, tone!"

"You don't think this trip to the Philippines is more important? Can't your trip wait? You wanted to discover more about the country and yourself, right? What could be a better way than to actually investigate your roots? You have never even been, and this is the perfect time."

Her mother held up both hands, voice softening. "Let's slow down here, please. You just got the first piece of information, which might not even be accurate. And going to Louisiana is not the same as going to another country." She gestured at the envelope. "And frankly, now I'm wondering what more is playing into this decision."

Dread settled upon Diana. She sighed, looked away. "So you know."

Her mother nodded.

"How did you find out?"

"The internet." She heaved a breath. "What happened?"

"I went against policy and accepted a patient that I shouldn't have. It caused a little bit of havoc on the floor, and then social media . . ."

"Social media did its magic." Her mother frowned.

Diana shrugged it off, laughed lightly. There wasn't any need to put her mom into a panic. "But it's all good. Every business goes through this, and it just so happens that I'm in the crosshairs, but Aziza and I chatted, and there's no worries."

"So you haven't been fired?"

"No, but I'm taking some time off, to let the dust settle."

"And your preoccupation with our history, your need to do all this right now, has nothing to do with the dust that's unsettled at work?"

She frowned at the implication. "Yes, okay, that's why I'm a little on edge. But I want to go to the Philippines right now because I have time, which, yes, is due to this fiasco. What I don't understand is why you don't seem to see the importance of this. This is a big deal. Why won't you come with me?"

"Because I don't want to. Period. End of story. If this is all true, and that's a big *if,* I trust my mother's reasons for keeping this away from me. I trust that she made a decision to protect me, to protect you. I was an advocate for her wishes up to the moment she passed, and if she didn't want me to know something, I have to believe her reason for it was good."

Diana was dumbfounded. She had been sure that her mother would come on board after seeing the pictures, that she, too, would have been swept up in this mission to piece together the missing part of their lives. In elementary and middle school, Diana had hated that part of the curriculum where she had to chart her family tree. While others drew branches, her tree was as sparse as an eastern redbud during the wintertime.

But they were at a standstill. It was clear in her mother's expression: Margo wasn't going to budge, choosing her nebulous three-quarter-life crisis trip over something that could change their entire lives, over solving a mystery seventy-five years in the making.

Diana guessed she was going to do as she had always done: she would take charge.

"Then I guess you and I will go our separate ways in a few days," Diana declared.

New Guinea
June 2, 1944

My dearest Leora,
   I received a letter from you today! I held it up
to my nose, and I swear I could smell the scent of
your skin. I read your words over and over again
last night. I tucked it under my pillow, a comfort
as I slept, and I have folded it carefully to keep
with me at all times. You're a good-luck charm,
and I'll tell you why.
   You are now reading a letter from a promoted
corporal. It's true! One of the corporals fell ill,
and the lieutenant saw that I am a quick
learner and I've been helping other soldiers.
This is just the first step for us, sinta ko. Ignacio
(you remember my mentioning him—he had the
bunk below me on the ship) jokes that I will be a
sergeant major when I return. I pretend to laugh
about it, but what if it could be true? Can you
imagine me with a sergeant major's rank? That
would really be something.
   How is everything at home? Your letter
mentioned the unrest among the farmers. Some
of the soldiers have received similar letters.
There is talk of future protests.
   We've talked about my feelings on the matter,
and you and I agree workers have a right to
demand better pay, but it doesn't mean that

I don't worry about you. I want to protect you. I know you don't like me saying so. You have the strength of a soldier, but with us apart and unmarried, I just pray you stay safe.

I hate to ask anything of you, but will you speak to my father? Will you remind him that I will return? He has not written me back, not even at Camp Beale, where mail came in regularly. He is upset, I know. While he gave his blessing, he wished for me to stay, to fight the fight there, for equality, for rights.

If you can, please remind him that I love him. He has to understand that I am doing this for him and for our cause. For the home of our birth and for the home of our adulthood. It's twofold, you see. I believe that. Going back to the past, to the homeland, even if I don't remember it well, will make me a better person, a better man. I will return to you with a stature no one can deny, and I will be worthy of you.

I must go. Tonight I will dream of you.

As always, iniibig kita,
Antonio

Chapter Ten

Margo milled around Diana's office doorway. She was technically packing and had a small stack of shirts in her arms fresh from the laundry to place in her suitcase, but when she heard her daughter click on the mouse, her curiosity distracted her from the task at hand.

Diana had been on the computer on and off for the last couple of days, sleuthing. She'd received a list of social media profiles from the investigator's report that might belong to the family members of Flora Reyes Cruz, and true to her stubborn nature, she was going through the list one by one.

"Ma, I can hear you and your fuzzy slippers back there. Your hair must be standing on end from static," Diana said, not turning.

How her daughter could tease her at a time like this, Margo couldn't understand. Margo had been on edge since Diana's declaration that she would be leaving for the Philippines, with or without her. Now, none of Margo's plans were on her mind. Instead, she was worried about her daughter's itinerary, the speed with which she'd bought her ticket, and her spreadsheet of places to visit despite not having a contact in Manila besides her travel agent.

That is, unless her current efforts turned up a contact for a Cruz family relative.

Which would make that relative Margo's relative, too.

Margo's heart rate doubled.

Oh God, Margo could have relatives.

And Flora Reyes was alive.

Alive.

Margo shook her head as an avalanche of thoughts cascaded around her. Flora Reyes might be the woman who had seen her father last. This might be the woman who had been married to her father. The woman who had kept her father from her. And her daughter was going to confront her.

"Can you?" Margo said now, curiosity peeking around a corner of her mind. "Can you reread the PI's letter?"

Diana turned, the note in her hand. "Sure. 'Enclosed are the following items that connect Flora Reyes to Antonio Cruz: a marriage certificate to Flora Reyes, a newspaper clipping connecting the couple with a mention of their family members, and possible Facebook profiles of their granddaughter, their next of kin. Enclosed is a potential business address in the name of the family. While a trusted partner in the Philippines has provided this information, I suggest making contact and conducting a DNA test for proof of relationship. As discussed, I will wait for further instructions on how to proceed.'"

"So he's not really sure, then?" Margo said, with a spark of hope in her chest. Her life would go back to the way it was if this all weren't true.

"Ma." Diana looked up. "This is them. I can feel it."

"But we aren't sure," she said, forcefully now. "Because if this is true . . . if these people are . . ."

Diana stood, guiding Margo into the chair while taking the clothes from her arms, and turned her so she faced the table of pictures. The ribbon cutting photo, the photo of Antonio and Flora, a close-up graduation photo of Flora, and of a third woman Diana's age, with a bright smile and Diana's eyes. The first time Margo looked at these pictures, she'd casually flipped through them, but now, she examined them intently.

"It's not too late, Ma. You can change your ticket."

"No." Though Margo wouldn't be able to put this out of her mind forever, she couldn't back out on her friends. And she refused to subject herself to this . . . this alternate reality. She'd lived her life in the moment, and that was what she was going to continue to do, not grasp at this potential scam. She turned to her daughter. "Diana, what if . . . what if this is all a lie? A lie made up by your private investigator, and no one's waiting for you on the other side. What if it's a . . . what do you call it? A catfish?"

She smiled. "I thought of that. I didn't tell the PI that I was going to the Philippines. And, I could say the same of you: you might be on a wild-goose chase with your wayward friends. It's the same kind of risk, isn't it? We're going to places we've never been before." Under her breath she said, "Though I still think you should come with me."

"Hello?" A low voice echoed from the hallway. "Dr. Cary? Mrs. Cary?" Lenny, their contractor, materialized in the doorway holding a rusty pipe. His presence no longer surprised Margo. Despite his weathered appearance, he was the epitome of honest and jolly, not to mention another person to chat with during the day while Diana worked.

"That's not a good sign," Margo said.

"Not horrible, but not good, either." He grinned, accentuating the folds on his dusty face. He lifted up the pipe. "We found this behind the wall in your master bathroom. It's looking bad, and I suggest we replace it."

Diana sighed. "Well, we don't have a choice, do we? Can you text me a quote?"

"Will do. Expect it in a bit. Sorry. It's these—"

"I know . . . old houses."

"Right." He nodded and turned out of their sight.

As his footsteps quieted, Margo was struck with another thought. "Diana, isn't this too much? The time off, the private investigator, this trip? You have student loans, your mortgage to think of, and now the pipes need replacing."

"You don't need to worry about it. I've made everything work before, haven't I?" she said bluntly.

The implication shredded Margo's motherhood card, a reminder that, yes, in fact, Diana had paid her own way. As a photographer, Margo had made just enough to live, to rent out the downstairs flat of a town house in Old Town, to give Diana the basic necessities of life, but everything else? The clothing Diana had wanted, her varsity jacket, her college applications, not to mention college itself, and medical school—Diana had done it on her own. It had all worked out in the end, with the two of them achieving exactly what they wanted in life, but Diana was right—Margo didn't have the say-so to worry, to double-check on her financially.

Diana pointed to her laptop screen, snapping Margo out of her thoughts. "Besides, there's no way I'm backing out now. I've found a relative, and her name is Colette Cruz Macaraeg."

"Hey, are you okay?"

"Oh, ah . . . yes." Margo looked up from her phone's screen, which had gone dark, to see Cameron sitting next to her, a carry-on bag between them. The rideshare van to the airport rumbled through the street—they were a mile from Reagan airport, where they were meeting Roberta—and she had just posted the picture of herself and Cameron loading the car up with their luggage. She had started to scroll through her notifications when her mind had wandered, far enough away to be noticeable.

A gray eyebrow rose, and his blue eyes gleamed. "Uh-huh. I don't believe you. Here I am chatting my butt off about our exciting trip, and your mind's a million miles away."

She couldn't deny it. She was caught, so she updated him on Diana's plans, of the foolishness of her wanting to fly across the world to meet complete strangers. Margo couldn't get her daughter's face, or how detached their goodbyes had been, out of her memory. They had hugged (though stiffly) and said their requisite *I love you*s. There hadn't been any outward hard feelings, but right now, it felt like the first day she'd dropped Diana off at day care, like she was missing an appendage. "I just wish she had listened to me."

"About the safety of traveling alone?"

"About everything! About moving too quickly. She and that Colette, who is supposed to be my niece. My niece, the daughter of my already deceased half sister named Marilou. Can you even imagine that, Cam? A sister!" Words tumbled out of her mouth and Margo was keenly aware she wasn't making any sense. "That is to say if that was truly Colette and not some phony person. Anyway, she and Diana were in communication most of the night. How I know this is because Diana kept walking from her bedroom to the kitchen and back, typing away at her phone. But my God, if the PI is right, and if they are, in fact, cousins by blood, then that puts a new spin on everything, right?"

"More than a spin. That's a tornado-force wind, Margo." Concern flashed in his eyes. "So what are you doing here? Why aren't you traveling with her? Don't you want to go, too?"

"No," she said softly. And then in a louder voice: "No! Of course not. I think this is a mistake. Even if they are really family, they're still strangers—we don't know what they might want or think. My family is Diana. My family is you and Roberta. My family was my mother. Of what importance are these strangers in my life?"

Cameron turned in his seat and leveled her with a stare. "You meeting new family doesn't negate the family you have, you know that, right? Nothing would be lost. But I get it. It's scary as hell."

"I'm not scared. I'm hesitant; I'm dubious. Besides, this trip has been the light at the end of the tunnel that kept me going last year. I've wanted to be able to breathe, and now I'll finally get to. Is that horrible? Does that make me an ungrateful daughter?"

"No. No, it certainly doesn't make you ungrateful." Cameron took her hand. He didn't do it often, and Margo was surprised at how soft his was. Both their hands were wrinkled, with the occasional spot, and she relaxed into his touch, as simple and gentle as it was.

"Margo, you've been through a lot. You loved your mother, and it was this love that made it hard to take care of her in the end, but you did it anyway. You *do* need to breathe. You shouldn't feel guilty for wanting to take care of yourself. And I support whatever you want to do. We're all in this together." He squeezed her hand. "We'd miss you, anyway. Our TALWAC with Cameron YouTube channel name won't work without Thelma. Anyway, it already has hundreds of subscribers."

"You think I'm Thelma?"

"You're changing the subject." He handed Margo his phone, and sure enough, below their first video, shot by Roberta after their last coffee date, was a series of comments. "I think this idea of ours has legs. Heck, it has wings. And I think it may fly." He gave her a side-eye. "But yeah, if I had to choose. Thelma."

"Wow. You might be right," Margo said, ignoring the blush creeping up her neck as she scrolled through the encouraging comments, recognizing handles from her Instagram followers. In real time, the subscriber count increased before her eyes.

But as they disembarked curbside at Reagan airport and walked the short distance to the airline terminal to pick up their boarding passes, Margo wondered: *What would Leora do?* Would her mother have left for this trip knowing Diana was going to the Philippines? Would she, too, have given Diana leeway to do what her heart desired, despite the threat of danger, physical or emotional, that loomed on the horizon?

The answer came to her quickly.

Yes. Yes, Leora would have, because she'd allowed Margo this same leeway in her young life. Leora had taken the reins of motherhood whenever Margo needed the time to breathe, to create and capture moments. Despite not having a partner, Margo had the unconditional support of her mother. Leora had known that the faster she let Margo go, to catch the wind's draft, the faster she would come home.

Right now, though, Margo didn't feel like she was flying with the current. Instead, every step felt like she was up against it.

part three

Twilight

Find a part of yourself hidden in the twilight.
—Fennel Hudson

New Guinea
June 28, 1944

My Dearest Leora,

I miss you. I'm worried that you aren't getting all my letters and V-mail. You haven't responded to some of the questions I asked in some letters. I, however, spoke to my sergeant, and he said that letters can turn up in the wrong order. I hope that's simply the case.

How are Mrs. Lawley and the shop? Sometimes I imagine you at work behind the treadle machine, working on a beautiful dress, like the first time I saw you. You were a sight. You were biting your lower lip as you worked the fabric through the Singer. You looked so determined, and I knew then that I wanted to meet you.

We have a few months here in New Guinea. Then some of us will stay, and the rest will go to the Philippines. I admit, my darling, that I'm nervous to go back to the Philippines. Will I get to visit my old home? Who of my neighbors are still there? Will they recognize me? Am I too much of a stranger now, older, wearing another country's uniform? Will they treat me like a traitor or a hero? Am I a traitor or a hero?

There are rumors that when we land in the

Philippines, there won't be much downtime. That the country is crawling with the Japanese and my people are under duress. I don't know what this means, Leora, or what it entails, though some of the soldiers look to me for advice. But who am I to give them guidance? Though many of them are young, they are not naive. None of these soldiers from America come from a life of luxury. Their hands are torn from fieldwork, faces hardened by the sun. They aren't innocent, by any means.

And yet, I still feel protective. Me and them, we are all in between—in between two countries where we have endured hardship, even hate.

I apologize for this dreary letter. Take heart, my joy is the sunset that looks close enough to touch, where it feels like the sun is setting all around me. Above, around, and seemingly below as it reflects off the water.

Again, no matter what happens there with the protests, Leora, you must keep yourself safe. I know you. You will want to defend me, defend my father. You have a good heart, always seeing the best in people. But you can't take part in it. Keep to Mrs. Lawley, to the shop, and I will return to you soon.

I can hear you cluck in disapproval at my attempt to tell you what to do. I know well enough that Leora Gallagher will do exactly what she wants. And I love her for it.

Until next time.

Iniibig kita,
Antonio

Chapter Eleven

That afternoon, Diana placed her keys into Sam's hand. She singled out each one. "My car. My mom's car. The front door. The front door dead bolt. The mailbox." Then she flipped a spiral notebook open. "These are the phone numbers of my contractor, the alarm company and code, and my lawyer. My will is in the safe—"

Sam scoffed. "Diana! You're going on vacation, not shuffling off this mortal coil!"

"I know, but just in case."

"Let's just put it out into the universe that I won't plan on calling your lawyer because you'll be back safely here in a week, okay? But, I will be blowing your phone up if your contractor happens to do something tragic to your home."

"I trust Lenny. There shouldn't be any issues, but if you ever feel something is awry, I have no problem with you telling them to hit the road until you can get a hold of me." Diana took a breath. "I'm sorry. Let me know if this is too much."

Sam leaned back on her barstool. "Nope, I'm good. But how about you? You look like you are in pain."

"Do I?"

"Face frozen into a half smile. Eyes widened, unblinking. It's a slightly panicked look."

"Great, just great." Diana laughed, unsure how to take it, and because her friend had just accurately pinpointed the sum average of the last week's emotions.

"Okay. Let me rephrase that question. Do you have everything?" Sam put a hand on Diana's forearm.

Diana nodded. *That* question was simple enough. "I have my passport, my wallet, phone, and some clothes. Everything else I can get there. Carlo is on his way to pick up Flossy, which I know he's thrilled about, but I'm going to miss her. And to be honest, I hate giving him the upper hand." At the sound of her name, the dog bounded from behind the couch with her stuffed bunny, which she carried by its ear. Diana bent down and rubbed the space between her eyes, her spot.

She looked up at Sam. "I know that look. You're wondering why I'm getting on a plane and flying to another country where I don't know a soul."

"That is a correct deduction."

"It's simple. It has to be done. Worst-case scenario: I get to visit a few sites. I know so little about where I came from, and I've nearly let the opportunity pass me by."

"It's just . . . it's not as if things are going well in the work front." Sam nodded at the television, turned to local news. "With the hospital and all, and the media coverage . . . I don't blame you for wanting to get out of here. You are coming back, though, right?"

Diana barked out a laugh, though Sam didn't join her. "That's silly. Of course I'm coming back. To quote my PI, 'This is just a fact-finding mission.'" She grinned at her friend, then down at her phone, which flashed another notification. Irritation buzzed through her. "But I'm not going to lie, this VIP issue is all so annoying. Just when I think everyone's forgotten about it, someone shares the article and tags me."

"Have you heard from Aziza?" Sam asked.

"Yes, but just to say that she'll see me when I return." The way her boss seemed out of touch was a little disconcerting. Usually a day didn't go by without some kind of communication from Aziza, even if it was a simple forwarded work email.

Another text notification flashed on the screen. Her mother.

I forgot my hair dryer

"Give me a sec." Diana picked up her phone to return the text. "She's been nonstop with her texts since they landed in New Orleans. Scratch that, her texts started on the plane."

"She's worried about you," Sam replied, as she hopped off the barstool to refill her coffee.

"If she was worried about me, then she would've come with me," Diana mumbled.

"Ah, you're applying the *if, then* argument. You know that that doesn't work with emotions, right?"

Use the one from the hotel, Ma.

I don't trust it. It's one of those hair dryers that have one speed.

Loud.

It's going to kill my hair.

Air-dry, then.

Diana turned to her friend. "Sometimes I don't understand her. And I don't understand this . . . thing they're doing."

"You mean their trip."

"More like their scramble to reclaim their youth. It's silly! They're just doing whatever the hell they want."

A grin slipped onto her friend's face. "I'm detecting a little anger in your voice."

"Not anger. Frustration. Do you see this?" She gestured at the boxes still sitting in her living room, though pushed to the side. "Months, this has all been here, and yet . . ." She shook her head. "I'm surprised and not surprised. Her priorities are much like her outfits, wacky and a little out of step. I grew up in a chaotic home, you know? She was always in a flurry, always late for deadlines, tardy for everything. She doesn't commit to schedules. It's like she thrives in this constant state of the unknown that she sometimes creates for herself. Like this trip. She could come with me and truly find out what happened to my grandfather, but she chooses another excuse to avoid reality."

Sam brought the coffee cup to her nose. "Have you taken a look at her Instagram feed?"

She shook her head. The Instagram feed—why did everyone always mention it?

At first, Diana hesitated in her answer. She didn't want to be the kind of woman who judged; she strove to be fair and open-minded, especially with online habits. Just because she didn't have the inclination to post her entire life didn't mean that her mother had to feel that way, nor her friend. As it was, Sam was very open in her online life, though in her case, more about her work and her political stances. The thought of being so transparent online gave Diana tingles down her neck. Nope, no way. That was not her style.

"I mean, doesn't it seem silly to you that a senior citizen has a following that large? I feel like she should be knitting, streaming shows, taking walks every day. Settling into her life."

"Technically she's taking a walk today, just down Bourbon Street instead of around the block. But what I mean to say is that her feed shows that she's way more focused than you think. Maybe—just hear me out because I know you already have a rebuttal—maybe you simply have a different process for achieving your goals. After all, she did take care of your grandmother for a year. That is far from noncommittal."

"Are you always such a devil's advocate?" Diana laughed, and stood up from the stool. She refilled her coffee.

"You know me. I'll give it to you straight. Anyway, I'm grateful. You leaving will give me some much-needed alone time, a week when I'm not in my housemate's hair."

Diana gave her friend the side eye. Sam and her housemate, Liliana, had had drama since she moved in, but Diana was convinced it was because of unrequited love.

"I don't want to hear it, Diana."

"You should just tell her how you feel."

"Feel? As in tell her how it drives me crazy when she stomps through the house with her outside shoes on, even after I told her that studies have shown that the bottoms of shoes contain more germs than a public toilet?"

"Yes, that's precisely what I mean." She heaved a breath.

Sam would come around in her own time.

"All right, bottom line, my house is your house. It always has been." Diana looked at her watch. She had to be on the road soon, and of course the last piece of this travel plan was running late.

Did you expect any less? The man was unreliable. She had excused these behaviors for too long in the past—how he was late to everything, a procrastinator, and, oh, that he had a penchant for looking at other women.

As if hearing her thoughts, the doorbell rang with one long chime. Then it rang again, an impatient cry. "I wonder who that could be." She rolled her eyes as she got to the front foyer. She peeked through the peephole and pulled open the door. "Carlo."

Her ex stepped in and looked around. Upon seeing Sam at the kitchen counter, he nodded. Sam lifted her mug, but the expression on her face went stone-cold. They never did like each other, which had been inconvenient, though both were gracious during get-togethers. "Looks like you're really ready to go," he said.

"Yep." She bent down to a basket in the foyer. She lifted it into her arms, eager to get him gone. "Here you go. Her food, some toys, her bed, and her blanket, of course. Oh and her vet paperwork."

"I don't need all this. I have everything I need at my apartment."

She offered the basket. "But this is her stuff. It'll make her feel more at home until I return."

"Fine, Diana." He took the basket into his arms, then turned to walk out the door, hesitated, and faced her. "Do you have time to . . . talk?"

Here we go. She turned back to her friend, who graciously pretended to scroll through her phone. "Sam, do you mind grabbing Flossy and bringing her out to us in a little bit."

"Of course. What are aunties for?"

Diana followed Carlo outside to his car, parked on a side street. It was a Tesla, his dream car, and another sore spot for Diana. He gifted the car to himself on their fourth Christmas, when Diana had been *really* sure he was going to propose. Which he didn't.

She hissed under her breath as she neared the damn thing.

He popped the trunk open and packed the basket into it. "So what's really going on?"

"What do you mean?" She hadn't mentioned anything except that she was taking a short trip to the Philippines.

He shut the trunk. "Look, I know I don't have a say here, but this feels extreme and sudden. Our trip to Williamsburg two years ago prompted a month's preparation. And didn't we have a fight a few days ago about my visitation rights? At the time, you clearly didn't agree with Flossy staying with me, and here I am packing all of her belongings in my trunk. And with your story running on the news last week"—he ran his hand through his hair—"I'm concerned. Can you blame me? We're not together, but you and I . . . you will always mean something to me. Can you tell me what's going on, as a friend?"

She sighed, feeling herself give way. Carlo had been a lousy boyfriend in the end, but there had been good times, times when he'd been her best friend, her staunchest confidant, and her number one fan.

So Diana told him. They both sat on his bumper, and he listened to her, arms crossed, as cars bumped along the cobblestone street and the occasional wind whipped between them.

"This feels like such a risky thing to do, Diana, and I'm not talking about the logistics. But I'm not going to harp. Sam and I might hate each other's guts, but I'm sure she's given you enough grief."

"That she has—"

"But to make *myself* clear: I have a passport, okay? If anything happens in Manila, I can come anytime. If Sam needs me while she's staying here—"

She was starting to regret having asked Carlo for a favor. "I have it covered, but thank you."

His face switched to a look of pain. "Right. Of course you do." He set his palms on his knees, then hefted himself onto his feet. "You always have it together. You've never needed my help. For what it's worth, it wasn't me who left first, you know. It was you. When your granny died, you cut me out completely. You ghosted me, maybe not with your body, but with your mind—"

Diana sighed again. "Carlo."

"I'm sorry. I don't want this conversation to go south. I know I fucked up, but there was more in the lead-up, more that I think we could have fixed—together. That we could fix now. I love you, still." A barking dog took their attention before a blob of white fur charged at Carlo's legs. He bent down to pick Flossy up like an infant. "My offer stands, okay? I can be on the next plane out."

This moment was a picture, and it swayed her still-bruised heart. Diana's mouth, the traitor, answered only with "Okay."

Diana had needed the entire three hours at Dulles airport to make it to her plane because of security. The line at the ticket counter itself was a mile long, with passengers with their baggage and *balikbayan* boxes, large gift boxes filled with American snacks and gifts, tied with twine. By the time she settled into her seat— she'd splurged on business class—Diana was already exhausted and looking forward to the Tagalog lessons she'd downloaded onto her iPad.

Except her mother had other plans. A text chimed in as Diana fastened her seat belt.

How was the Flossy hand off?

At the reminder that she'd left her most precious pet with her ex, Diana's belly dropped at the reality of what she was about to undertake. It was like the moment after a tough delivery, one in which the handbasket had been steps from hell, when the gravity of said emergency came in like a tidal wave.

But she wasn't going to admit it to her mother.

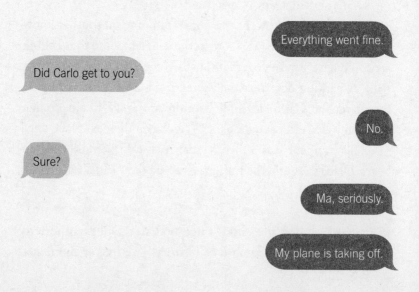

Everything went fine.

Did Carlo get to you?

No.

Sure?

Ma, seriously.

My plane is taking off.

It wasn't taking off. In fact, passengers were still boarding.

> I love you, sweetheart.

> Don't forget to take your Dramamine.

> Text me when you get there.

Annoyingly, Margo was right; Diana had forgotten. When she opened the purple pouch where she kept her nausea aids, next to the Dramamine tablets were a couple of Hershey's Kisses. She pursed her lips as a sliver of guilt ran through her. Growing up, there hadn't been expensive presents at Christmastime, no big birthday parties. But there had always been Hershey's Kisses. They were Granny's favorite, too, chilled in the refrigerator for the exact moment that one needed the sugar rush or a reminder that life did have its sweet moments.

Like now.

She sighed.

> Love you too.

> Thank you for the kisses.

She looked out the airplane window. The runway teemed with planes sliding into their respective gates, of the ground crew slinging baggage into carts. The sky behind it was orange.

Soon, she would be seeing this view from the other side of the world.

Unwrapping a Kiss, she ran through plan B in her head. She'd scheduled sightseeing trips that could take her away from the Cruzes if her meeting with them was too painful or awkward. The plane ticket Diana had purchased was also fully refundable and changeable, which was a good plan C, if everything deteriorated and she had to get out of the country.

Plan D was only a fleeting possibility. One that involved Carlo, of taking him up on his offer. Of finally agreeing to that vacation he was always talking about; maybe he could meet her in Manila, away from Alexandria, where all their struggles could remain.

A beep sounded through the cabin, followed by a man's faraway voice through the speaker. "Ladies and gentlemen, welcome to North American Airlines flight 2598 headed for Ninoy Aquino International Airport in Manila, Philippines, with a stop in Tokyo. This will be a completely full flight, so please be patient as we load all passengers."

Diana took inventory of her things. Neck pillow, check. Blanket, check. Magazines, check. Phone, check. She clicked her phone awake, readying it for airplane mode, faced with the picture of Flossy in an impeccable sit, mouth open slightly in what Diana swore was a smile. In a surge of bravado, she dialed Carlo's number, pulled directly from memory. What she was going to say, she wasn't sure yet, but maybe, just maybe, a sliver of what had been might still be intact. He did say that he loved her, still.

The other line rang once, twice, three times. Just before she took the phone away from her ear, it picked up in the middle of the fourth ring. The trail of a woman's laughter sent familiar shivers through her. Then Carlo's voice, saying, "Give me that, silly."

The phone muffled in what Diana assumed was the handoff, a space of time long enough for her to, again, remember that they'd broken up not because of her—as he'd insisted time and time again—but because of him. Because he couldn't keep it in his pants, couldn't be the partner she deserved.

She pressed the red button to hang up.

Chapter Twelve

The jostle of the plane as its wheels hit the runaway startled Diana from her hazy nap, and she blinked her heavy eyelids awake. Her mouth was dry, throat parched from the stale air, and she rotated her stiff neck.

"Once again, this is Captain Noriko. Welcome to Manila, Philippines. It is now ten forty-three p.m. and eighty degrees Fahrenheit, or twenty-six degrees Celsius, with sixty percent humidity."

Passengers groaned in response.

"We thank you for choosing us as your preferred carrier for this trip."

Manila, finally. Although, through the window, Diana wouldn't have been able to tell if they were still in the United States—the scene outside was typical of every darkened airport, with flashes of reflective gear marking the workers on the runway, the dim lights showing the track of luggage being pulled from planes to the conveyer belt and back. Diana had lost sense of time since leaving DC the previous day and an extended

layover in Tokyo, the trip filled with the occasional nap interrupted by announcements by the pilot and the rumble of the
food and drink cart passing through.

Excitement zinged through her as the cabin stirred awake.
There was no turning back. She was here now, unequivocally.

After the plane taxied to the gate, she stood, and her legs
thanked her for the blood rush with pins and needles. Nervousness rolled through her in waves as she checked her small shoulder tote's contents. In her haste, she'd packed lightly: plane items
and one suitcase of clothing. Now, Diana was thankful, because
the exodus for the door had begun, and God knew she would
have forgotten half the things on the plane, so nervous was she.

Ninoy Aquino International Airport was a bustle of people,
and she followed signs to immigration and the baggage claim
area. At baggage claim, familiar passengers milled as the baggage
turnstile beeped and started, and one by one the bags jostled
down onto the main conveyer.

Growing up, Diana had not traveled extensively. Short road
trips had been more her mother's and her grandmother's speed,
on the Greyhound to New York City, on trains for two trips to
Disney. Granny had been wary of planes; she had a fear of
heights, a tendency to shy away from being too far from home,
though the two women thought it was worth it to witness Diana's
glee at seeing her favorite movie characters come alive. As an
adult, she'd done plane trips to conferences within the United
States, weekend getaways with Carlo that didn't take them away
from work for too long. So the airport itself was overwhelming.
But the people—Diana could not resist staring at the Filipinos
around her.

Her cheeks heated at the thought, at how foolish it sounded
even in her head. She couldn't help it—she looked for the simi-

larities between her and the woman next to her, who was about a decade younger. The idea that there were people not just of her race but potentially of her lineage—previously completely unknown—swirled in her head. What was the probability that some of these people around her waiting for their own baggage shared her DNA? She had never thought once of the possibility before, and now, the opportunities seemed limitless.

The phone, which she had turned on before disembarking the plane, now rang. The number was unfamiliar, but she answered it.

"Ate Diana?" the voice said.

Ate. Older sister. It gave her pause, this word. This assumption. "Colette?"

"Yes, it's me. Are . . . are you here?"

"I am. I'm waiting for my baggage now."

"What are you wearing? For when you come out? I will be looking for you, with a sign." Her speech was easy, as if Diana weren't a stranger. It relaxed her a tad, and she let out a breath.

"I'm wearing cropped jeans and a blue shirt with red poppies."

"Okay. See you soon. I can't wait!"

"Um . . . me, too!" Diana said, caught up in Colette's enthusiasm, but it was quickly replaced by panic. They had messaged each other almost nonstop before Diana left DC, and their correspondence mimicked hers and Sam's: without pretense. Still, her mother's warning flashed in her mind. The person she was messaging could've been anyone.

"This is fine. We're fine. Deep breath, Diana." Except that the thumps and scrapes of luggage and balikbayan boxes being pulled from the conveyer belt became a cacophony. Doubts came back in a full tidal wave: What if these people were not who they said they were? What if this was all a lie, too? What if they were murderers?

She texted her mother and Sam in a group text, as promised.

> I just landed. Colette is here to pick me up.

> Here is my location.

Sam's answer came quickly.

> Got it.

> Remember that you can walk away.
> Follow your instincts.

Baggage claim and customs were each a relatively painless process. But when she walked to the arrival lobby and toward the meet-up area outside the double doors of the air-conditioned airport, Diana was hit with a fight-or-flight reaction. Despite the dark night, the heat was suffocating, confusing to her body, which had, a little more than a day prior, left the cool DC springtime behind. The air was sticky and stifling, and her lungs tightened as she breathed in the smell of motor oil and gasoline from the bumper-to-bumper curbside traffic.

She spotted the sign to the meet-and-greet area. Across the pedestrian parking and down the ramp she went, following the sound of voices until they became a roar. Other passengers disappeared into the mass of people on the other side of the barrier. People were holding signs, some calling for their families and friends, others in uniforms ushering people and their luggage into cabs and cars. It was a total overload of Diana's senses.

Then, out of the waves of sound, she heard her name like a hummingbird's trill. And then she heard it again: "Diana!"

She jerked to the right and walked to the edge of the sidewalk. The air whooshed as cabs and cars sped by. She willed her eyes to cooperate despite feeling discombobulated, then she saw it, a bobbing sign with her last name in big block letters. GALLAGHER-CARY.

Then she heaved a breath, urging her legs to carry her as her heart whirled in anticipation.

A figure came around the corner of a group of people: a woman who looked a decade younger than Diana with a shoulder-length bob and long bangs, and a smile that exuded confidence. The sign was in her hand. "Oh my God. Gallagher-Cary?"

"Yes?" Diana asked more to herself than to the woman as she scoured her face for familiarity. Did she look like the picture from her Facebook photo? And sure enough, slowly, her brain puzzled together the similarities.

"Yay!" Colette leaned in and threw her arms around Diana, who hesitated at the forward gesture. She wasn't in the habit of just hugging anyone, family or not. "Ate Diana, it's so nice to meet you. Oh my God. I see some of my mom in you. It's weird and cool at the same time." The woman pulled back and canvassed her face, smile widening.

"And you're . . ." Diana faltered, surprised at the belly poking her. "You're having a baby!"

"I am!" Her hands flew to her belly. "I'm seven months to-morrow, in fact!" She cleared her throat. "Oh, and *ate* means 'older sister.'"

"I know what that means, and some common Tagalog terms. Some words. I have nurse friends who are . . . and my mom knew some phrases, and then of course Rosetta Stone." Diana stumbled through her explanation, apologetic.

"The family speaks English, and I'll help, Ate." Colette smiled. "Anyway, I have a car for us. Let's get you home." She took Diana's bag automatically. "Follow me."

"Actually, I've rented a car. I can go get it and follow you," Diana said.

With that Colette threw her head back and barked a laugh, then simmered down to a giggle. "Have you ever driven here, in Manila?"

"No, but I've driven in busy cities before."

"It's not the same, trust me. Also, you're tired. Better just ride with me." She was already walking away with her bag, leaving Diana to follow like a lost puppy who had just found its mother.

"Wait." Diana halted in her tracks. "May I . . . can I see some ID?" She felt silly asking for it, as if it was a true fail-safe.

"Of course. Silly me." Colette dug through her bag and pulled out a black wallet, from which slid a Republic of the Philippines driver's license from a card slot. And sure enough, it said Colette Cruz Macaraeg. "Shall we go?" Colette asked brightly.

"Okay." Diana relented. Colette was nice enough, but it all felt so sudden. When they reached a luxury car parked at a curb, a man who had been leaning his back against it stood and scooped up Diana's bag, stuffing it into the trunk.

"You're really coming in at the best time of day. Besides it being a little cooler, you get to see Manila Bay at its best, at night," Colette said, getting into the car, and Diana followed suit.

As they got on the road, Colette took charge of the conversation. She asked Diana basic questions about her flight, the travel she had planned. Nothing too difficult to answer, thank goodness, because Diana was trying to take the skyline in, and how different it felt being with this cheerful woman who was supposed to be her blood relative. But it hadn't sunk in yet.

She was also gawking at the audacious drivers around her who were sometimes ignoring traffic rules and lines on the road.

"This is Manila Bay, Ate Diana," Colette said, pointing to the left. The bay's water glistened in the distance, broken up by the outline of the winding road that seemingly drove out into the water, and the sway of palm trees. "And Las Cruces is coming up."

The car slowed, then took a right into a curved driveway among the towering buildings that lit up the night sky. LAS CRUCES HOTEL was etched into marble at the entrance. Guests in beautiful cocktail dresses entered and exited the front doors, reminding Diana that she had not brushed her teeth in almost twenty-four hours. She ran her fingers through her hair, pressed them under her eyes, swollen from her lack sleep. She must look like a zombie.

"There is a wedding planned this weekend, and we have most of the large party staying here and starting their celebrations early, but we placed you on the twenty-fourth floor to get away from the noise—I hope that will be fine. It even has a balcony. We can meet up tomorrow, if you'd like, but I know you might want to get settled and look around, so I'll keep that open, okay? I do have a meeting set up the next day for an early lunch, when we will do the DNA test and make our plans."

"Do we . . . do I get to meet Flora?" Diana's voice cracked.

"Yes, though not here. It will be at Sunset Corner—"

"Sunset Corner?" Diana asked, flashing on her grandfather's letters.

"Yes, our home in Forbes Park in Makati. Lola Flora is too old to get around, and we'll have to make sure that she's well enough to see you. I hope you don't mind that that part isn't set yet. I figured we should get the DNA test done here, where it's easiest, and then make the call."

"I think it's a good idea," Diana agreed. "One thing at a time."

The door next to Colette was pulled open by the valet. The sound of traffic filtered into the car. "Oh, and here, your key." She fanned out two hotel key cards and handed her one. "I hoped in the last minute that Tita Margo would come, so I reserved one of our suites in both of your names. But I'll go ahead and bring this extra key to the desk since you don't need to check in. You're family, after all." She smiled.

I'm family.

The thought gave Diana pause until Colette motioned her out with a hand. She then chased the clatter of Colette's footsteps up through the double doors.

She was met with a grand marble entryway with an open view upward to skylights. To her left and right, baggage handlers assisted customers, and a long bar was the centerpiece of the reception area, with uniformed concierges huddled over maps and brochures with guests.

"You can call for room service or the front desk for anything," Colette said over her shoulder, waving a hand. "Just in case you're hungry in the middle of the night, they can deliver food at all hours. Or you can simply come down to Tipanan. It's our bar, which is open till about two a.m. They serve food there, too."

The floors switched to flagstone, and a canopy of real palm trees draped over them, changing the vibe from cold and lavish to cozy and comfortable. Just beyond it were three alcoves, all with signs labeled with different floors.

"Here you go. For floors twenty through forty." Colette looked down at her hand, to her lit-up phone. She gave it a concerned look as she pressed the elevator button.

"Oh, and bring your travel itinerary when we meet? We just want to make sure you're getting a good deal, you know? Your trip is quite short, and I want to—" Distracted, she looked at her phone again. She shook her head. "I'm sorry. Work calls, and I have to leave you for now."

"This is more than perfect," Diana said. "I'll get settled. I have your number. I'll text if I have any questions."

"Great!" She nodded to the bellhop behind them, then kissed Diana on the cheek, and just before the elevator doors shut, said, "See you soon, Ate."

Upstairs, Diana gasped at her expansive and modern suite with two king beds and windows that overlooked Roxas Boulevard and the Manila Baywalk. She picked up the amenities binder and ran a finger over the embossed logo on the leather front. Las Cruces. Cruz. Antonio's last name.

She was related to this, too.

Diana picked the leftmost king bed and perched on it with a heavy feeling in her chest. The gung ho adrenaline that had coursed through her earlier was now but a trickle. She felt the way a pregnant woman looked after being admitted for labor, when realization settled in about how much work was yet to be done.

It was about to get serious.

New Guinea
August 14, 1944

My dearest Leora,
    Now that we have been in country for a while
I can tell you that New Guinea is unlike what
I imagined it would be. I thought it would be
desolate. I thought that the people would be
harsh and cold. But I was wrong, so wrong.
    How beautiful and lush this little country is!
Flowering trees, tall green grass, and swaying
palm trees occupy the island. The insects are
loud and boisterous. The people are friendly
and helpful. I wonder how they feel about all
us outsiders on their land, foreign people fighting
other foreign people. I wish we all didn't have
to be here, to step on their grounds. This entire
island is their home, understand? There are
no doors, no windows, no real fences to mark
property because this entire island is theirs. At
times, I feel like a trespasser.
    I can't really say more about what our plans
are, what our mission is while we're here, or these
parts will be censored, or my letter may not make
it to you altogether. But I'll say this: we are on the
move, and I'm sorry I've been scarce in my writing.
    I have seen a lot in the weeks we've been
here. Some not so good, but I try not to dwell on
it. This is war. We are here to fight.

But you needn't worry. I am with my brothers. Not brothers by blood, true, but brothers at arms. Months ago, I didn't know they existed, but now I can't imagine life without them. It's much like how I feel about you. Just as the scent of cigarette smoke reminds me of the nights we snuck out to meet at the dance hall, the inside packed with people smoking and dancing, my brothers are like the other parts of my brain. We work together well. Many times, I don't even have to look to know who is on my left and who is on my right.

In your last letter, you asked me about them, so I will tell you.

Raul hails from Louisiana. He was a farmer. He has a wife and a son, and reminds me of my father as a younger man. He is very serious, though he talks in his sleep. We all give him a hard time about it, that one day we'll write down what he's saying.

Ernie is from Illinois and a lawyer. Yes, a lawyer, sponsored by a Jewish family. He's older, almost forty years old. He eats everyone's leftovers, but he's also adept at spotting the right plants we can cook to enhance our supplies. He's very smart and has picked up some of the language of the native people, which is helpful because they are like our eyes and ears.

Ferdinand is from Seattle. He worked in the

fish canneries. He is the best shot out of all of us. I know that must scare you, but his eyesight is a godsend. He can spot anything moving in the trees, including the wild animals. Beyond the enemy, sinta ko, we also have to watch out for beasts because we are prey!

And finally, Ignacio, who is more brave than I have given him credit for. He might be the smallest, but he is fierce and loyal. He offers his food, his bed, to anyone who needs it. He is calm when there are too many decisions to make.

I hope one day you will meet them all.

Your letters are my comfort. Today, I received four! I had to put them in order to read them. I welcome them with open arms.

I admit I'm a bit of a braggart. I think I got the most letters out of anyone in the squad today. I hope you don't mind, sweetheart, but I read one aloud this evening. Not the personal parts, of course, but the everyday news from town. My buddies miss home. Or what they thought of as home. It's funny how home can hold both happy thoughts and sad memories. That even if they had experienced the worst in America, what they remember are the good things.

Your letter helped them, too. Your descriptions of our world: the trees, the grass, the blue of the sky. It helps the men, because some have received no letters at all.

Not to say that we aren't looking forward. Ignacio continues to promise me a home-cooked meal when we make it to the Philippines. I've taken it upon myself to watch over him. In the last two weeks, he seems to need help in everything. Please don't mention him in your next correspondence to me. I wouldn't want him to know I was writing about him. Please, just keep us in your prayers!

I must run.

Iniibig kita,
Antonio

Chapter Thirteen

*M*argo stared intently at Diana's message on the phone screen while the rest of the world erupted around her in applause. Seated on a padded chair on the balcony of their B and B, just steps from the French Quarter, she lifted her eyes to a group of partiers who seemed to be heading out for their first round of festivities. And yet, she didn't feel part of the chipper environment, knowing her daughter was now spending time with this Colette Macaraeg.

"If you don't eat your beignet, I will." Roberta, typing with one hand, gestured with the other at the plate in between them, piled generously with the fritters and covered with a mountain of powdered sugar. (Thank goodness Margo'd chosen a white crocheted dress, the powdered sugar was a mess.) The cherry on top: two paper cups of café au lait next to the treats. Margo had gone out to grab them while Roberta tended to the comments of yesterday's review of the Hop-On Hop-Off bus tour. This snack would be their last before they packed up and headed to their next destination: Los Angeles, California.

"I'm sorry. Diana just landed, and I'm worried about her," Margo said sheepishly, though that was only the surface of it.

"How is she doing?" Roberta lifted her eyes to her.

"So far, so good." She smiled in an attempt to exude optimism, but all she felt was unsettled.

"Where is she staying?"

"Las Cruces Hotel, this posh high-rise right by Manila Bay. Apparently, the family owns it."

"Ah," Roberta said.

"Anyway, this looks so good. Yum." Margo willed the conversation to move forward by sliding one onto her plate. She knew she had been holding back since arriving a day and a half ago. They were in New Orleans, for God's sake, she needed to get with it. She'd wanted to come here since she was a child. This was a photographer's dream, with the city's multitude of cultural textures. From voodoo to superstition to the religious undertones to the party-town aspects, the loyalty of its residents, and the fervor of tourists. Since arriving, she had gone overboard snapping pictures for her account, but she just wasn't feeling the joy in the process.

Speaking of . . .

"Wait a sec, lemme snap a shot," Margo said, just as Roberta was about to take a bite out of her fritter. The woman grumbled playfully but set it down on her plate.

Margo angled her camera to get the entire delicious display into view and uploaded it into her feed. Instantaneously, notifications rang out from responses to the photo, emojis of hearts and heart-eyes. But it didn't have the same effect on her—it didn't make her grin. A feeling of satisfaction didn't come. But she pushed those thoughts away as she noted the time on her phone.

"We're due at the airport in a few hours. Is Cameron done with the video edit?"

"Did you have any doubt?" a male voice answered from the doorway that connected their room with Cameron's. He stepped out onto the balcony, looking more relaxed than Margo had ever seen him. In the last couple of days, she had witnessed him shedding several layers of formality, from his polo and jeans to polo and shorts. And now, after a trip to the local gift shop, an eclectic-patterned short-sleeve button-down, shorts, and sandals.

She gasped because he was so . . . sexy. Then she flushed at the fact that she thought the word *sexy*, and then she was mortified that she thought Cameron was sexy. Not handsome, but sexy, and not in a suit but in a casual, everyday outfit.

Truth was, while there hadn't been any more handholding since arriving in New Orleans, she wondered if there might be more in their future.

As in, hopefully all the time.

"What's that look for?" Cameron asked.

Margo snapped to, and she cut her gaze back to Roberta, who eyed her through narrow lids. "Nothing. I was just thinking of . . . Anyway, let's see the video. Our fans are waiting."

Cameron set the laptop on the patio table. He scrolled and tapped to open the editing program. "Ready?"

"More than," Margo said, setting her focus on the screen, to rev up her anticipation for what would be their second video here. Since arriving, despite her lackluster enthusiasm, they had been productive. Their first video caught fire, their subscribers multiplying and their accounts' cross promotion causing followers to jump on their video bandwagon. This video, of them on the bus, mixed with shots of the local foods they'd eaten, would no doubt be a hit. It was fifteen minutes of an all-around view of New Orleans, the sweet-spot time frame for a short attention span.

But as she watched, the only person she thought of was her daughter, whose attention she had not been able to grab at all. Of all the people in the world whom she would have loved to have seen this video, it should have been Diana, not a bunch of strangers. And now, more than ever, she felt less accessible, in the Philippines.

Where Margo should be.

No. No, that was wrong thinking. *This* was where Margo was supposed to be, exactly where her mother instructed her to be—discovering new places and new ways of understanding who she was.

"So, what do you think?" Roberta asked, in anticipation. "Good, right?"

"Not just good. It's great. It's better than great. Great work, team." Margo took a bite out of her beignet and shut her eyes to savor the sugar rush. She was in New Orleans, eating a beignet, damn it. Who would want anything different? With a full mouth, she said, "Let's post it."

Their flight to Los Angeles was that afternoon at two, which put the threesome at the airport at a little before noon. Bone-weary from all the walking they'd done the past couple of days, Margo pulled her hard-shell suitcase with one hand and held a to-go cup of tea in the other as she headed to the check-in line. As much as she was on social media, there were still habits that she clung on to: banking in person, snail mail, and checking into a flight in person.

"Over here, North American Airlines," Margo called behind

her. Roberta and Cameron were picking up the rear, though Roberta had her phone to her ear.

"Margo."

Margo turned, now behind the last person in line at the counter. Roberta gestured for her. Margo scrunched an eyebrow and shook her head. Another family had gotten in line behind her, and she didn't want to lose her spot.

Roberta gestured again with her hand. "Come here," she whispered.

Margo heaved a sigh. She wasn't a stickler for things, but the last thing she wanted to do was rush through security. But she left the line anyway.

"What's wrong?" Margo asked.

Cameron spoke this time. "Nothing. Except that this is the wrong flight."

"Um. No, it's not," she said matter-of-factly, then scoured her brain again. Was she wrong? She pulled the information from her memory. "North American flight 1241 to LA, right?"

"It *is* right, for us, but not for you."

"But we're on the same flight."

"No, we're not. Or, we won't be, soon." Roberta's eyes flashed with mischievousness. "Cameron and I will be going on this flight, but you're going on Pacific Airlines, to the Philippines."

"What . . . are you talking about?"

Her friend rolled her eyes. "I mean, I called the airlines and there's a flight to the Philippines with stops in San Francisco and Taiwan that leaves in a couple of hours. There's a seat available on that flight. And I think you should go."

Margo shook her head. "That's nuts!"

"Not nuts. It makes perfect sense. You're not in this," Roberta said.

At her friend's implication, Margo's shoulders slumped. Roberta was right. "I'm . . . sorry—"

Roberta threw her arms around Margo. "We don't need your apologies, Margo. We would feel the same way. But we also know you won't go unless there's no other choice. You're scared. So we're telling you that you have to go. You don't need to worry about us. We have each other. You have your passport and your credit card, and you know what hotel she's staying in. There's nothing stopping you."

"This feels . . ." *Wrong? Sudden? Exciting?* Margo couldn't put a finger on it, because she was utterly speechless.

"Like exactly what you should be doing. C'mon," Cameron said, then grabbed Margo's suitcase and rolled away from the North American Airlines line, toward Pacific Airline's ticket counter. Roberta hung back.

After getting in line, Cameron said, with a low voice, "You can do this."

"But our trip."

"We . . . I . . . will be here when you return. We'll work it out, okay? You can meet us at whatever location we're stomping through. Until then, we'll keep going with our TALWAC plans. Maybe you can even do your own photos and videos."

"I don't know. I don't know if I can do this. It's so far away. The expense. It will be too much of a surprise." She bit the inside of her cheek to try to push down this nagging indescribable feeling. "What if . . ."

"What if what?"

She spit out the first thing she thought of, trusting her lips and vocal cords and brain. "What if they don't want me . . . again."

He laid a hand on each of her shoulders as he'd done a million times before, and it grounded her. "I don't have any wise words for this, Margo. I can't even imagine. But I know that your daughter wants you there, and I know you want to be by her side. So I say, fuck them."

A laugh burst out of Margo, breaking the tension that had pulled her taut the last few days. She nodded, and then, strengthened by his conviction, echoed, "Fuck them."

Cameron's smile grew to the size of New Orleans.

The line in front of Margo jumped forward, and she and Cameron were swept along like a wave.

"Next customer, please," said an airline attendant. They moved another foot in line.

"Ready, Margo?" he asked.

"I guess?" She darted her gaze from the attendant to Cameron, and with it came a surge of bravado. Roberta was right. He was right. She inhaled deeply. "I am. I'm ready. Thank you, Cam. And please, tell Roberta . . ."

"Bert will be fine. It's me who you should feel sorry for. She's going to be a bear to live with." His lips quirked, and as if realizing that he still had her bag in hand, he passed the handle to her. "I'll . . . I'll miss you."

"I'll miss you, too." It dawned on her then that she spoke to or visited with Cameron almost every day, individually and with Roberta. This would be the farthest they'd been apart, and for a moment she was forlorn.

"Next," the attendant said.

They were now at the front of the line. Cameron shifted, awkward now, and Margo wasn't sure how to say goodbye. This seemed to warrant more than a wave, so she leaned in, and so did he. She lifted her head to kiss him on the cheek, which wasn't uncommon. But he tilted his face forward.

And her lips collided with his.

Or was it the other way around?

But she didn't care. The touch of his lips muted everything else around her. The grumble of the other passengers, the audible sigh of the airline attendant—it all became white noise. There was just her and this man she had known all her life and this kiss that she now realized should have happened long ago.

"Wow." Cameron's cheeks pinked after she finally stepped back, though it had been hard to.

"Yeah," she could only say.

Now *that* was something they had never done.

Someone behind her cleared their throat, which brought her back to the present. And with a final nod, she rolled her suitcase to the counter and faced the terminal agent.

"How can I help you?" he asked.

"I'd like to buy one ticket to Manila, Philippines, please."

Chapter Fourteen

*D*iana was running. Her footsteps echoed on the asphalt; her breaths kept half-time with her heartbeat. The sky was onyx though her path was brightly lit by cars and jeepneys—open-mode transportation with two bench seats facing each other, decorated in bling and lights and painted in graffiti—packed in fours across two lanes, with passengers all staring at her.

Her skin burned from their gazes. She could tell that they knew that she didn't belong here, in Manila, in the Philippines.

Then her surroundings changed like the fall of a curtain at a play, and she was running through the halls of Alexandria Specialty. Looking down, clogs had replaced her running shoes. She was all alone here, and she passed the closed doors of patient rooms with mothers in labor, all pushing at the same time. The one room she had to get into—she could see it right in front of her—fell farther and farther away despite the length of her stride. She didn't know what was behind that door but only that the answer was there. The truth. But the muscles in her legs began to burn; a cramp radiated up her thighs. The panic escalated in her chest as she reached out for the doorknob; it was so close.

Until it wasn't, because she was no longer in the hallway but outside, on the Mount Vernon Trail. Cement at her feet. Above her, a plane descended, on its way to Reagan airport, the sound of its engine roaring through her ears. It was close, even too close for Gravelly Point.

As the plane passed, wind whipped through her hair. She shivered at the sudden cold. She looked down at herself; there wasn't a stitch of clothing on her. She was naked, with her glorious farmer's tan. The scar from a tumble when she was six years old, her uneven breasts, the sag of nearly forty-year-old skin— despite not having children and pounding the pavement four times a week.

Time stopped. Everything halted: the plane midair; the biker who just passed her; the child midskip, holding a balloon. Time stopped for everyone except her, and her body continued to change, skin sagging so that her breasts dragged with gravity. She lifted her fingers; they were wrinkled like her mother's. She touched her face, leathered and folded in places. The underside of her chin was another chin. Then the point of view shifted again, and she was out of herself, looking through a fish lens. Still, she recognized the image. Herself, except elderly, back in her home, sitting in a robe but with no one in sight but the dog at her feet.

Diana jerked upward but was dragged back, constrained by something. Her eyes flew open, and all at once her hearing turned up to high, and she was bombarded with voices and an incessant bell. She blinked to orient herself. Against her neck was a white, fluffy terry-cloth towel. The voices were from a movie playing on the television. And the ringing bell was her phone alarm.

Diana thumbed at her phone to turn off the alarm and swallowed a golf ball–sized lump in her throat. Sitting up, reality returned to her. She was in Las Cruces Hotel. She had taken a shower after settling into her room and ordered room service. Her overfull belly and jet lag had kept her up the whole night, until finally she shut her eyes at 6:00 a.m., as the sun came up. She now squinted at the time on her phone, eyelids still heavy.

Eight p.m.

She had slept a full day away.

She stood then, launched by the volition to do something. Relaxation was not in her vocabulary, and a part of her felt guilty about what she had missed. It was a vicious cycle, sleeping after an exhausting day and then wondering what more she could have accomplished had she stayed up a little longer.

She caught sight of her face as she passed the dresser mirror and jumped back at her wild hair and the dark bags under her eyes. One would've thought that taking on-call and night shifts would have had her acclimated to the constant switch from day to night, but with all the decisions she'd had to make—as if everything had all amounted to this one trip—she felt as if she had been hit by a Mack truck. Damn stress dreams. She'd had them growing up, right before each school year started, around college finals or boards. They'd all been some form of her running, of everyone looking at her, of finding herself naked.

She was supposed to be an expert at managing stress and change. Her job was all about going with someone else's flow. By God, it wasn't like women gave birth exactly when Diana predicted. Precipitous births were actually her favorite events, when all she had to do was truly usher along what nature had taken control of.

And yet . . .

Diana's phone buzzed in her hand.

It was Carlo. Actually, she'd removed his picture from her contacts and renamed him "The Asshole" after they broke up, and seeing it now made her laugh. She was delirious, obviously. She declined the call, then opened her text box.

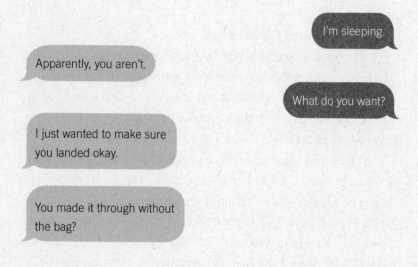

I'm sleeping.

Apparently, you aren't.

What do you want?

I just wanted to make sure you landed okay.

You made it through without the bag?

Diana pressed her lips together. The first flight they'd taken together, she'd thrown up at takeoff. Of course he'd brought it up, to remind her that they *had* something.

I took Dramamine.

I saw that you called.

I can explain. The person who answered was just a friend.

She thumbed the screen with more force, admonishing her past self for calling him before takeoff.

I don't need an explanation.

Night.

But Flossy misses you.

The next text was a snap of Flossy snuggled up against his chest. He carried her like a baby, belly up, and her sweet face lolled to the side, tongue hanging out.

Damn it. The guy knew how to get her, knew just how to keep her on the line.

How is she doing?

Truth? Awful. She's had two accidents in the house. It's like she knows you're gone.

I'm not gone.

> You know what I mean.
> I miss you.

> I'm here for you.

> No, you're not.

But she didn't send it. Instead, she deleted that last message, one letter at a time. What was she doing, entertaining the thought of him? Why did she continue to give him the benefit of the doubt, when his only saving grace was that they'd had a few good years?

The tension had built up in her legs. They wanted to go; her muscles craved lactic acid. She peeked out the window. Below was the Manila Bay coastline. With its slow-moving and constant traffic, though with fewer pedestrians at this hour on the baywalk, it would've been the perfect time to run. But running in an unfamiliar city might not be the best decision.

On the bedside table was the list of the hotel's amenities. She flipped to the back and saw that the fitness room was open, so that was an option. With a quick scan down to Tipanan, her tummy growled. Food and a nightcap sounded like the better plan. But as she opened the door, a man in a suit passed, reminding her that she was in sweats and a T-shirt, which was probably not appropriate for this fancy hotel. She weighed how important getting out of this room was against her opposition to changing clothes.

Her tummy growled again, sealing her decision.

Diana pulled a sundress from her suitcase and shook it out. She gathered her hair in a bun and changed out of her pajamas but didn't bother with makeup. She stuffed the phone in her dress pocket along with her coin purse and walked out of her room.

Tipanan was packed with a mix of wedding attendees and hotel guests. Diana relaxed; she and her outfit fit right in with the raucous mixing bowl of people and noise. And to her relief, she found an empty seat at the bar.

She signaled the bartender. "Can I have a food menu and a pinot grigio, please?" As she waited, she willed herself to relax, focused her gaze on an older couple by the window who were having a private conversation. They appeared to be in their sixties, both with gray hair and an air of calm around them. Each held a drink in their hand, but they didn't take their eyes off each other, not even when they sipped their drinks. They were a couple with an obvious connection, a couple with a history.

Her heart squeezed, but for what, she couldn't put a finger on. For a nuclear family she had lost long ago? The chance at her own version of a family? Was it silly to yearn for something she knew, after almost four decades of life, might not be for her? Her granny hadn't married out of choice, nor did her mother remarry after her father passed. Diana knew in her bones that there were no promises in life, no guarantees, and no set plans for anyone.

"Get a room already, right?" a man grumbled to her right, a barstool between them.

She spied his profile just as her wine and a menu were placed in front of her. He was unshaven, though his dark hair was close-cropped. He lifted the beer to his lips for a protracted pull, and when he placed the bottle down and pursed his lips, his cheeks caved into dimples.

Diana sipped her drink, relished its pop of flavor, and the bit of attention she'd just received. She hadn't been with a man for at least six months; she was probably a little lonely. But she was on vacation, right? She could be whomever she wanted. "Oh, I don't know. I think they're really sweet."

"*Pfft.*" His head jerked to accentuate the point. "Until one of them finds out that the other was sleeping with their best friend. Yeah, right." His eyes darted toward her. "Theoretically, of course."

"Ah." She now recognized that slouch he was sporting as well as the cynicism in his voice. She grinned at him, not out of pity but out of understanding. "Or, maybe, one of them sleeps with another doctor during their nights on call. In the call room. Over the course of a year. Theoretically." Goodness, she hadn't even had half her drink and she was spilling her business. The jet lag must've have been worse than she thought.

He turned to her then, solidarity in his eyes. He was lean, with broad shoulders and a square jaw, which he clenched before he said, "And the one leaves the other to take care of her children while they explore this midlife crisis."

"And they call back after a while and say, 'I actually think it's you I want and not that other woman.'"

"And the other says, 'I would rather live alone than live a lie.'" His voice was redemptive, eyes flashing.

"And then they find themselves having a drink all by themselves because . . ."

"Because they can and why not?" He raised his beer to her.

Why not? she mused, and raised her glass in response.

They both sipped, then set their glasses down on the bar simultaneously. He glanced askance at her. "You're a visitor. From the States?"

"Yes, and you?"

"Spent many years in the States, but this is home now. What brings you to Manila?"

"Just a vacation." She left it at that. There wasn't the need to say any more, though her instinct was telling her otherwise. "Are you here for the wedding?"

"You could say that."

So he was being private, too, which was fine enough. "I'm . . ." she faltered. "Ana."

"Nice to meet you, Ana. I'm Crew." He offered his hand, which she took, noting his firm handshake. "May I?" He gestured to the open barstool next to her.

"Please." She nodded, and he slid next to her and sat face out, while she faced the bar. This close, she could smell the slight scent of his cologne, of pine and citrus. From his white shirt, rolled up to his elbows, peeked a tattoo, its green hues muted against his dark brown skin.

"So why aren't you with the rest of the party?" She glanced up as a group began to take shots.

"I'm a little distracted thinking of work."

"Hence the look."

An eyebrow shot up. "The look?"

"The frown. Like you've just been lowballed in a deal."

He grinned this beautiful crooked grin, and Diana had to check herself and glance at the drink in front of her. No, she hadn't downed the whole thing, but her body was heating up like she had.

"You hit it right on the head," he said, bringing her back to earth. "In fact, maybe you can help me with this dilemma."

She turned toward him then. There was a charge between them, but she met his eyes and kept contact even as she took another sip of her drink. She swallowed the liquid courage. "I've got you."

He smiled. "Let's say you've been placed in charge of a big project. A project very important, not just to you, but to the whole team. And something unexpected happens." He accentuated his words with his hands.

"Unexpected like . . ."

"An external force appears, out of the blue."

"Is the force people or a thing?" This was reminding her of grand rounds as a med student. It was kind of fun.

"People."

"Okay . . ."

"Do you fight that external force, because it's obviously nefarious? This party wants something undeserved. Or should you agree with what the rest of the . . . the team, wants to do?"

"And that is . . ."

"To allow them a piece of the pie. Hell, a free-for-all."

Diana tried to piece the information together—she was great at puzzles—but her foggy brain failed her. "Crew, it might be that my wine has gone to my head, but I have no idea what you're talking about."

He laughed. "All right all right. Fine. I suppose since we don't know each other and I'll never see you again, I could probably be more specific—"

"This is the kind of suspense that would make me not put a book down, you know?" She grinned against her glass.

He laughed, looking down at his beer for a beat. His gaze softened. "You have a beautiful smile, Ana."

"Oh no," she said, still in the mood to joke, though her cheeks heated at the compliment. "You didn't just go there."

He winced. "Too much?"

"No. I mean, yes, that was cheesy as hell, but thank you."

"How long will you be in Manila?"

"So we can talk more about your work?"

"Maybe? Or I can give you some tips on places to visit." He leaned in closer, and Diana spotted a tiny mole just above the Cupid's bow of his lips. "Because let me guess. You're probably going to visit a couple of historic places and then jet on to an all-inclusive resort with an unencumbered view of the water and mountains to watch the sunset. And I'm here to tell you that while that's all wonderful, there's way more to see."

She dragged her eyes away from his oh-so-sincere face. This was minor flirtation, but she was so out of practice, already out of her league. "Well, the offer sounds tempting, but—"

"Let me guess. Despite the theoreticals, there's someone else."

"You're . . . you're not wrong," she said, half laughing. "But it's not what you think. First, I am actually really good at putting a travel plan together. I have spreadsheets. And second: it's complicated."

"The *c* word. Well how about this, Ana?" He waved the bartender over. "Let's keep it as simple as possible, then. How about we have something to eat and drink, and you can talk to me about your spreadsheets, and I can give you my thoughts on your list."

"Hm." She hesitated. She was in another country, out of her comfort zone. And yet, here she was *in another country,* making a new acquaintance with this hot guy, and she had no other responsibilities that would need her attention till tomorrow. No patient, no boss, no Carlo, and no family drama. "Oh, sure, why not."

New Guinea
August 28, 1944

My dearest Leora,

My love, is it true? Is this really true?

I've just received your letter. My hands are shaking, and I can't stop smiling.

Are you sure?

I'm sorry, of course you're sure. Did you tell your father? Was he upset? What's going to happen now? Are you okay? And when . . . when will our baby be born?

I will write my father immediately, so he can give you my pay. I'm not sure what you will need, but you can use it for whatever you need and want.

Oh, Leora. I'm going to be a father! You're going to be a mother! You have just made me the happiest man in this small country.

You mentioned feeling ill—is that normal? I wish I was there to help you with everything. I want to see you grow, see our baby grow. Damn all these people here, because the only person I should be watching over is you, my dearest Leora.

We must hang on to faith. Take heart that I will see you again, soon. I will see our baby. You have my word. And my word is my soul.

The two of us, Leora. Now the three of us. Can you imagine it?

We are on the move again, sweetheart. But even if time passes, and you might go without hearing from me, I'm with you.

Iniibig kita,
Antonio

Chapter Fifteen

*M*argo padded down the hallway of the twenty-fourth floor of the Las Cruces Hotel, gripping the hotel key in her hand. She yearned for her daughter, for the hotel room, for sleep. She had been traveling for what felt like a week, the thought of Cameron and his kiss the only things to make her smile through the chaos of changing her travel. Margo was only too grateful that the hotel attendant downstairs gave her no problems when she gave her and Diana's name. It was as if they had been expecting her.

Finally, room 2440. She took a deep breath. Diana was sure to be surprised. Margo didn't get a chance to text or email once she got on the plane, and while in the hired car to the hotel, her phone calls went to Diana's voice mail.

Margo knocked.

Then she knocked a little louder.

From inside the room, Margo heard a thump. With an intake of breath, she listened for it again.

Thump.

She blinked away the sleep in her eyes, gathered her wits. The sound *did* come from inside, from Diana's room, right?

Next was a muffle, and another large thump, and Margo let go of her suitcase handle. It *was* coming from the inside, where her daughter was alone, or supposed to be. All the scenarios played out in her head, and she transformed from noncombative to mama bear. And even without a weapon in her hand, she didn't hesitate as she reached to swipe the door key. Her old eyes squinted against the bright room lights then landed on Diana.

In bed.

With a man.

There was a stray arm here. A bare back there. And clothes, oh goodness. Clothes on the floor, sheets everywhere.

"Oh my God!" Margo heard herself gasp.

"Oh my God," Diana yelled. "Mom? Crap! *Mom?*"

Margo slapped her hand over her eyes and padded backward, into the hallway, until she felt her back up against the wall.

Her daughter was in bed with a man. Could they have just been sleeping?

She rolled her eyes at her own naivete. *No, dummy, she wasn't.*

But this was her Diana. Her Diana, who was probably mortified and embarrassed, probably more than Margo was at the moment.

Hand still over her eyes, Margo heard Diana and this man share a few words, and then she detected the shuffle of footsteps. She caught a whiff of cologne that surely wasn't her daughter's fragrance.

Her face lit on fire.

"Mom?" Diana said now.

Margo lowered her hand tentatively and opened her eyes. Diana was at the doorway, wearing pajamas, her hair piled neatly on top of her head. She stepped aside, a gesture for Margo to enter. As Margo passed, Diana said, "I can't . . . I can't believe you're here."

"I know. Me either." She spun around at the entryway; all her thoughts were at the tip of her tongue, and they leaped without encouragement. "I just couldn't let you do this on your own. I was scared. Am scared. But whatever happens here, we're a team, you know?

Diana's face broke out into a smile, the kind that made it all the way up to her eyes. She slinked an arm around Margo's. "I'm sorry I was a little hard on you."

"It's okay. I needed to hear it." She sniffed, tears brimming. This was the most emotion she'd seen from Diana in a long, long time, and she relished their close proximity, this moment. "I was wrong not to come in the first place."

"I just wished . . . you hadn't seen that."

"Diana." She looked at her daughter in the eyes. "You won't get a lecture from me."

Diana started, as if she were a volcano about to explode, then paused. "I won't?"

"Am I scarred for life? Yes. But will I judge you? No. You're a grown woman. I trust you to make your own decisions."

Diana crossed the room and sat on the bed, and Margo followed her in. "I don't normally do that, Ma. But it felt . . . and he was . . . I mean, it's been a while since . . ."

Margo finished Diana's sentences for her. Margo understood, and well. "You felt comfortable and safe with him. A connection, right?"

She nodded. "Like he could read my mind. It's not serious, of course, but tonight, he just made me laugh. Even when you walked in and after, there wasn't any weirdness at all. Is this TMI?"

Margo swallowed. "Look, I've always said that you and I would be honest with each other, that you could tell me everything, and I meant it." Though, without admitting it, the idea of her daughter telling her *everything* sent a flush through her. Just when she thought that she couldn't possibly learn more about motherhood, something like this happened.

"Well, nothing's going to come of it. When we said goodbye, we made no plans to see each other again."

"Okay, but if something else comes up, we're going to have to figure out a plan. Deal? I wouldn't want to barge in on your privacy again."

"You don't have to tell me twice. I think I'm as traumatized as you are."

part four

Dusk

Dusk is the time when men whisper of matters about which they remain silent in the full light of the sun.

—Simon Raven

New Guinea
September 5, 1944

My dearest Leora,

Yesterday, my sergeant gave me a telegram from Sister Agnes from St. Anne's Church. It only had two sentences. Fourteen words that have changed my life.

My father is dead. His heart was weak—I knew that before leaving. And he died in his sleep and was discovered after he didn't show up to work at the restaurant.

My grief is overwhelming, as thick as the brush here, as confusing as the dialect the people speak. All this time, I worried for his safety from other people. From the corrupt who wanted to take advantage of him. I did not think that he would die of natural causes.

I wrote to Onofre separately so that he can check on where my father was buried. I know I cannot risk you and our baby, but can you try to find him, too? Tend to his plot? Though he did not approve of us, he knew you are a good person. He knew that I love you.

I am depleted. My legs are heavy, my eyelids weighed down with stones. I am so sad, and I am mad at myself. Could I have stayed? Should I have? First with my father, and of course with you and our baby. Now that he is gone, I feel like

I've lost the connection to my home. I am fighting aimlessly in this limbo, in between two countries, in between two parts that make up me.

Iniibig kita,
Antonio

Chapter Sixteen

a sliver of light peeked through the blackout curtains, slic-
ing Diana's dark hotel room in half. It extended all the way
across to the bathroom now—Diana had been watching it for the
past forty-five minutes. She barely slept.

How *could* she have slept after her botched escapade with
Crew? She'd almost made a monumental mistake with that man.
Not that he was horrible or gross or overreaching, but because
casual sex wasn't for her. Because of this very reason, her penchant to overthink.

Thank God her mother had intervened.

She slapped her hand over her mouth and let out a little
scream.

Oh. My. God.

She turned her head to the right, to the second king bed in
the room. To the woman lying with her arm slung across her
face. Her mother was here. Her mother had seen. Her mother—
the Goody Two-shoes of her friends, a woman who rarely

cussed, the woman who thought *Dirty Dancing* was too dirty to watch at the age of fifty.

Her alarm rang. She patted her mattress and found her phone, then scanned her most recent notifications: a Bed Bath & Beyond coupon (always a joy to receive), her dinner subscription box asking if she'd consider coming back (what part of *no, thank you* could they not understand?), and a text from Carlo, which she promptly ignored.

Her body relaxed as she came to Sam's text.

> How are things?

> If you can say that I almost had sex with a guy I met at a bar and my mother walked in on us before it happened as good, then it's good.

> Diana.

> Do you need a phone-a-friend?

> Maybe. What are you doing? How's my house?

> Nothing important. And everything's fine. The housemate's over watching a movie.

OH REALLY. LILIANA?

It's nothing. Don't change the subject.

I'm so proud of you right now!

?

You got out of your head! I was against this trip but I change my mind.

You are the worst.

Will there be a second attempt?

No!

Just because Margo saw? She's grown! Don't worry about that.

OMG. I just realized. Margo is there?

Diana bit her lip, took a breath.

Margo is here.

I'm not here for pleasure. I'm here for business.

I mean, doing both might not be so bad.

We'll see. Today is the DNA test.

Egads, GL! Keep me posted okay? And see that guy.

Diana scrolled up to the next text, to number she didn't recognize:

Offer still stands. I'd like to see you while in town. —C

She flushed from the tips of her toes to the top of her head, then admonished herself. Crew had been exciting and new, but nothing more. She only had a few days in the country, which was just enough to sort through the most important thing in her life right now: her family's past.

Even if he was the best kisser, and had magical hands, and said things to her that Carlo hadn't had the imagination to say.

She exhaled a cleansing breath and left the message unanswered, then jumped out of bed. First things first. Three hours until their meeting with Colette, and she would need every second to gather her composure.

Hot Stove Café was located in the northeast corner of Las Cruces Hotel's first floor, marked by heavy, dark wooden double doors, where the hostess greeted them with zeal.

"For two?" She nodded at Diana and her mother, who was a half step behind.

"We're . . . we're meeting some folks here. Colette Macaraeg?"

"Oh, of course. Follow me." She led the way past empty wooden tables with shaded lamps hanging overhead. As Diana wound through the dining room, her stomach came to life and she drooled at the smell of cooking food. More so, her eyes ate up the view of the baywalk through the back windows.

"Wow, I love that," she said aloud.

"There's more to see in here," Colette's singsong voice answered as Diana and her mother were led into a private dining room. Colette stood beside the round table that was set with colorful, cheerful tableware, mouth open in shock. "Oh my God. Are you . . . ?"

Behind Diana, her mother answered, "Margaret Gallagher-Cary."

"Tita Margo. It's nice to meet you, finally. What a wonderful surprise, and what a gorgeous skirt. The chevron pattern is stunning." She took Margo's hand and placed it up to her forehead. A sign of respect to elders, called the *mano,* the gesture took Diana aback. It felt so intimate.

"It's nice to meet you, too," Margo said.

As if remembering, Colette turned to the man next to her. "Both of you, this is my husband, Philip."

"A pleasure," he said, shaking both their hands. "Ate Diana, I'm sorry I didn't get to meet you when you first arrived, I was out of town."

"*Always* out of town." Colette breathed out. "Which should be interesting when the baby comes."

"I'm an attorney," he added, then wrapped an arm around Colette's shoulders, squeezing. "And I promise I'll be home more, *mahal*."

"Fine. Okay."

Diana warmed at the couple's back-and-forth, then stepped aside as a member of the waitstaff excused herself and created another setting on the table.

"Here, sit to the left and right of me, Ate and Tita." Colette pulled out the chairs for them and signaled the hostess to bring them water. "Are you settled in, Tita? And did you rest well, Ate Diana?"

Margo gave Diana a conspiratorial look. "I think it's safe to say that after the initial surprise of my arrival, we slept well."

Diana's face burned up like a furnace. "Yes, exactly."

"That's wonderful. Wow, this is such a gift, to have the both of you here. Soon, Johnny Pascual, who's administering the DNA test, will join us. And my brother seems to be running late. I'm sorry." Her smile was sheepish. "He has an ex-fiancée, and her children have become like my brother's children, since they were together forever. But she has a habit of taking advantage of it. She took off on some trip, and, well, it's tricky." She lowered her voice. "He loves the girls, but the lines are blurred sometimes. Or actually, erased altogether."

"No need to say more," Diana said, well versed in a myriad of family dynamics. Her longtime conclusion had been that all families were dysfunctional.

"So there are children? So I am like a grandmother figure?" Margo's hand fluttered to her chest.

"Oh my goodness, yes. I didn't even think . . . yes. You'll be addressed as Lola, is that all right? Or however you prefer."

"No, no, Lola will be fine." Her mother's eyes misted, and

Diana had to look away. She understood that Margo's reaction was due to the idea that she was a grandmother in general, but Diana couldn't help but feel a little disappointed she wasn't the one who'd made her mother's eyes water like that.

"I'm sorry, but I think I need a moment. Is the bathroom—" Margo said.

Colette sat up in her seat. "Are you okay?"

"Yes, yes. Just a little makeup running, and I don't want to be a mess when the children are here. Just point me toward it."

"It's straight ahead."

"Thank you." Margo turned to leave just as a server came in with a tray of sparkling water bottles and orange juice.

"She'll be fine," Diana reassured Colette, though she worried, too. "The last day has been a doozy for her." *For more reasons than this.* But she gestured to the meticulously decorated table. "This, however, is amazing. Thank you."

"It's no problem. You both are family, like I said." She frowned. "What's wrong? You look upset."

Diana shook her head. They both had been so open online, and Colette was gracious and hospitable. *Relax.* "No, it's just—all of this is . . . surreal."

Colette sighed. "I feel the same way. But there's nothing to do but embrace, it, right? This is a blessing. Frankly, I always wondered if Lolo had family elsewhere. He was in the States until he was in his twenties." Her face became solemn. "Honestly, though, it's still a shock. After you contacted me, I spoke to my lola and confirmed that my lolo enlisted from California, from Marysville. But I . . ." She looked away.

"What is it?"

"Here's the thing: my lola? She's old and secretive and sometimes mean, but she wasn't always that way. Time did that to her.

She doesn't like to talk about the past at all. She's pretty tight-lipped."

Diana took a breath. "Okay."

"And, I wanted to tell you that . . ." Colette halted when the double doors reopened and a staff of three carried in dishes and placed them on the lazy Susan. Behind them followed two little girls in matching flowered summer dresses. They ran around the table and threw their arms around Colette, who peppered them with kisses. Margo walked in shortly afterward, a wide smile on her face, and took her chair to wait for introductions.

"Where's Tito Joshua?" Colette asked the older child.

"I'm here." A man's voice followed just beyond the doors. "Johnny's outside on his phone. *Mukhang serioso*. Must be about business. Anyway, he apologized and said we should get started with the meal because he'll be a while. Girls, what did I say about running indoors?"

Diana had the cold bottled water to her lips, and glancing up just as Colette's brother walked in, she sputtered.

Because this gorgeous man, now fresh-shaven and in slim-cut slacks and an oxford shirt was Crew, from last night.

"Joshua, this is Diana Gallagher-Cary. Our cousin," Colette said.

Cousins.

The word pushed Diana into a full-on coughing fit.

"Oh my goodness, are you okay?" Colette patted her on the back.

"Yeah, um. You." Diana's voice cracked and she stood. Did she . . . had she . . . "You said your name was Crew."

He halted at the door when they locked eyes, and like a hic-cup, he started up again. "I . . . because my friends call me Crew. For Cruz." His eyes darted around the room to Philip, then to

Margo, then Diana, finally halting at Colette. In a way Diana had experienced only with good nurses in the delivery room, a message leaped between them. But Diana didn't understand what he was trying to say. Because she didn't know him.

If she had, she wouldn't have gotten into bed with him.

"Wait. You said your name was Ana," Crew—no, Joshua—said with a raised eyebrow.

"Um . . . Ana for Diana?" Diana croaked. "You said you were part of the wedding party."

"I was, am, I mean! I manage the hotel."

"Joshua. Josh!" Colette yelled. "No, you didn't! Of all people, Josh."

"We didn't," Diana and Joshua said at the same time.

Margo giggled. "Oh. Oh my."

"Oh my God, Mom. This is so embarrassing." This was too much. This was oversharing. This was crossing the line. She didn't need to know this.

"Wait, wait. Stop!" Joshua said above the flurry of voices, and the room went silent. "Diana, I *am* her brother, but we are not blood related. Which means you and I aren't related." His body seemed to deflate. "Girls, why don't you go get a toy from Ate Carolina. Remember? At the front podium?"

The girls ran out at the word *toy*, and Joshua closed the doors behind them. He gestured for Diana and her mother to sit. Joshua took the seat across from Diana.

"I am adopted. My mother was Colette's nanny, and her mother took me in as a child. I've never known my life without Colette and her family."

"Our family, Joshua."

"Yes, well, but in this case, there is a definite line, and Diana and I did not cross it. In more ways than one. Anyway. This has got to be the most awkward situation I have been in, and God knows I've been in too many to count." He turned to Margo. "I am sorry about early this morning."

"It's okay," her mother said.

"Let's not talk about it anymore, else you will put me into labor," Colette interrupted, a hand on her belly.

Diana didn't even have the mind to ask if the woman was serious, because amid the shock of finding out the man she'd nearly slept with was an almost-cousin, she remembered a line in their conversation:

Do you fight that external force, because it's obviously nefarious?

Joshua thought Diana and her mother were out for the family's money.

As more food was brought into the dining room, Diana pushed the awkwardness and her questions aside in favor of her sudden hunger. The contrasting colors of each dish popped out tantalizingly, and her appetite grew as Colette described each one: *karekare*, or oxtail stew; *sisig*, which was marinated and fried pork; a noodle dish called *pancit*; and fried tilapia. "Simple dishes for this first meal. I hope you're not afraid to try some new things."

"Are you kidding?" Diana spread the napkin on her lap. "You're looking at a walking stomach."

"And I did try my best," Margo piped up, before taking her phone out to snap a pic of the food. "I had a few friends teach me some dishes over the years. I made some mistakes, but I think I got a couple of dishes reasonably right."

Diana reached out to her mom's hand, behind Colette, heart squeezing. She'd taken it for granted how her mother had tried to be everything: mother and father and grandfather. "Yes, you did," she said. "Your *arroz caldo* was the best. It kept me alive through med school."

"You'll have to show us how you do yours, Tita Margo. The restaurant recipes are family based. Maybe we can do a special that's based on your version."

Her mother's upper lip quivered. "Really? That's sweet. But you don't have to say that."

"Let's serve it up," Joshua interrupted, like a crack of the whip. He hadn't said much since they had started their meal. With a child seated on each side, he'd paid attention to their whims, their questions. Now, he perched at the edge of his seat, scooping food onto their plates. It was sweet, especially knowing that these were his ex's children, that his affection for the girls hadn't stopped just because his relationship with their mother did.

Still, Diana thought he was being curt to her. The worst, though, was that she couldn't be upset that he lied because she had, too.

Diana inhaled each dish to smother her barrage of thoughts, mixing the rice and sauces with a spoon and fork. She took cues by watching what Joshua and Colette added to their dishes, like *bagoong*, or shrimp paste, that gave it a burst of saltiness, a perfect contrast to the deep flavor of peanut sauce. Soon, Diana was high from a full belly of carbs, and despite the conversation focusing on Diana's plans, which would now include her mother, she started to zone out. Margo, too, had gone silent, a sure sign she was nearing food-coma status.

While they waited for Johnny, Joshua excused himself from the table to smoke with Philip, and her mother took a walk with the girls in the lobby area. Finally alone, Diana asked Colette, "You didn't finish what you were saying, about Flora?"

Colette bit her lip. Inhaled. "I should just come out and say it . . . Lola Flora doesn't know about you."

The words startled Diana out of her well-fed stupor, her spine becoming ramrod straight. "What do you mean?"

"I didn't tell her. Well, let me back up. I told her that you contacted me, that we were in conversation, but I haven't said anything about you coming. Or that you're here. I thought . . . I thought it would be better to present you, in person, or soon after I announce it."

"This doesn't sound like a good idea at all," Diana said as Joshua's words rang in her head. "Joshua thinks we're trying to infiltrate your family."

"Ignore him." She smiled. "He didn't agree that I should keep it a secret from Lola, although he can't deny how important it is that you're here. It's time to set things right."

Diana sank back into her chair. "God, we might be giving an old lady a heart attack."

"It will be a shock, at first. But I also knew if I waited too long, if I had given my lola or the rest of the family the choice, the idea would have been dead in the water. If the family found out before you came, they would have done everything in their power to keep you away. No one wants a scandal. Anyway, I want to bring you to her tomorrow night. Before everyone else comes over."

"Everyone else?"

"The rest of the family."

At Diana's raised eyebrows, Colette mumbled something beyond her hearing.

"Before the rest of the family comes where?"

Colette heaved a breath. "To her one hundredth birthday party."

"What?" Diana shook her head to clear the carb sleepiness from her brain. "You want us to break this news before her hundredth birthday party?"

"At the party." Colette nodded like she'd just agreed to chocolate for her ice cream rather than dropping the biggest news in her family's generation. "The DNA test will be back in time—Johnny will see to it. Though, with what we've exchanged, the pictures, the letters . . . in my eyes, the DNA test is mainly a formality."

Diana nodded, agreeing. Her instincts didn't doubt that she and Colette were related by blood, though the rest of her emotions had yet to catch up. "But can't we wait until *after* the party is over?"

"With a big extended family full of very opinionated people, it's all about timing. And getting ahead of everyone is probably the best move."

Joshua and Philip returned, each taking a seat. Joshua glanced at the two of them. "You told her?"

"Yes." Colette smiled reassuringly. "Until tomorrow's party, Ate, by the sound of it, you have your days fully planned sightseeing."

"Just a couple of highlights this first trip. Today, to Antonio's grave, which is more for my mom." Diana confirmed, though she was still stuck on Colette's news. Good God, Flora didn't know about them at all? How would she explain this to her mother?

She nodded. "You'll need help and some company. Joshua can assist."

"Oh, I don't know." Diana flushed.

"I insist. Right, Joshua? This place might be intimidating to some people. And he's really got nothing to do."

"Speak for yourself." He scoffed. "I've got a hotel to run, and have you seen her spreadsheets?"

"What spreadsheets?" Colette waved the thought away. "I'm sure the hotel can manage the next few days. And I'll join in when I can." She took a sip of water.

"Philip?"

Philip raised his hands, "Work, buddy. Because I actually have a boss."

"Look, I don't need any help," Diana insisted.

"No! This is no trouble at all." Colette frowned at her brother. "Joshua is just being a bear. Your ex should be picking up the girls soon, and you have the most flexible time out of all of us, Josh. And c'mon." She pointed to her belly.

His smile was tight. "Fine."

"Great!" Colette beamed just as Margo returned with the girls and a man just steps behind her.

"Johnny!" Colette greeted Johnny with arms up, an invitation. Johnny bent down and kissed her on the cheek and shook Philip's hand. "This is Johnny Pascual, my dearest friend. He owns DNA-Corps, a DNA and ancestry lab in Makati. You missed the meal. Are you hungry?"

"No, I'm okay. I'm so sorry I'm late. But I'm ready to get started. I just met Mrs. Gallagher-Cary in the lobby. It's so nice to meet you, Diana. Colette's told me so much about you."

Diana took a deep breath. "It's so nice to meet you, too, though now I suppose it's time. Are you ready for this, Ma?"

Her mother sat down tentatively in her chair. "Ready as I'll ever be."

Chapter Seventeen

*M*argo, in fact, had not been ready. When Johnny swabbed her cheek, she didn't really understand that it might truly connect her to the Cruz family. When those little girls called her Lola, she hadn't taken the title into her heart completely. And even as she witnessed her daughter's interactions with Joshua—admittedly another uncomfortable moment—she had not comprehended that her daughter was truly attracted to him. It was as if Margo was having a lucid dream, alternately solidly in the moment and unsteady, like right now, riding onto Manila Memorial Park.

Margo rolled down the window, letting in the warm air and the scent of grass, as the car passed rows of headstones.

Once places of fear and of sadness, over time she began to see cemeteries as places of gathering and of quiet celebration, even behind tears. Looking out now at flowers being laid on tombs, of a random teddy bear perched on a headstone, and at a gathering of visitors, this place felt more like the continuation of life rather than the end of it.

But to think that all that time, her father had been here. It didn't seem real. Her whole life, she'd accepted her mother's explanations about Antonio Cruz, and they'd been enough for her.

Should Margo have insisted on more, like her daughter had?

"Here it is." Joshua broke the silence and directed the driver to pull over. Diana exited the vehicle first and came around to Margo's side, though Joshua beat her to the car door. He helped her out of the car, thank goodness, for even if Margo hadn't needed the assistance, his firm grip grounded her. "It's a ways down," he said.

I like him, she wanted to say to Diana, to whisper in her ear. *I like him because he can read between the lines.* The car ride had been full of tension because of what Margo could only presume was a misunderstanding between them, and she wanted to ease her daughter's angst. Diana hadn't made a mistake with this man, because he was good.

But right now, Margo wasn't a mother but simply a daughter.

They passed the rows one at a time, and Margo read the names as she walked by, looking at bouquets of small fake flowers. Around one raised cement edifice, a family congregated with flowers and food, in celebration of life. Tiny gifts and expressions of devotion from the living to the dead, to nurture the love they had for that person, to stoke the grief that continued to burn.

How did her mother mourn? Had she found peace and closure? Margo, so young when she first asked about her father, simply chose to accept he had given her mother the best of himself before he left for the war, but not once had she seen Leora grieve for him. Did she leave flowers somewhere special to her? Did she build an altar? Or did Leora simply swallow it all, forget?

"We're turning left down this path," Joshua continued.

The immediate landscape changed around them, and then they were flanked by mausoleums. Some enclosed on all four sides, some without walls. All were made of cement or some kind of stone, structures etched with images of the Santo Niño, Our Lady, or Jesus on the cross. One building was built with a Roman influence, another Chinese. Each prominently displayed a last name.

These were family plots.

Margo gripped Joshua's elbow with greater force upon realizing where they were going. He squeezed back but pushed on, despite her legs fighting against the forward motion. And then she saw it. A bold CRUZ etched on black stone, right above the entrance of a mausoleum.

All her life she had been a Gallagher. It was her mother's last name. She associated it with her mother's hard work, her unwavering resiliency. Margo was raised with pride in the name, and though it wasn't common at the time, she even hyphenated her name when she married her husband, refusing to give up what seemed like her only tie to family.

Now facing the raised tomb, Margo felt him. Antonio. His presence, his spirit, whatever it was. But in this acceptance came a rumble from inside her, like a volcano that had been sleeping for a century.

Finally, Joshua stopped at the foot of the tomb. Margo raised her eyes to the inscription.

Antonio Cruz

CPL

US Army

World War II

August 2, 1918–January 6, 2010

Father, Husband, Friend

Her knees buckled. Margo knew that he had died a decade ago—the date was in the information the private investigator had provided. But Margo hadn't accepted it. The entire concept of having and then losing a father she'd never known seemed unbelievable. Except now, the name on the marble was indelible proof, the dates undeniable.

There was a stark difference between reading a fact and then actually witnessing proof.

And here was hers.

The man buried in this tomb was her father, Antonio Cruz. And she could have visited him, could have seen him, could have gotten to know him. Had she realized he was still alive, had she sought the truth, she could have met him. Could have heard his stories, held his hand, sat on his lap. Could have been comforted by him.

She crushed the wet grass with her knees; the ground dirtied her flowing skirt. The pain of regret threw her body forward, tears bursting forth in an endless waterfall.

A body hovered behind her, then arms slipped around her shoulders. Her sobs wracked her chest, helpless against the sounds of her daughter's soothing voice, the caress on her back.

Any other day, Margo would have been embarrassed by this spectacle. Even in her most impulsive state, she was never this distraught; she had been brought up by a mother who put great emphasis on acting right. Being right, especially because they'd stood out, the two of them, markedly different. Even as a young child, Margo knew what they looked like in the land of nuclear families: Like they were a set of china missing a piece. Margo had felt the brunt of it from other children, from the questioning looks of other mothers. From the inquiries about her skin color, her lack of a father.

This man, when alive, would have made them whole.

And the curiosity that she'd felt transformed to anger.

Silent on the way back to the hotel, Margo noted that Diana and Joshua jumped into a conversation as if they'd been friends for years. While he gregariously spoke like a tour guide, pointing out the different sites as they passed—the SM mall, the famous Manila Hotel where General MacArthur stayed pre-WWII, and Rizal Park—her daughter chatted with such gusto that Margo saw through this charade. Even on her most agreeable days, Diana was a contrarian. About everything.

"You know what, Ma?" her daughter said now, voice pointedly airy. "I think we should cancel the rest of our trip here in Manila. We should just find a nice all-inclusive resort somewhere. What do you think, Joshua?"

"Oh . . . ah, sure. I know of one in Bohol that's quite serene. Luxurious amenities, and the food is incredible. Gorgeous views and pristine waters. I would just need to make a phone call."

Oh yes, they were trying their damnedest to sway the day from morose to cheerful. They tittered and tattered about choices of locations, modes of transportation, and it all blended into the background of noise as the car joined the traffic. But it wasn't going to be that easy. Margo's clothes were dirtied, her makeup smeared by her tears, and her heart was bruised.

She brought her fingers to her head as she sorted through the facts of her life, all the while being jostled as the car weaved, stopped, and started through the long drive back to Las Cruces. Snippets cycled like an old-fashioned movie reel. Hurt though she was, this couldn't be it. Just as the epilogue of a book, even if incomplete, sparked interest in the unwritten next chapters of those characters' lives, there was more to that grave site, and she deserved to understand it all. But first things first. "Shhh. There's too much information to process. Hold on. What time are we seeing Flora tomorrow?"

"Noon," Joshua answered back.

Diana glanced at Joshua. "You should tell her now."

Margo eyed the couple, suspicion rising. "Tell me what?"

"Well, um . . ." Joshua cleared his throat. "It's Lola Flora's one hundredth birthday tomorrow, and you will be meeting her at her party."

The breath left Margo's body, and she leaned back, stunned.

Diana twisted in her seat, and in her eyes was resolve, an idea. "Okay. This is what we're going to do. We don't have to go to the party. The DNA test will come in, and we can just be on our merry way, do some sightseeing on our own. Or . . . or! We can just go home. I can change the tickets so we can be on a flight tomorrow morning."

Confusion crawled up Margo's chest. "Go home? Why would we want to go home?"

"You said so yourself. This is all too much."

"Oh, Diana, if I took that stance, I wouldn't have made it this far. It was always too much, this life. This won't be the stumbling block to take me down."

"Mom."

"For once, dear, listen to me." She waited for her daughter's shock to settle. "I admit that I hadn't prepared myself for that. I didn't believe that any of this was true." She took a breath to keep the tears at bay. And out of respect for Joshua, she kept the rest of her thoughts to herself. Flora Reyes was the woman who wrote the letter to her mother. Because of this woman, Margo had missed out on a lifetime of memories. Because of her, Diana had grown up without a grandfather, and Leora had lived her entire life alone.

When Margo spoke again, her voice was resolute. "Now that we're here, we're going to follow through. We're going to find out about everything. You brought me here for the truth, Diana, and I intend to get it."

New Guinea
October 9, 1944

My dearest Leora,

Where are you? I haven't received a letter from you in two weeks. My worry has reached its peak. I've written Onofre but haven't received word from him, either. Every night I wonder how you are doing and where you are. I imagine your belly growing. And while I lament every second I'm not at your side, I hold on to our memories tightly.

Do you remember when we first met?

I do. My father was working for Manong Imbito at the restaurant, and I was just shy of twenty. Manong's feet were in too much pain, so I needed to deliver a sack of grain to Mrs. Lawley as payment for service. It was a long walk to her shop. A pebble lodged in my shoe. By the time I arrived, my face was caked with dirt and my arms screamed in pain. You were there, though, mending clothing, and you shared a piece of candy with me.

I kept that candy for a long time, sinta. Kept it in my pocket until it became sticky. I held on to it whenever my days were full of struggle. Whenever I wondered why people acted the way they did, why people chose wrong over right.

I kept that candy until the day I saw you walking with a group of friends. Do you remember that day, too? I sprinted across the road to say hello. I know your friends must have teased you, but I could tell you were happy to see me. Soon we found ways to meet, and we read to one another. You shared everything you learned in school. You made my days better. Those days we met at the golden hour, when the sun was just setting and Marysville actually looked beautiful, I forgot all my struggles.

Oh, Leora, write me back. Tell me you are doing well.

I know my letters are starting to sound the same. But this war, the fighting, it feels unimportant when I finally sit down and want to tell you about it. Much of it is grim. Much of it I can't talk about. But all I know is that I look at things differently. Sometimes for the better, other times worse. The only thing that remains true is the sunset, which comes every night without fail.

Soon we will have our marching orders. So much time has passed. Will you wait? Can you wait? Is it fair for you to wait? Even with child, is your life better without me? Have I made it worse?

My heart yearns for you. Why didn't I take advantage of every night we slept in the same town, Leora? Why didn't I do more, give more? At least back then, you were within my grasp. No day was difficult or useless because you were nearby. Now there is this ocean, the creatures under it, the sky above it. And there are days, weeks, months between us. Is it fair to love someone this much, to keep you even when the world has made it impossible? Is it fair that you are doing this alone, that you are facing this struggle all by yourself?

Iniibig kita, Leora Gallagher. I love you, and I'm sorry for leaving. Please write me.

As always,
Antonio

Chapter Eighteen

The next morning, Diana ended up on the treadmill. She had grand ideas of running on the baywalk, getting up early despite the jet lag, to shake off her nervousness for the day's events. But after lacing up, pulling her hair into a ponytail, and heading out the front door of the hotel, she'd crashed into a wall of humidity. The air was thick; the smell of rain hung in the air, except the sun was high and bright. Pedestrians milled about; there would have been too many to weave through, and her racing thoughts took her out of the mood before she stepped onto the sidewalk. She hadn't been ready for it, this extroversion, this effort. So she spun around and navigated herself to the hotel gym instead.

Finally in the air-conditioned gym, she got into her stride. The treadmill faced an exterior window, with a section of busy Roxas Boulevard below her. From high up, the view was colorful. A haphazard line of cars with the occasional bus, dotted with jeepneys, vying for space. Horse-drawn carriages for tourists meandered among them. Beyond the waterline was the outline of barges, and for a moment she imagined they were transport carriers, taking young men to war, idealistic and some-times sad men like her grandfather. She imagined their weeks of being out of touch with family, the necessary acceptance of the unknown. Today's military still did this despite social media to ease the distance. Diana saw some of these soldiers in DC: wearing their uniforms on the metro, sometimes running in their unit shirts on the Mount Vernon Trail. Soldiers hoping to make the right decisions, and wondering if the things they did would matter generations from today.

These emotions were evergreen; Diana, too, felt them. It was why she chose her profession, why she was here in Manila. She wanted to make a difference; she wanted the truth, but it seemed that despite her concerted effort to do the right thing, she had led her mother into a mess.

Diana's legs kept time against the rolling mat underneath her; her pink shoes stamped down the worry of what might face her at Alexandria Specialty when she returned. That maybe—maybe—it hadn't been a good idea to come here after all. Yester-day was traumatic. Watching her mother fall to her knees had been the worst of it. Even now, Diana shut her eyes for a brief moment in a small wish that it hadn't happened at all.

One of her steps came off too short and she stumbled, her eyes flying open. She reached for the emergency cord and the treadmill slowed as she steadied herself, arms out on the hand rails, shaking her head.

Pay attention—you could have gotten hurt.

When her vision refocused on the scene in front of her, she caught the reflection of someone else walking into the gym. Pressing a towel to her forehead, she disembarked.

She turned to face the exit, out of habit, and the guest.

It was Joshua, hair askew, wearing wireless headphones. He

was in a tank and shorts, and to Diana's dismay, looked just as good as he did the other night, naked, in her room. It was ridiculous and silly and immature—it wasn't as if there weren't good-looking men in DC, or like her workplace wasn't staffed with men—but this one was, objectively, handsome. He made her slightly giddy. All at once, snippets of their escapade flipped like a slideshow in her head, and she gripped the towel to remind herself that despite not being related, they were for all intents and purposes, cousins. She might have been impressed with the way he handled himself with her mother yesterday, but it didn't solve this . . . whatever this was . . . between them.

From across the room he raised his hand in acknowledgment, and she did the same. Her heart drummed a faster beat in both excitement and dread.

She couldn't allow this awkwardness to go on the entire time she was in Manila. They would be seeing each other later on today. He would be at every turn of the corner.

It was time to address the elephant in the room.

It was time to talk about their night and move on from it.

He had taken a seat on a workout bench and took off his headphones at her approach. "Hey. How's your mom?"

"Better. Rested as soon as we got back last night. She was quiet, but okay." She relaxed at his question. "I just wanted to chat about—"

He shook his head. "No need. It was a mistake. If I had known, I wouldn't have—"

She was struck by a double-edge sword. She, too, regretted that it happened, but his statement came off like it hadn't meant a thing to him.

She admonished herself. It *didn't* mean a thing. "I wouldn't have, either."

"So how do you like the Grand Suite? Enjoying the free stay?"

She caught the edge in his voice, and thank God she was adept at dealing with the grumpy, the whiny, and the confusing. Sometimes, all at once. Right now, he was trying to egg her on, and for what reason, she didn't fully understand. "I do in fact. Comfy beds, great view."

"Only the best."

She changed the subject. "I wanted to confirm about today. What time should we expect you?"

Grabbing his water bottle from the floor, he squeezed a stream into his mouth, flippantly, making her wait. "Eleven. Is that enough time to get yourself ready?"

"Yeah, I think so." She peered at him. "What's with this tone?"

"What tone?" He turned away, setting his water bottle down and tucking his hand into a black lifting glove. She opened her mouth to answer, but in perfect timing, he ripped the Velcro tab open. She closed her mouth and tried again.

"That—"

Rip.

She steeled herself. "Does this have anything to do with what you told me, the other night? About nefarious intentions?"

"I don't know what you're talking about."

"Because you sure are acting like I kicked your cat."

He frowned at her. "Is that some American phrase?"

"No, it's my phrase. It means that for someone who doesn't know me, and as someone who you almost slept with, you have a pretty sour attitude toward me. For the record, my mother and I don't want anything from your family but the truth." She cackled. "When you left that night, I was disappointed it was cut short, but now I'm counting my lucky stars."

He shrugged, then lifted a weight and rested it on his thighs. A dismissal.

She walked away, waved a hand in his direction. If he wanted to play this game, then she would be all in for it.

By noon, jet lag had hit Diana hard, and when they arrived at the Cruz family home, her headache was excruciating. It was not helped by the anxiety thrumming through her; today would be the day of truth. They would find out the DNA results; they would meet Flora, and hell, even the entire family in a few moments. With her mother by her side, it took all of Diana's concentration to follow the back of Joshua's striped short-sleeve oxford shirt as she stepped carefully over the paved walkway.

The home appeared from the shroud of trees, halting Diana in her tracks. Its beauty overshadowed the grandeur of Las Cruces Hotel.

Easily a multimillion-dollar home in the DC area, the family home was nestled in a thicket of trees in the Forbes neighborhood of Makati. It took about an hour's drive to get them out of Manila this morning, a stop-and-go that turned into a smooth flow, where pedestrian-laden traffic had given way to tree-lined streets and then a winding driveway and gate.

"Wow, what more?" her mother said as she sucked in a breath, mouth agape at the open architecture. She'd dressed in a neutral safari-green sheath dress today, but her jewelry stood out: a white round plastic-bead necklace and a tower of bracelets that jingled when she walked.

"No kidding, right?" Diana couldn't keep the snark out of her voice. The home was a beauty, there wasn't a doubt. It mimicked the *bahay na bato*, or stone-fashioned home, reflecting both Spanish and Chinese influences. Multiple pitched rooflines, tall and slim windows with panes shimmering, so it looked like capiz shells. The foundation was made of stone, but everything above was a regal wood. It was clear that despite its matriarch being a hundred years old, this home had been cared for meticulously.

There was so much . . . grandeur. The Cruz family had flourished like the citrus of the calamansi trees they'd driven past, burgeoning with fruit, when all the while, her own family, on a weak three legs, had its own struggles. Growing up, Diana had wished for this kind of life, where she wouldn't need to stop herself from asking for something extra.

This estate was like the VIP rooms: excessive.

It made her despise Flora Cruz more.

An instinct rose inside her like a wave, to turn around and run the opposite direction, to take her mother back to the United States, where they belonged, despite the lack of blood relatives. This whole thing had been a mistake. They had friends, good ones. They had a community waiting for them. Not these people who they wouldn't have known about had it not been for those letters Leora had kept secret.

"Here's the plan." Diana decided now, before they went through the double doors. She was going to recover this trip. Take away the sadness she'd seen in her mother. Get in, get out, and get Margo to a resort, where she deserved to be pampered. Joshua had already climbed the wooden steps, and the sound of people laughing sprinkled lightly in the air—it was now or never. "We just need to get the truth, and then we're leaving. We don't have to stay."

"I know." Her mother's voice was resolute.

"Joshua?" Diana called out now, and Joshua turned. The faster they got this meeting done with, the better.

His face registered an acknowledgment. "I texted Colette. She'll meet us in front."

Diana looked around for her cousin. "I don't see her."

"I mean, inside front."

An older man wearing blue jeans and a T-shirt opened the double doors. Diana followed Joshua inside to an open-air covered foyer, the floor made of gleaming brownish red rock. A fountain bubbled in the middle, imposing, a natural stopping point for strangers, but beyond it was a walkway to a second set of doors, with a small wooden crucifix nailed above the doorway.

The pitter-patter of footsteps echoed after the door opened, and Colette fluttered out, wearing jeans, a white tank taut across her belly, and a flowing white kimono-style silk jacket. Diana relaxed at her cousin's open-armed welcome. She hadn't realized how much she'd needed a hug, and she felt her body soften from its stiff posture. "Welcome, welcome. Okay, so don't freak out. We have a lot of people inside. A lot more than we expected." Her shiny lips wiggled a half-hearted smile.

"Oh?" Diana glanced at her mother.

"Yes, um. Sometimes my family doesn't like to RSVP. They just show up." She wiggled her fingers with a flourish. "And, well, that's what a hundredth birthday does. It brings everyone around."

"It's because they all want to be in her good graces, a.k.a. money," Joshua muttered on the side.

"*Naku*, stop." Colette rolled her eyes. "It's just the way of it. But they've all started drinking, so the mood is quite good. I'll introduce you and that's that. It's probably better they're all here, so there's no *tsismis*." She glanced at Diana. "Gossip. Better they all hear and see for themselves; that will lessen all the gossip later."

"How about the meeting with Flora?" Diana asked. "That will be solo, and soon, correct?"

"Yes, of course. We'll see her now." Colette nodded, pulling the phone out of her back pocket. "Ah, Johnny just texted."

She paused, then gasped. "It's the results of the test."

Diana held her breath and watched Colette's face switch from fright to joy. Her eyes widened and she giggled.

"Well?" Joshua said.

"Okay, here it goes. 'As requested, the following are the results for the relationship between Colette Cruz Macaraeg, Margaret Gallagher-Cary, and Diana Gallagher-Cary.' There's a whole crapload of numbers I don't understand. Yada yada yada. *Diyós!* Oh, here! 'In conclusion, it can be positively concluded that Margaret Gallagher-Cary is the aunt of Colette Cruz Macaraeg, and Diana Gallagher-Cary and Colette Cruz Macaraeg are first cousins.'"

"Holy shit," Margo said, and reached out to the fountain's sides.

"It's for real," Diana whispered. She had assumed the DNA results would show a connection; she'd even said it aloud to Colette. But now . . . now she was unsteady on her feet. These tests were reliable. Irrefutable.

It changed everything, again. Because now, knowing, for sure, that she was a blood relation to Colette and to some in that hundredth birthday party, she realized that she had every right to be there, too.

What would Leora do?

Would she stay, risk being shunned by the rest of the family as Joshua had treated them? Would she insist that her mother endure potential rejection from her newfound family members? Or would she leave, tonight, and tuck away the knowledge that this family didn't deserve either her or her mother.

Diana looked at her mother, who was a product of risk. Leora had loved someone she wasn't supposed to love. She raised a child all alone. Fear of rejection wasn't in her granny's vocabulary.

Here we go.

"Great. Just great." Joshua ran his hand through his hair, and it pulled the last tether of Diana's impatience. She would not tiptoe around him.

"I think I've about had it with you and your underhanded comments. I've forced myself to be patient, since we're stuck with you."

"Oh, you've been stuck with me?" Incredulity marked itself in his expression.

"Diana," her mother pleaded from behind her.

She lowered her voice but pointed to Joshua. "I'm sorry to sound like a child, but he started it."

He put up both palms and took a step back. "Whatever. You won't hear another peep from me."

"Good." She spun around to Colette, whose belly reminded her that everyone needed to stay calm, damn it. "Shall we see Flora now?"

Colette plastered on a smile that didn't quite make it to her eyes. "Actually? Change of plans. Her caregiver just texted, and Lola's not quite ready. You're meeting the family first. Is that okay?"

"Mom? Are you good?" Diana straightened her posture, bolstered now, and tipped her chin up.

Margo blinked back at her. "I'm okay."

"Then let's get this over with, shall we?"

The house—light-filled with high ceilings with touches of rattan against white walls—crawled with people; the mood was bright and cheerful. Laughter punctuated the guitar music in the background. From somewhere, a person sang. Servers mingled in the space, holding platters of hors d'oeuvre and drinks. Occasionally, a child ran through a crowd.

"This is what you call a small event?" Diana asked Colette, who flagged down a server. Champagne glasses were shoved into her and her mother's hands, and the next second, plates of food.

"Yes, comparatively. My *ninang* wanted it to be at the Ayala Museum, but when we were scheduling the party, the museum was closed for renovation. Having it here at home limited our guest list. But we invited the requisite people, including the secretary of the Department of National Defense, our bishop, and the one and only Pichi Lewis." She pointed at last year's Miss Universe chatting it up with women with stars in their eyes. "It's a mixed bag in here."

"Wow."

"Follow me. Let's find a space to sit." Colette led the way, splitting the crowd, and in her wake, curious faces turned, registering their presence. Diana's cheeks heated at the attention.

They found an empty small table toward the rear of the living room. Grateful, Diana felt magnetized to it and pulled a chair out for her mother before sitting down herself, attempting not to stare at the crowd but failing. Everyone but them looked so comfortable in the home. A couple at the antique piano looked at a painting on the wall behind it. An old-world scene right out of a history book, it showed a refined young woman in a Maria Clara dress with regal butterfly sleeves that stood nearly to her ears, the front of her hair teased into a beehive. A man stood next to her in a barong tagalog with the white undershirt beneath. The frame of the painting was gilded, ostentatious in Diana's opinion.

Diana's brain sparked, and she blinked at the painting. The man's face, though painted, bore a stark resemblance to her mother's, cheekbones high despite his unsmiling face and a widow's peak hairline.

"That's him." The sweep of her mother's voice took Diana from her thoughts.

Before Diana could answer, Colette arrived with two more plates brimming with food. After her, Joshua arrived with two more glasses of champagne as if he'd known that Diana would need it. She accepted the glass, downing half its contents in one sip.

Joshua's eyebrows shot up.

"You don't get to judge me," she said to him, before drinking again. The bubbles tickled her nose, but she refused to make a face.

"Not judging. Though you might want to eat something. The humidity can fool you, but you're probably dehydrated." He pointed to her plate, at the little hills and valleys of colors and textures. "Lola Flora's favorite foods. Do you know what this is?"

"Of course I do." She pointed out the lumpia, but stopped at that, not recognizing anything else. Petty, yes, but it killed her to admit anything to this man that might make her vulnerable, even if it was basic knowledge of Filipino food.

"The one with the egg is *embutido*," he said of what looked like a stuffed meat loaf. "That is *tortang alimasag*—stuffed crab."

"And spaghetti," she added, willing herself into the conversation with him.

"Ah, but not spaghetti as you know it. Filipino-style. Sweeter. And once you go sweet, you will never go back."

She narrowed her eyes at him, wary at his sudden friendliness—he had found another chair and squeezed himself between her and her mother.

God, this was awkward.

"Hey. Eat." Joshua passed her utensils and a napkin, then added at the last minute, under his breath, "Please. You look like you're about to pass out."

So she did, grateful for the instructions, in silence as Colette was approached by a woman in a white sarong, hair pulled back in a tight bun. Her cheeks were pink from rouge, eyes lined in a gray charcoal. Her lips eked out a tepid smile. "Colette, my dear."

"Ninang Vera." Colette kissed her on the cheek. "I'm glad you could come."

"I wouldn't miss it, you know that."

"This is it," Joshua said, under his breath. He busily cut his food with the side of his spoon. "Her godmother. Once Colette tells her, the news will take ten minutes to travel, tops."

"*Sino ito?*" Vera's fingers clutched her bag in front of her. "New visitors? I don't know them."

Colette cleared her throat. "Let me introduce you. Ninang Vera, this is Tita Margo."

Vera's penciled-in eyebrows plummeted, confused.

"Margaret Gallagher-Cary. Daughter of Lolo Antonio. And her daughter, my cousin, Diana. Both from the US."

Colette's voice was the ring of a cowbell, and silence descended around them. Passersby turned. Vera's right hand crawled to her chest while she choked out a greeting, as if her breath had caught in her lungs.

Another woman appeared next to them, wearing jeans and a polo shirt. "Ma'am, Manang Flora is ready to see you."

"Ninang, we have to go. But talk later, okay?" Colette huddled Diana and Margo together. "Let's go," she commanded.

They were a blob, Diana and her mother, shuffling through people and their whisperings. They went through a second set of double doors, down another wide hallway to a smaller living room and dining room with rattan furniture. And then a third set of doors, where the caregiver knocked. Moments later, she opened them, to a bedroom.

Chapter Nineteen

The door yawned open to a cavernous room. It was cozier, old-fashioned compared to the rest of the home, and the sun shone dimly through the windows. The AC wasn't strong here, the room was markedly warmer, though with the breeze from the windows and the sheers blowing gently, Margo could have pretended to be on some tropical island. Which, she realized, she was, except she wasn't at all relaxed. Her blood pressure was probably so high that her cardiologist would have had her own heart attack.

"Sit down here, ma'am." The caregiver, with a gesture, directed them to a seating area, where they found the silent woman, nestled into a chair with a blanket draped across her legs. Margo startled at this, reconfiguring the pictures from the private investigator and her own imaginings with the reality.

She had expected a formidable force, a wicked expression, a woman with hair made of snakes. Even after seeing Flora's painted picture on their wall in the living room, with her fancy dress and hard-as-nails expression, and knowing that the decades would have added wrinkles, posture issues, and a laundry list of aging's realities, Margo still wasn't prepared for this. This Flora was frail. Her bony hand rested on the arm of her chair, a ruby ring tilted under its own weight, a silver rosary entwined in her fingers. Her white hair was so thin, Margo could see the tan of her scalp, and her cheeks caved into her facial bones. Her eyes were deep sockets hidden behind glasses.

Margo had planned to spear her with curse words and accusations, but nothing left her mouth. The woman was a hundred years old today, and despite Margo's initial desire to spew hate, there was a vulnerability in that. There were times now when she'd catch her reflection in a mirror upon passing and do a double take. Inside, one felt evergreen, but the exterior can be such a jerk.

And seeing this woman, alive, when her own mother was dead felt more like a gift rather than a curse.

Against Margo's better judgment, her heart softened a little.

"Come. Don't be afraid." The woman spoke with a surprisingly energetic voice.

"She's not afraid," Diana piped up from behind.

Margo sighed and gave her daughter the look that said she would take care of it. She turned to Flora. "Thank you for seeing us . . . Flora."

She wasn't sure how to address her. Her age seemed to deserve some kind of title, but she couldn't bear to say *Mrs. Cruz*. Margo might have been polite, but she wasn't a fake.

"Please, sit." Flora pointed at the settee in front of her, and Margo obliged. She sank into the plush seating, taking in the expanse of the room, the religious wood carvings and paintings that decorated the space. Details that cost more than what she'd made every year. Everything she'd done to make ends meet:

working as many photography jobs as possible, applying for every discounted and free school food program, powdered milk, canned fruit and vegetables. S'mores over the gas stove, shoes that wore down over Diana's toes.

The fire of anger that had ignited at the cemetery now warmed and bolstered her with the thought that she'd done it all without anyone's help.

So she sat a little taller, raised her chin at this woman.

"Can I touch your face?" Flora asked.

"What?" The words pushed Margo back into her chair. She glanced at her daughter; Diana sported the same look of incredulity.

"I can't see very well, even with my glasses."

"Um, I suppose." She stood and went to the woman and bent at the waist.

Flora leaned in, her eyes canvassing Margo's face. "Colette told me who you are. And she said you even did a DNA test, but I have to know it's true." Her hand grazed Margo's face, gripped her chin, and turned her face to the side. The examination, surprisingly, did not make Margo cower. Instead, she took that moment to examine this woman back.

"Good-luck mole, I see." She pointed to Margo's beauty mark on her cheek. "And you like fake jewelry."

Margo smiled despite herself.

Flora's hands dropped to Margo's, and she held one with surprising grip, then turned it right side up. "You're fair, but you have his lips, his cheekbones. And his hands. You have his hands. But he had calluses. Tough ones that never seemed to heal, even when he stopped working. He always tried to plant things that I knew would never grow in our soil, but he kept trying. He even had seeds flown in."

This was all too much. Seeds flown in? Why wasn't Margo flown in? Why couldn't she have made the trip instead of inconsequential seeds? A single tear answered for her, without her permission, and she hated her moment of weakness.

Flora wiped the tear with her thumb. "Do not cry, *anak*." The old woman made her way to stand, pushing her hand against the armchair, shaking as Colette and the caregiver came to her side. Even Diana stood, probably from medical instinct because the woman looked, as she swayed, as if she were going to faint.

Margo, all the while, watched in a mild daze. Flora called her *anak*. Child.

"Wait, where are we going? What's happening?" Diana asked.

Flora's voice quavered. "We cannot waste any more time than what has already passed. I'm going to greet my guests, we will cut the cake, and then celebrate this new beginning." She raised her eyebrows when no one around her moved. "What are you waiting for? Let's go."

The group startled into action. A wheelchair was produced at their side. And as Flora tutted instructions to the caregiver and her granddaughter, Margo stepped into the background with her daughter, who downed the rest of her champagne.

Margo didn't drink—it didn't agree with her stomach—but for the first time in a very long time, she was tempted. Her emotions were in knots. She had had every intention of telling this woman off, and now she was about to follow her into the party and then what?

Cameron came to mind then, his words, the conviction in his expression at the airport. His kiss, a reminder that she was who she was despite all this, despite what would happen in the next room.

"Fuck them," she whispered.

"Ma, did you cuss?" Diana slurred. Her daughter clearly had already had too much. Her fourth glass of champagne was in her hand. Diana always walked with a kind of a poise; she ran with a purpose. She had to-do lists that were actually completed and checked-off, but right now, her limbs were like a baby giraffe's, too limber and loose. Not a good sign.

"Do you think all those people know by now?" Diana asked too loudly when they entered the main party room. "They shouldn't be staring at us. We should be staring at them. That's right, bitches, look. We belong here."

Joshua stifled a snort.

Oh, to clamp a hand over her daughter's mouth.

They made their way to the cake. Margo attempted to slip away from center stage. This was Flora's moment, despite the unfolding family drama. The band was ready for its cue, and the servers lit the candles. But Flora reached out to Margo's forearm and tugged her back into place. "Stay here."

Out of respect for Flora, and because the phones had come out of pockets and purses, she stayed. Margo understood the power of social media. It had only taken a few pictures on her Instagram account before one went viral.

Behind her, Diana hiccupped. "Are there really a hundred candles on that cake? I wonder where the closest smoke detector is?" She craned her neck upward. "Oh good, there it is."

A server handed a microphone to Colette, who set it below her grandmother's lips.

Flora's shaking voice echoed into the silent room. "Thank you for coming today. Even if I don't feel well enough to see all of you personally, I am so happy that you are here to celebrate with me. Today, I am one hundred years old. That is a lot of years. I have forgotten many details, but the big things stay with me. You all have changed before my eyes. The country has changed. I have changed, too."

"You've become more and more beautiful!" someone yelled from the crowd.

"Ah, Junn, you are too kind." Flora laughed and took a breath. "I'd better hurry up before I have to sit." Laughter permeated the crowd. Her caregiver made to get Flora's wheelchair, but she waved her away and continued. "When you get to be my age, you don't wish for material things, because none of that matters. We are but skin and bones. Fragile outsides that cover up what matters inside. Yes, even you, Manolo—you won't live forever." She eyed a man mid-pull at his beer, who stilled at being called out. Someone cackled.

"So I won't be making a birthday wish today, because my wish has come true. My wish was for the Cruz family to come together again, as you all have done every year for me, but it was always missing something, someone. But she has found us, and now I want to invite my daughter Margaret and my granddaughter Diana to cut the cake. With me."

A hush of words rippled through the crowd. From elsewhere someone gasped. Colette burst out into happy sobs.

"Margo, Diana," instructed Flora.

Margo followed, caught in the flow of the moment. The band strummed the birthday song.

"Just to be clear, it was me who suggested the PI," Diana cheered to no one in particular as she joined her hands on the cake knife. Together they lifted the knife. It sliced through the cake with ease, but as she caught the interested stares of the guests, Margo was aware that despite this joyful moment, their happily-ever-after was still to be determined.

The day-to-afternoon transformation of Flora's home was drastic. After the hours-long party, the big room was now devoid of people, and its comfortable plush furniture and greenery and various jugs and antique pieces were back in their right places.

Margo was still on edge. She'd survived the pointed looks and circling questions of Flora's guests. She'd even found a way to keep her daughter from saying something scathing, though she mostly had Joshua to thank for that.

"I trust you had a good time today?" Flora asked. They were in her private dining room, sitting at a mahogany table inlaid with gold leaf. The chair backs were carved into a flower design Margo couldn't help but finger as she sat down.

"It was wonderful."

"It's only wonderful with a good nap slipped in." Flora's face squeezed into a grin. "Escaping in the middle is the secret. Sometimes you just need a break." She eyed the bowl of rolls on the table. "Can you hand me one of those, Margo? My doctor wants me to give up bread, but I still refuse to give up my *pan de sal*. One a day is worth it." As Margo placed a roll on her plate, Flora's eyes flicked up to Joshua, then to his girls, dropped off by his ex earlier in the day, still in their party dresses.

"YOLO, Lola. You only live once," Joshua announced.

"YOLO," Flora enunciated. "*Halika dito,* children. Come." She turned to the children as they got in line to mano, bringing her hand to their foreheads. "Don't forget to greet Lola Margo, too."

Margo steeled her insides to keep her emotions from flowing out. She would never tire of this. She loved being a mother, and she could see herself spoiling these little ones rotten.

"Okay, everyone go to the living room and play," Joshua said.

"And if you're good, Lola will give you a snack," Flora added.

"Lola, it's too late for *merienda*." Joshua frowned. "They'll never sleep."

"Did someone say merienda?" Philip walked in with small paper sacks and held them up. Colette followed him, still with a bounce in her step despite being on her feet all day.

"I smell sugar," Diana said, as if suddenly awake in her chair. She'd had a nap sometime during the party, and her hair was slightly unkempt.

"*Banana cue*. Fried sugared plantains." Colette set sacks down in front of Margo, Diana, and Flora. "A snack, but since this is a special day, served before our meal."

"Perfect, because I have the munchies," Diana said.

Joshua took the seat next to Margo and sighed. "Nonstop spoiling. Whenever we come here it's like taking the kids to Disney—it's the happiest place on earth."

"It's different when you can send them back to Mom or Dad," Margo said, taking out the banana cue by the stick, though she hesitated in eating it. Bananas and sugar might not do well with her blood sugar. She'd already had a piece of cake, and pancit, and little precious steamed rice cakes called *kutsinta*.

"YOLO," Flora said, placing the tip of the banana cue into her mouth. She moaned.

Margo smiled and followed suit, taking a small bite. The dessert was heavenly; the banana was a perfect complement to the sugar, and she couldn't resist taking another bite. But when she looked up at her daughter, she found Diana slack-jawed, eyes darting back from Flora to Margo and back in disapproval.

Setting the banana down, Margo sipped some water and let

the treat wash down her throat. She eyed her daughter a message, to ask her what was wrong, and Diana responded with a look that she could not decipher, complete with hand gestures that made her look like she was cheating at Pictionary.

"Esme," Joshua's voice rose above the increasing squabble in the living room area, interrupting Margo's thoughts. "Share your toys, okay?"

"I don't want to." The older child's shoulders slumped a little.

"Hey." He gestured for Esme to come to the table. Once next to him, he wrapped an arm around her, brought her close. "Your sister just wants to spend time with you and play with you, just like how I always wanted with Tita Colette."

"Except he tortured me," Colette added from the opposite end of the table.

"Anyway." Joshua rolled his eyes. "Your tita shared all her toys with me, even her teddy bear. You should do the same."

"She might break it."

"Maybe, maybe not. But even if she did, you both would have had a good time playing with it together, right?"

"Okay, Tito."

He kissed the little girl on her forehead, turned her around, and sent her on her way.

I like him, Margo thought. The man showed such care toward these girls.

She stole another glance at her daughter. Despite the tension earlier between those two, there was something more, something unsettled between them. Curiosity, if she had to name it, and a little bit of play. He'd kept an extra eye on her today, took her side as she flitted through the crowd, as if knowing Margo had been overwhelmed herself. And the greatest indication of all— Diana had let him.

Sure enough, her daughter was now sneaking looks at Joshua.

As the cook brought in food from the kitchen, an older gentleman walked into the room. "Oh, oh." Next to her, Flora covered the banana cue with a napkin. "*Docktór*, please come in! Just in time. Sit here." She raised a shaking arm to the free chair next to Diana.

"Oh, no, Manang Flora, I don't want to intrude. I couldn't make it earlier but wanted to come to wish you a happy birthday."

"No, no. Come and stay. We're about to eat."

The man took a hesitating first step, but as if deciding he didn't really have much of a choice, strode to the table. As he neared, Flora said, "This is Dr. Troadio Sison. He has been my nag for decades."

A wary smile graced the doctor's face as he greeted those he knew and shook Diana's hand. When he turned to Margo, he said, "Though we know who's really in charge. Please call me Junior."

"Margo." She offered her hand.

"This is Antonio's daughter. My daughter," Flora said.

His eyebrows rose as he took a seat.

"You aren't the only one who was surprised," Margo said in an easy matter-of-fact way that astonished even herself.

He sniffed a laugh, though an incredulous, serious expression fell upon him.

Flora invited her caregiver to the room. "Edna, have dinner with us now."

"Okay, ma'am," she said, taking the seat on the other side of Margo.

And as she sat, Margo shook her hand. "I don't think we properly met."

"Edna Ramirez. I've been taking care of Manang Flora for a long time now."

"Family, I keep saying, the two of them," Flora said, then rang the bell next to her plate. "Junior is a neighbor."

"And how about you?" Margo asked Edna, intrigued. The relationship between the two was easy, but there seemed more to this than the traditional caregiver/patient arrangement. "Where do you live?"

"Down the hallway."

"She makes sure I don't sneak out," Flora supplied, then purposely glared at Dr. Sison. "I am watched everywhere, all the time."

At this Dr. Sison smiled. "I promise you, we don't always succeed."

The table laughed, including Margo, though her memory harkened back to her mother, always surrounded by people who cared for her. Friends who respected her independence and who stoked her feisty nature that endured until she was finally bedridden. They'd gathered at her dinner table much like this group was around Flora, the banter plentiful.

No one could tell Leora what to do, either.

Across the table, Diana rolled her eyes slightly, unimpressed. Margo would need to have some alone time with her soon. She was seeing her daughter's walls go up, brick by brick.

Two women came into the room with platters of food. They were not dressed in the same clothing as the servers who assisted during the party, and Margo once again wondered the extent of the Cruz's wealth, at the history that brought Antonio's family to this success. Where had it begun? Or was this opulence from Flora's family?

Why didn't Antonio return to her mother?

She heaved a breath to snap herself out of that last question, which she had been asking herself since she read his letters. Besides wanting to be with Diana, that curiosity ultimately put her on that plane to Manila.

Thank goodness Joshua's girls led grace, and their voices shoved her out of her circular thinking. Thank goodness, too, for the food. While Margo was still stuffed from the party, the meal itself was so tantalizing that it found a different part of her stomach. Fried fish, *lugaw*, a rice porridge, *tocino*, fried eggs. All savory and hearty, and she could have eaten two helpings of each.

The table descended into relatively comfortable conversation while everyone ate. Shortly, Dr. Sison bid the party farewell when he was called to visit another patient.

Once everyone was served coffee and tea, Margo leaned toward Flora, compelled from the entire day's experience. "Thank you for hosting us for this dinner. This is delicious."

"Breakfast is my favorite meal at all hours. And I expect for you to visit every day while you're here." Flora stirred her cup of tea. She watched Margo, making her feel more like five instead of seventy-five. "Since we have quite a bit to talk about, some personal and also business to discuss. Don't we, Joshua?"

Margo's heart began the quick trill of a hummingbird's.

Joshua cleared his throat and said something under his breath.

Flora raised a hand. "Joshua, why don't you take Diana to the little house."

"Now?" he asked, frowning.

"What's the little house?" Diana asked. "And why shouldn't my mother come, too?"

"Because I have a few things I want to talk to your mother about, privately, and you might find the little house interesting.

There is some . . . thing . . . for you to bring back. Is that okay, Margo?"

Margo glanced at Diana, whose pointed look was pure objection. To keep the peace, her answer should have been a resounding *no!* She and Diana had to stick together. But if Flora could explain everything, truly everything, then Diana would have to concede.

She pulled her eyes from her daughter. "It's okay with me."

New Guinea
November 18, 1944

My dearest Leora,
    I haven't received a letter from you in 68
days. Every mail call, I hope for a note from
you. Every morning I pray for you to contact me.
Every night I wonder what you have been doing.
Onofre says you no longer live at home, and I
can only guess that you have told your father
about our child. Though he has seen you at Mrs.
Lawley's and has been leaving letters in the
usual spot, he has not found a letter from you to
send. I can't do anything else but trust that all
is well.
    I will be in the Philippines soon. The men are
nervous and excited. We have lost people, Leora,
but my friends are still here. And soon, we will
land together as a family. Ignacio is especially
excited. It is his joy that's giving some hope, since
mine is slowly fading as the days pass.
    But I will keep writing. I will keep writing until
you tell me otherwise.

Iniibig kita,
Antonio

Chapter Twenty

*S*o she says jump, and you say how high?" Diana asked as she paced after Joshua in the hallway outside of Flora's suite.

"Yep." He reached for his pocket and deftly popped out a cigarette box. He kept walking, leaving her to chase after him, which, of course, she did. "It's called respect for elders."

Diana harrumphed.

She had been dismissed, which put her in a mood. That woman back there with Flora? That wasn't her mother. Her mother included Diana in everything. Every doctor's appointment, every decision, even if simply for support.

Diana didn't have a choice but to follow Joshua, tail between her legs, with the hope that she would be able to glean her own information about those letters.

But if she was being honest, she hadn't minded escaping from the dining room. It was too close for comfort in there, with everyone shooting questions across the table to get to know one another. As if it was a casual gathering of friends, not a reunion of a broken family unit.

When they both stepped out through a back-patio door into the warm night, Diana inhaled deeply, closing her eyes. Too much time had passed since her last outdoor run, and she missed the freedom of it, of letting her arms dangle at her sides while careering down a hill, or challenging her legs to lengthen their stride.

And then she smelled smoke.

She scrunched her nose and opened her eyes. Joshua was up ahead a few feet. His back was to her, and a sliver of smoke trailed up from where he stood.

"You know that's bad for you, right?" Diana called out.

"That's interesting because I don't remember asking your opinion on it," he said, turning. The backyard spotlight cast a shadow over his face, but she caught a trace of a smile on his lips.

"Doctor's prerogative to educate you on the consequences."

"Ah. Doctorsplaining." He blew out a smoke ring, which she waved away. "And what would a doctor say about attempting to lick icing off a cake knife."

"Whatever, totally different!" Her face burned with embarrassment. She was never going to have champagne again, ever. Not only did she lose her verbal filter, but she also lost all composure. "I was being safe. It just looked so good, all that icing clumped together."

He pursed his lips as if to stifle a laugh.

"Ha ha."

"Thanks to me your lips and tongue are still intact," he said, before he stilled. His eyes flashed with what she recognized from their first night as desire.

And yep, she felt it, too. She shifted her feet. Scrambled to fill the quiet between them. "Well, thank you, for stripping me of the knife. My lips and tongue appreciate it."

Stripping? Oh my God. Was she still drunk?

"My pleasure." He stepped in closer, pointed with his free hand. "Aaand, speaking of lips, you have something on your cheek."

That didn't make any sense at all to her, but she rubbed at her cheek.

"Nope, it's still there . . . to the left . . . a little lower." And yet, despite his directions, she was failing. "May I?" he asked.

"Yes, please. Just take it off."

Oh my God.

The man was kind enough not to point out her Freudian slips, and simply brushed his thumb against her cheek. "There you go."

"Thank you," she said, as another wave of awkwardness washed over them. She needed to straighten this conversation out, take her mind and language out of the gutter and redirect it toward the task at hand. "So, why were we sent out here?"

"I'm supposed to show you something."

Her mood plummeted. "I'm not sure what you could show me that could properly justify what was done to my mom and granny. I don't understand this dynamic. How everyone's acting so calm, so casual in there . . . when she did what she did to our families."

He took a drag of his cigarette, and blew out smoke exaggeratingly away from her. He matched her stern expression. "What *did* she do to our families, Diana? Why don't you tell me?"

She growled at this loyalty, but in his expression she noted a true curiosity. "You really don't know?"

"No. Not that whatever you say will make me think that Lolo and Lola were fully responsible for whatever you claim."

How did that happen—how could he make her swoon one moment and then leave her frustrated the next?

Diana didn't mess with complicated personalities for this very reason—it took too much headspace, took too much work. Much of why she and Carlo had vibed was because they hadn't needed to fight over their relationship. Their decision to be together was logical. They were easy. They were predictable.

Of course, they also ended in disaster, so maybe she wasn't the best at judging character after all.

Bottom line: Joshua was like a mother in labor, angst and sharp emotions on the outside, but vulnerable on the inside, and maybe, Diana just had to wait it out. She had helped women in labor for hours. She could stand there for a minute longer.

To find out the total truth about her family history, she would have to.

"Well?" he asked.

She met his eyes. "Antonio Cruz was a father who didn't take responsibility for his child. And Flora Reyes aided and abetted his crime. Because of this my granny was left to care for her child, alone. And my mother suffered because of it."

He shook his head. "And that's the final story."

"Obviously not. Hence the reason why I followed you out here. Otherwise, I would have convinced my mother to blow this joint, after seeing all"—she turned toward the house and raised a hand at it—"all this."

"Nothing is as easy as it looks. All that?" He pointed at the house. "That, and the parties; that is what everyone sees. But I believe every family has secrets, Diana." He dropped the cigarette and, with a shake of his head, ground the butt with his shoe.

"Oh, what a relief." She waved away the smoke that wafted in her direction.

"I would be more worried about the air pollution in Manila than that cigarette."

"Right, but wrapping your mouth around a chimney of tar doesn't help, either."

"All right, all right, Dr. Cary. Let's go."

She tried not to grin. "Where?"

"Can't you just come without having to ask every question under the sun?" He turned, obviously expecting Diana to follow.

She scrambled after him. A path emerged adjacent to the cement fence line of the property, hidden behind lantana bushes. Diana ducked and weaved, following Joshua's back and the contrasting tiles dug into the ground amid the grass.

"Are we doing something illegal here? Because I don't do illegal," Diana said, and then corrected herself, remembering that, in fact, she was on vacation because she did break the rules. "I mean, not totally illegal anyway."

"Nope—they still own this part of the property." He stopped, turning. His face sported a pained look. "Are you ready?"

All of this angst and anticipation was not her style. "Yes, I was ready back there. What is it?"

With a hand, he raised the bottom branch of a lantana bush that had climbed the side of the cement wall so that it encroached onto the path like an overhang. Diana ducked underneath, her hair catching in the leaves.

What she saw took her breath away. It was a house—a farmhouse bungalow. White wooden exterior with a slightly pitched black roof. Black shutters and a wraparound porch with two rockers next to the front door. It seemed familiar; Diana dug within the recesses of her brain to remember.

"It's a California bungalow–style home," Joshua said, and shuffled past her. The grass was sparse here, the ground muddy in parts; he sidestepped it. "It's built with cement walls to with-stand tropical storms, but it's made to look like it as much as possible."

"Oh God, it is." A picture flashed in Diana's memory, a photograph of her granny next to her great-granddad in front of the Gallagher home in Marysville. Behind it was an expanse of fields, and a never-ending sky. It was one of a handful of photographs her granny had, after traveling across the country.

"What . . ." she began to ask, but didn't know where to start.

"Lolo and Lola made their wealth out of real estate. They were great at it. He saved while she invested. Hotels, restaurants, resorts. They bought and sold over decades, looking for a place to settle down, and they decided it would be here in Forbes. Lolo Tony had this built when they moved in. I remember him being really stubborn about the details. I used to watch from the back porch of the house." He pointed back toward where they came. "Before Lola insisted on putting a cement wall up. C'mon." He gestured and climbed the porch, opening the door. It squeaked a melancholy sound, and out came the scent of wood.

She'd expected a living-museum quality home, rickety insides with cobwebs, maybe old-fashioned equipment, a farm table and antique furnishings, a porcelain wash basin. But the inside was simply a home with real walls and wooden floors. The living room had a couch and a TV on a stand. A small glass-top breakfast table sat in the middle of an eat-in kitchen. "Oh. This is surprising. Was this like his man cave?"

"You could say that. This was where he worked, where he read, and where he went when he needed to get away, which was most times. If someone asked for him, Lola would say, 'He's behind the wall,' in her feisty way, and we'd know he was here and not to be bothered. Except by me, of course, because I was the favorite." A grin graced his face, then it faltered a little, "Probably because we were both kind of the same. We didn't belong anywhere or to anyone, truly."

He said it in such a tone that Diana's heart softened, not only for Joshua, but for Antonio.

No. She couldn't let that happen.

She followed him into the galley kitchen. It was simple and clean, though missing a refrigerator. Running a hand along the countertop, she found it free of dust. "Someone's still cleaning it?"

"I don't want this house going to disrepair. There's more."

The floorboard creaked as they entered the narrow hallway, into the first bedroom to the right, where a window greeted them. A desk looked outward onto the view of the back of the property, and farther away was a hint of a cement fence.

"This was his favorite spot, because it faces west. He even had the ground ahead leveled so he could have an unencumbered view, or as best as he could get with the next house being so close."

"Of course. The sunset."

"It was his thing," he said.

"*Their* thing," she corrected. "Leora and Antonio's."

"Really?"

She nodded.

"Lola Flora told us when we were little that Lolo had gone through a lot in the war. There were some things that we knew we couldn't ask or talk about. As this house was being built, we just accepted it—that's what we do, you know, in our culture. We accept the truth of our elders, sometimes without question. Even when this place was upside down with workers because he had to have this house built, no one dared to ask him why. And I have a feeling Lola Flora didn't ask, either. There was always a bit of distance between them. They didn't even sleep in the same bed. Then again, that was old-school, right?" He grinned, then opened the drawers.

"When he died, he left me in charge of this house, among other things. Until then, no one had access to this home except the maids. Lola Flora didn't step foot in this place—she was getting too old, and by then, I think, you get to a point in a marriage when you just accept things for what they are. But who am I to say—I've never been married." He shrugged. "I decided to finally go through the contents of this house recently. At first, it felt like I was intruding. You might not be able to tell, but every part of this place is my lolo. I can feel him in here." He pulled out an attaché case, rectangular and leather with a three-dial combination lock. He presented it to Diana. "I've been working on this combination lock for a while now and was just short of having it cut open when you reached out to my sister. I'm sure this is what Lola Flora wanted me to show you. I guess she thinks you might be able to open it."

Diana accepted the briefcase. Her fingers tingled at the cool leather, and she gasped when goose bumps trailed up her arm. Her gut was telling her that the truth she wanted lived in this case. She examined the lock, thumbed the dial. "No, but my mother might."

Leyte, Philippines
January 28, 1945

My dearest Leora,

The Philippines is as beautiful as I remember.
Everything is familiar and strange all at once.
It's like I'm reliving life. The smell of food cooking
over charcoal and wood, the way the wind feels
against my cheek, warm and wet—it's sublime.
Today, Ignacio and I dared each other to climb
a coconut tree. The young boys in the barrio are
experts here. They shimmy to the top without
even a rope around their bodies, gripping tightly
around the trunk. They are adept in cutting
coconuts down with one fell machete swoop. They
make it look so easy and exhibit such a freedom,
despite the war around them. I envy them
sometimes.

Anyway, I barely got a quarter of the way up,
even with a rope tied around me and the trunk.
The tree wasn't tall in comparison to the rest,
but I didn't have the right technique, or maybe
I'm not as strong as I think I am. Ignacio and the
kids had a laugh, because he got up to the top
without a problem though couldn't quite get a
coconut down without effort.

I laughed along with them, but inside, I
wondered: How could I not get up there? Why
couldn't I? In the moment, I felt like I didn't belong.

Well, it's nothing that didn't pass quickly. When I drank the coconut water, it was all better. One day, when all this is over, and we're together, I'll have a coconut cut down and you can drink its juice, and we can crack it open and peel the coconut meat from the fruit itself. There is nothing like it.

Maybe it's because of my old memories coming back from when I was a child, or the fact that we are again on solid ground, but the island is a sight to see. The sky is blue despite the rubble on the ground. The water is warm and inviting, and there are so many Filipinos. Men and women and children. Some frightened, others upset, but there is also happiness. The people— my people—are resilient and joyful. Despite the destruction of this war, I am greeted with open arms. I'm treated like family even if I'm wearing an American soldier's uniform. I'm one of the good guys, but am I really? These people have seen worse times, and I, in this uniform, am part of that, too.

It's all so confusing.

It's even more confusing because I feel like I've lost my center, you. Our letters tethered me, and whenever I got lonely, all I simply had to do was to close my eyes.

When you told me you were with child, this tether became a rope. It kept me alive, Leora.

Ignacio has been helping me count the days.
You should give birth to our baby soon. Will I know
when I become a father? Will it be a boy or a girl?
Will the child look like me, have my dark skin?
And will he or she have your eyes?

   During the loneliest nights, I have succumbed
to doubt, that maybe you don't believe that we
can make a family. That it's too hard. Maybe
you believe the world isn't ready for a Pinoy and
a white woman to be together. That I will only be
a hindrance in your and our baby's life.

   But I haven't given up. I still have faith.

   Please write me.

Iniibig kita,
Antonio

Chapter Twenty-One

Margo listened as Diana's and Joshua's footsteps faded into the background, then said to Flora, "I don't usually feel the need to send my daughter away if there's something serious to talk about."

"Yes, but they will bring back something important. And I need to talk to you, alone." She coughed.

Edna shot to her feet, and concern flashed onto her face. "Manang, are you okay? Let's put you in bed to rest. It's been a long day."

Flora waved a hand though her breathing had become slightly labored.

"You're so stubborn sometimes, Lola. Tito Junior said not to push it," Colette added, now at the edge of her seat. "I'm texting him now." She took out her phone and thumbed the screen.

"Anak, one doesn't get to one hundred years old without being a little stubborn. I am old. I am allowed to be sick. Something has got to kill me."

"COPD is not a joke." Edna frowned.

"You have COPD?" Margo scooted closer.

"It's nothing. A tinge of it started earlier this year," Flora answered.

Edna rolled her eyes. "A tinge, heh."

Margo agreed with the sentiment. "COPD is serious. . . ."

Flora clucked. "I'm taking my medicine, anak, and I have my heart and lungs listened to whenever any of these children call the doctor. Right now, I have something to say, something about your father and me."

Margo's thoughts ground to a halt. She leaned in, intent on every word, as was everyone else in the room: Edna, Colette, and Philip silent in their chairs.

"I met Antonio in Tacloban, my hometown. It was destroyed, both by the Japanese and the Americans when they leveled the ground. We hid in the mountains, but many of my friends died. Family. Neighbors. We didn't know who to trust, or who to thank. That is what happens in war. We weren't sure who to turn to. We just had to survive, to eat, to live somehow. I was twenty-five, young, though not very optimistic. I knew how to use a machete. I was the eldest of three sisters, and responsibility came with that."

Flora's eyes glazed over in memory, and she continued, "Antonio was part of the First Filipino Infantry Regiment, which split up after they arrived in New Guinea, and he was moved to the Sixth Army. In New Guinea, no one knew how entrenched the Japanese were. Antonio said that the country was beautiful but so dangerous, though he never spoke of what happened there, or in Leyte. Not aloud.

"The things Antonio said in his sleep . . . even after we married. He used to call out Leora's name."

Her mother's name coming out of this woman's mouth sent

a shiver through Margo. In her own research as a young woman, Margo hadn't found much about the First Filipino Regiment. At some point, in the hustle and bustle of life, she'd put the effort aside, settling for the very basics of history of World War II in the Philippines. Then again, it had been easier to just accept what was told to her. Less painful than digging into the real truth. Her father had been an enigma in story form.

Flora broke out into an incessant cough.

Edna tutted, pushed her chair back, and strode to her side. "Time for bed."

"I'll help." Colette stood.

"No, you won't." Philip gently coerced her to her seat and joined Edna.

Margo stood to help, too. She took Flora's other arm and helped her up from the chair. The woman was so light and fragile that Margo feared too much pressure on her bones would crush them. Earlier, in her beautiful garments and amid the lure of festivities, Flora was a regal matriarch. Now, she was simply an elderly woman who struggled to walk to her bed, shuffling in her slippers.

"I'm here." A low voice rushed into the space. Dr. Sison had a doctor's bag in hand. As Flora perched on the mattress, with Margo still on one side, he settled his bag on the bedside table. It was only then Margo noticed the oxygen tank, discreetly tucked behind the bed, a long tube attached to it.

After they'd both settled Flora in bed, the woman's eyes shut. Margo shared a glance with Edna, who was looking at her lovingly, which struck a cord of regret. That was how Margo had looked at her own mother at the end of her life, when there was little left to do but preserve her dignity at a time when her body was failing her.

Margo didn't have to pick up a stethoscope to know that Flora was sick; she could hear the crackles of her breathing Still, Dr. Sison did his duty; he listened to her heart and lungs. Gave her the customary warnings and guidelines, and even admonished her for pushing herself today. "And please, you should use your oxygen."

"I already use it when I'm asleep," she countered.

He sighed.

"I'll think about it."

Dr. Sison grinned. "How about right now?"

"Fine," she said after a dramatic second.

He pulled the tube out and affixed it onto Flora's nose with care, then glanced at Margo in triumph.

"Oh, is everything okay?"

Margo looked up at the sound of her daughter's voice. She halted briefly at the door, then entered, holding a briefcase in her hand. Joshua followed right behind, hands stuffed in his pockets.

"I'm dying," Flora piped up, making all of them jump, though she still had her eyes closed. "I'm dying, but it's okay. Now that you are here, Margo. You and Diana. Joshua, did you give Diana the briefcase?"

"Yes, Lola."

She exhaled, and coughed. "Good. Open it, and I will see you tomorrow afternoon. And I will tell you more."

Leyte, Philippines
February 24, 1945

My dearest Leora,

I don't know if it's any use to write, but here I am, penning another letter. I can't stop myself. I think of you when something significant happens, good or bad. Today, a terrible thing occurred. I lost a friend who I considered my brother. I thought I could protect him but I couldn't.

Everything has changed. I have changed, and I feel like I'm at the edge of a large divide, unsure whether to jump. In the past, I would have looked to you for advice, for encouragement. You have always been the one who made quick decisions. You were always more practical than me. Me and my sometimes-wild dreams—you always reminded me what was real. Without you, I don't know what to do.

I have to make this decision on my own. For all that I may do, I am sorry, Leora. I have tried my best. Know that I love you, and I love our child.

Yours, forever,
Antonio

Chapter Twenty-Two

That night, with a stiff cup of coffee in her belly, Diana sat cross-legged facing her mother, the briefcase on a coffee table between them. Neither one of them had made a move to open it.

"I feel like the wrong combination will set off a bomb," Diana said. Her initial feeling of entitlement to this briefcase had passed, replaced by fear. The last three days had upended her poorly imagined expectations. She had this version of a re-union in mind, a cerebral *Here is your cousin and the wife of your late grandfather, and the entire family history will be bestowed upon you* scenario. Not a party, not an almost one-night stand, and then now this object between she and her mother that, going by Flora's implication, might reveal the truth they wanted.

This trip had been like peeling an onion—one eye-stinging realization after another. She didn't know how much more she could take.

She would need a vacation from her vacation.

Correction: there would be no time for a vacation after this. The unknown waited for her back in Virginia, too.

Diana gnawed on her lip to clear her head. If she weren't so intent on being lucid for this, she would've had a stiff drink instead.

"Speaking of bombs. You looked like you were going to hurl one at me earlier today at Sunset Corner."

"Did I?" Diana pressed her lips together. She knew she couldn't blame being tipsy for her behavior at dinner—her champagne high had been long gone.

"Do you want to talk about it?"

"It's nothing."

"It didn't look like nothing."

So she shook her head. "Everything was coming all at once, is all. I was surprised that you got along with them so well, I guess."

What else could she have said? That she wanted to forbid her mother from talking to Flora? That it was traitorous? What would that have done? If her mother had been a jerk toward Flora, then they probably wouldn't have this briefcase here now.

"It's a lot for me, too. I had to keep remembering that this wasn't just about Antonio or Flora, but about my mother, too. But Flora said something that rang true today. She said my father was a brave man. That bad things happened, but he was brave. It gave me such comfort to hear that." Her eyes fluttered upward, meeting Diana's gaze.

Diana nodded. As usual, her mother's optimism always showed through. She forgave and forgot. But Diana didn't forget. Carlo had been a heartbreak, and even now, six months postbreakup, she could still feel the bruises deep in her heart muscle.

"This doesn't excuse her, or anyone, for that matter, Mother. She wrote that letter to Granny. It was that letter that kept her from him. And I swear Flora's stalling, sending us back here to the hotel. Why couldn't she just tell us what's up?"

"Patience, dear."

Diana rolled her eyes. A lecture was coming. She waited one second, two . . .

"I know you can't understand it, but decades have passed without me knowing, so giving the woman a day or two to sort out her own story is all right with me. But the mere fact that both your granny and Flora said that my father was brave, that must have meant that it was true. And maybe there is a reason for all of this."

Her mother was bargaining, rationalizing. And rationalizing, though it might make someone feel better, wasn't wise to enable. Not in medicine, and surely not in love. But Diana couldn't say any of this. "What combination should we try first?"

She took a deep breath. "How about Granny's birthday."

"That would be too easy." But Margo was already sliding the lock to 3–0–3. With a flick of her thumb, it popped it open with a snap.

"Whoa."

Margo's eyes widened.

"Here we go," Diana whispered as she shifted to her mother's side and she lifted the top. The distinct smell of leather and old paper wafted from the case. Inside were sketches, old maps, pictures. But what caught Diana's eyes were the letters interspersed with the trademark V-mail envelopes, and she fished them out. A quick glance—some were from Leora Gallagher, with her distinct handwriting and California postmark. A familiar flutter started in her belly, of nervousness.

More letters.

In complete silence, they both took turns reading each and every letter, and just as Diana predicted, her entire world was remade again.

Diana's running shoes brushed against the hotel hallway carpet. The tips of her ponytail bounced against her neck, her earbuds in, though no music streamed through them. She had dressed herself for a run, a good fast and hard run on the hotel treadmill to clear her head, to immerse herself in the predictable.

Her mind was filled with words, endless words in rotation. Her classmates in school had envied her for having a great memory, for knowing not just the facts but the page she learned them on. Diana cataloged information into files, and then into drawers, labeled and tucked away in her head until she needed it.

But that skill was a problem when she tried to forget.

With the letters now in her head, Diana knew she needed to sweat it out, despite her run this morning. But as she approached the door to the gym on the twenty-eighth floor and peeked into the window, she found the room dark. The gym was scheduled to close at 11:00 p.m., and upon checking her phone, it was only 10:59.

She looked down to her phone, and texted the only person she knew here who had any kind of pull: Joshua.

Hey.

Something wrong?

She half laughed at both his ability to be empathetic and in-sulting at the same time.

> No. Yes. We opened the briefcase.

> Really? Want to talk about it? Room 2837.

> Um, no. I was texting because your fitness room is closed before it's supposed to be.

> ?

> Can you open it?

> It's after eleven.

> *Now* it's after eleven

> That's my point.

Diana growled, out loud. She didn't even care who heard her. All of her pent-up energy had to go somewhere . . .

Psst.

Diana looked up, curious at the noise, then dismissed it.

> Seriously can you open the door?

And there went another *psst* noise. It came from behind her so she turned toward it.

Joshua was standing in the hallway, hands on his hips, at the opening of his room, just a few doors down. He was in sweats and a white V-neck tee. And dark-rimmed glasses—he had been wearing contacts all that time?

"I heard your growl all the way down here, Diana."

"I'd appreciate you opening this door for me." She pointed to the lock.

"Sorry, can't. It's against policy. And anyway, I don't have the key."

"But you own this building."

He shrugged. "I still have to follow the rules."

She huffed. "Fine. Thank you for nothing." She turned to go.

"Diana, let's have a drink. Coffee? Tea?"

She halted. "Because you want to know about the briefcase?"

"Yes, why else?" He smiled charmingly, his teeth bright in the dim hallway. Their relationship had gone from strangers to lovers to extremely complicated in a matter of forty-eight hours, and she wasn't sure how to take that smile. Friend or foe? The guy who kept her company during the party, or the man who was suspicious of her presence?

But right now, she needed to talk things through with someone else besides her mother, and Joshua was the most convenient person.

She just had to keep her head on straight if she was going to be alone with him.

"Fine." She walked toward him. He gestured to the open door, and she entered his brightly lit foyer.

A book sat on the hallway table, opened facedown, next to his keys and wallet. A vision of him reading on a couch, and her curled up next to him flashed in her head, because what was sexier and more comfortable than that?

"Are you alone?" she asked. Her face heated with the understanding that she hadn't planned this well. She was attracted to this man, and whenever she was around him, there was this push-and-pull electric charge that rendered her off-balance. And what if the girls were there, and she was this woman stranger coming to their father figure's door so late at night like this was some booty call?

She flushed, hot all of a sudden, though she swallowed a fleeting thought of them together in bed.

"Yes, all by my lonesome."

"You know what? It's late," she said. "We can talk about this in the morning when we head out." The next trip on her agenda was a Corregidor Island cruise and tour, which both Colette and Joshua would participate in. After, they'd planned to make another visit to Flora.

"Oh, no. You pulled me out of a dark night of the soul, so we might as well talk about it now."

"A dark night of the soul?"

"The black moment?"

When she shook her head, he continued with a smirk.

"The climax of the book, when all is lost?"

She cackled. "I know what a black moment is, I just have never heard it called the dark night of the soul. That seems a little, I dunno . . . extra." She unsuccessfully tried to keep a grin from slipping onto her face. The guy was a reader, as she was. Carlo hardly read, and aside from the medical journals he kept up with, he rarely picked up a book and had complained that her reading light was bothersome when he was trying to sleep.

He frowned. "Are you making fun of me?"

"Yes. That's . . . cute."

"Great. I'm cute. Come on in. I actually just turned on the kettle. Coffee or tea?"

"Coffee is fine. Thanks."

She stepped out of her shoes and lined them up with his to the side of the door, then followed him deeper into the hotel room, to the combined kitchen and living room. It was neat and uncluttered. Hand-drawn pictures hung on the refrigerator, and framed pictures of the girls were sprinkled everywhere in the room. Two teddy bears sat atop an armchair. A family apartment at first glance, although he was, for all intents and purposes, a bachelor.

She hopped up on the barstool and faced him as he busied himself with a French press.

"What are you reading?" She spied a second book on the kitchen counter.

"A thriller. The gruesome kind."

"Tough guy."

"Don't you forget it." The kettle whistled and he turned off the stove. "Lolo Tony was a reader and it was our thing. He gave me books as presents. Along with hands-on work, he called reading true education. Though I read many genres, I prefer fiction. Even romance."

"Really?" Her lips wiggled into a grin. There *was* a soft spot in him.

"Is that weird?"

"No." She scoured her mind, thinking of her own book selections. "I read across genres, too, but mostly nonfiction."

"I am not at all surprised." He poured the hot water into the French press, grinning. "With you being a fan of the truth."

"And by you reading romance, you believe . . . what?"

"What else? But in a happily-ever-after." The nutty scent of java filled the room, and Joshua prepared their cups.

In the silence, Diana mulled over what the words *happily ever after* meant and in what context.

"Join me on the couch?" he said, finally, and she followed.

The coffee was a surprisingly welcome treat after the day she'd had. It grounded her from her overconsumption of champagne, from her heavy heart with the newfound letters.

"Don't you believe in a happily-ever-after?" He turned his body to her and slung his arm over the back of the couch. "I assume that's why you're so quiet."

"Oh, ah . . ." Caught by his sudden question, she shook her head. "No. I mean, in response to your question, I'd have to ask if there's really such a thing? Life is comprised of hills and valleys. Triumphs interspersed with lows. Isn't a happily-ever-after a happenstance, or when one decides to take a snapshot of their life while standing on a hill?"

He leaned back into the couch. "That is fatalistic."

"I'm not being fatalistic, Joshua. It's realistic. Of course we all live for the hills. I'm just saying that not all stories end on a high note, and even if they do, it doesn't mean it'll last. I mean, look at all this, what's happened to us. To both of us. Where would you say we are in this drama called the Cruz Family?" At his silence, she took a sip of her coffee. "Obviously I'm in a valley, since I'm hanging out with you." She raised an eyebrow to punctuate her joke.

"Hey, I didn't force you to come to my door."

Her cheeks warmed, properly put in her place. She opened her mouth to speak, but he beat her to it. "But I'm happy you came." He paused. "I'd been meaning to say that I'm sorry. At the gym, then at my lola's house earlier in the day, I was rude. . . ."

"No, it was me."

"I was trying to reconcile who you were—are—with that night."

As his face dipped down minutely, a section of his hair flopped forward over his forehead, reminding her of him on top of her, seconds from sex. A thrill ran through her with the memory. She looked away from him. "Same. And we're on the same side."

"Same family actually," he half laughed.

"That's right." And, wanting to move on from the awkwardness, she said, "So, the briefcase . . ."

"Can you share what's in it?"

"Documents and letters from my grandmother to Antonio. Seeing proof from this end—that the connection was real—I'm not going to lie: I was stunned by it. As if the DNA test weren't enough."

"Did the letters give you answers?"

"Not totally. But they were heartbreaking." Pairing the letters together, Diana could have imagined their correspondence, both bent over their pieces of paper, hopes and dreams laid out in the words they wrote. Still, they didn't tell a complete story. "My mom—I don't think she really gets it. She read all of them with this stoic face, like it's not seeping in."

"Give her some time. It hasn't sunk in with me, either. It's a lot to process."

"Time isn't the problem. It's about my mother's ability or desire to face issues, to make decisions. Did you know that if I hadn't insisted that we come here, to Manila, this reunion wouldn't have happened? It's the same with a million other things." Just saying it unnerved her, and at the next second she admonished herself. It was unbecoming of her to talk ill of her mother.

She pushed herself higher on the couch.

"You're going?" He sat up.

"Yeah. Speaking of my mom, she's probably wondering where I've gone." A lie—her mother was sound asleep. This little coffee break with Joshua had been perfect. Until now, when unease had taken over her once again, fueled by caffeine. She had to get out of there before she got angry, upset, or maybe cried, which would be a disaster.

"Look, I love my mom, despite all I've said. I don't want you to get it twisted. Anyway, thank you for the coffee and the chat."

Diana moved to the door, with Joshua following behind her. Before he turned the knob, he said. "Um, so tomorrow, the Corregidor tour—still a go?"

She sighed, her mind cluttered. "Yes, we're still on. It will be a great distraction before seeing Flora tomorrow."

"Great."

Diana turned from the door. She took two steps and halted, just as he shut it. It could have been attraction, or need for comfort, or this surge of energy, but it felt one and the same.

She didn't want to go.

She turned to face the door. Her right hand tingled with the temptation to knock.

The door opened, as if reading her mind. Then Joshua opened the door wider. An invitation.

It would be her decision.

Logic and emotion warred within her. What exactly did she want? What was holding her back? What did she have to lose?

Nothing. She had nothing to lose, because what she thought was real had revealed itself as a facade.

She crossed the threshold and crushed her mouth to his. Their clothes fell by the wayside as they stepped out of socks and pants, and as shirts were peeled off. Without breaking their kiss, he walked her backward to the bed, and she perched on the soft blanket still in her underwear. She helped him out of his, the sight of him taking her breath away. She lay back, and he, in one swift movement, slid her panties down and off, and she gasped in surprise, in pleasure.

It wouldn't be the last time that night.

part five

Night

When it is dark enough, you can see the stars.

—Charles A. Beard

Marysville, California
April 17, 1944

My dearest Antonio,

I'm writing this letter under the pecan trees at the Ludlows' orchard. When Onofre found me with your letter in hand, I ran straight to this spot and tried to remember us here months ago, before you left for the Army. I know it's only been two weeks since you left San Francisco, but every minute without you is a hundred days.

Things are different without you here. I am different, though the strikes have continued and the entire city is feeling the pressure. The tension is thick, but all I can think of is the last time you held me, before you left. Is that foolish? Do you find it silly that while there is so much fighting in our little town, all I can hold on to is my sadness? I'm convinced everything would be better if you were here. That you and I could find a place where it's okay to be us, without the jeering, without the quiet side conversations from our friends. Without fearing my father's disapproval.

Onofre and I have made a plan for your letters. Mrs. Lawley's shop is on his way to the barbershop, where he works, and on the days he receives a letter, he will slip it under the big rock behind the house.

Your letter arrived wrinkled and dirty, but I have read it time and again. I want to write you about everything that's going on, but the newspapers say we have to keep our letters cheerful. They remind us that what you need to know are the little things going on in our lives, the comforts of home. They say that we shouldn't burden you with our thoughts and fears. I definitely don't want to do that.

I miss you, though. I want to hear you laugh, or see your crooked, dear smile. I picture it at night. While I tend to Mrs. Lawley or try to sew a seam, I think of you. My father asked yesterday if something was wrong, and I wish I could have told him. This secret between the two of us was fine when you were here. I could talk to someone about it—you. But now that you're gone, I feel full to bursting.

I want to get this letter out to Onofre soon, so I will have to end it here. I will write when I can. I love you with all of my heart, with every sunset.

I remain here, and yours,
Leora

Chapter Twenty-Three

Margo glanced at the list of individual unread texts from Roberta and Cameron and in their collective group text while on the balcony at Las Cruces Hotel. It was already a balmy ninety degrees, but the sun was positioned just right so the balcony above her provided shade. She was still working on her first cup of tea. This would have been a perfect time to catch herself up, to read through not just her texts but also her emails and social media responses. This would have been the perfect moment to call Cameron to discuss their kiss and where that would go. But she couldn't do it. She hadn't been able to engage online since she left the United States, with not one shared photo, not one text.

The outside word seemed irrelevant, and the virtual world more so. The only thing on her mind was this glaring hole in her identity that'd always been covered with excuses and acceptance. She'd reread her mother's letters to her father again this morning, and while the words were legible, she couldn't comprehend their meaning. What struck her was Leora's neat, straight penmanship, the flair of a curlicue when she crossed her *t*'s. The flow of her sentences, such a familiar cadence. While she read those letters, Leora's spirit was ever more present, and for a moment, Margo could take joy in pretending that her mother was still alive. And then, just as quickly, the feeling dissipated.

The grief she thought she had begun to manage after Leora died had returned in full force, doubled now that she was grieving over what could have been with her father, too.

But she couldn't stop there. Because those letters didn't tell the entire story.

In front of her, next to her cup and saucer, was a pad of paper embossed with the hotel's logo, scribbled with dots and petals, stems, and leaves. A field of daisies in blue ink. Now, she picked up a pen, and in between flowers, wrote out questions:

Why did he choose you and not me?
Did he love me?
Did he love my mother?

Her pen stilled at what she'd written. Since she and Diana had found her father's letters, she had only harbored these questions within herself, never expressed them. There was a misconception that an artist always bared their soul in their work. Margo, despite years of photographing people at their most vulnerable, always kept a little of herself away, tucked behind where she hid her deep-seated fear of rejection. That fear was probably why she shielded herself behind her camera, pointing the lens at others to keep herself out of focus.

Now it was time to face these questions, and quite possibly, receive unwanted answers.

A door closing woke her from her thoughts. She saw the outline of Diana walking through the room, preparing for the day. The plan was for them to meet Colette and Joshua at the dock for the tour of Corregidor Island, a national historical marker of World War II. Though her father was still in the United States when MacArthur left the Philippines as the Japanese occupied Manila, the island was a memorial to both Filipino and American soldiers.

After wincing at the sheer number of text messages, she opened a new one to Colette.

> Split up this afternoon? You and me to Sunset Corner and J&D to Corregidor?

> We are on the same wavelength.

> I will tell Joshua that I will stay?

> I will break the news to Diana.

> Good luck!

"I'll need it," she whispered, then entered the hotel room. Margo folded her written note and popped it into the wide opening of her bag.

Steam billowed out of the bathroom. While outside it was humid and muggy, inside it was a constant sixty-eight degrees, and it still warranted a warm shower.

"I needed that." Diana's hair was ensconced in a towel, body shrouded in a fluffy white robe. She walked to Margo's side. "But

I'm ten out of ten going to end up falling asleep during the car ride." She tipped her head down, and the towel spilled open, tresses tumbling out. "I'm starving now, though. Want to grab something to eat at the bar before we head out? I'm not planning on blowing out my hair—just going to scrunch it with gel and go."

Margo waited a beat, then another. "Diana, I think we should change our plans."

Diana flipped her hair up; tiny droplets of water hit Margo in the face and made her giggle. "Change them? Why?"

"I want to see Flora. I don't think I can wait the day to discuss the letters with her."

"Then that's what we'll do." Diana's lips pursed in disdain, likely as much at the change in plans as the fact that they were changing for Flora.

Margo shook her head. "I mean, maybe I should go alone."

Diana walked into the bathroom and shut the door with her change of clothes in her arms. From the inside her voice echoed. "She doesn't like me; I get it. I drank too much champagne yesterday and was probably really sassy, but when I'm around her, I get so angry."

"She never said she didn't like you, so don't assume that." Margo checked herself in the mirror and readjusted her polka-dot bubble-sleeve top, eyeing the bathroom door, choosing her words wisely. "I think a more intimate conversation alone will suit her better. It might suit me better, too, so she and I can have a good heart-to-heart. Understand?"

"I do, I guess." The door opened, and Diana walked out wearing a black-and-white floral-print romper.

Margo couldn't help but smile. "You're so adorable in that."

Diana looked away, bashful. "Well, you did get it for me."

"It's perfect on you." Margo scoured her daughter's face.

Diana seemed different today. Light, loose. It could have been the warm shower, or simply, because she wasn't in her usual scrubs. "What do you say? We wouldn't want your outfit to go to waste. You can go out, and I can handle the old lady." She winked.

Make it like it's her idea, Leora had said once. Diana had been at the sour age of four—because the terrible twos had been a misnomer in Margo's experience. Twos were glorious. At two, their words weren't quite as formed, unlike the fours, where they had enough logic and will to create chaos on purpose—and Diana had decided in the middle of the market to throw a tantrum over the wrong kind of apple. Only the red varieties were acceptable to Diana, and Margo had reached for a Golden Delicious.

Leora had been there, and in a whisper reminded Margo that her little one wanted choices—that was all. Choice was its own power. Leora had picked two green apples, and presented them to Diana. "We have to have green apples for the dessert, Di, but you can pick which green apple you want. Will you do that?"

And her daughter, hiccupping from the last of her tantrum, chose the Granny Smith.

Right now was the green apple choice.

Diana leaned against the bathroom doorway. "How will I know you're okay? Do you have a plan on what to say? I know how you are, Ma. You'll get around Flora and fall for the trap—you're too nice to people."

Margo winced at the implication that she was a pushover. "Well, I figure, I'm okay now, aren't I, and I feel like the worst part has passed. And I . . . I'm going to go with what feels natural to say. Though I promise to demand the truth." She lifted her eyes to her daughter slowly.

"Hm . . . we'll definitely the get the answer faster if Flora feels comfortable, and she is most comfortable with you. And I don't want to waste these tour tickets. Joshua, Colette, and I can still make a good day of it," Diana began. "But I want you to promise me that you'll bring your A game. Practice these words, *Out with it.* It's what I tell my med students and interns. Like, bottom line up front."

Margo scrunched an eyebrow down. "Okay, but that's not really my style. I'm more like a 'Can you clarify?' kind of woman."

"Nope. Just say it, Ma. I won't leave until you do. Out with it."

"Out with it," Margo said, in a normal voice, feeling silly.

"Louder. Out. With. It."

"Diana, this is—"

"Out! With! It!" Diana yelled. "Out! With! It!"

"Okay! Fine, fine! Out! With! It!"

Her daughter's grin was smug and refreshing. "See, that wasn't so bad, right?"

Margo's heart was pounding so hard from all the yelling, but Diana was right. It wasn't bad at all. She laughed. "No, no it wasn't." She swallowed a breath. "Though our neighbors are probably calling the front desk as we speak."

She shrugged. "We know the owners, so . . . but remember, that if you feel weird at all—"

"I'm out of there. Promise." Margo held a hand up like a Girl Scout.

"Okay." Diana clapped her hands together. "I guess I'd better text and update Colette—"

"Actually, she mentioned accompanying me if I felt the urge to see Flora earlier."

A knock on the door caused Diana to turn. She headed toward

it. "Oh?" She opened the door to that handsome Joshua on the other side.

"But there's always you and Joshua."

Her daughter turned to her and rolled her eyes. "Sneaky, Ma, sneaky."

To that, Margo simply shrugged. "Caught red-handed."

An hour later, Margo had arrived at Sunset Corner to find that Flora was napping.

"Tita, do you want to go to the mall so you're not bored? You'll be impressed at how big it is. You can get your steps in, maybe buy some souvenirs? Whatever you'd like," Colette said.

They were standing in the kitchen, and Colette had just handed her a cold glass, frosted and filled with ice and what Margo suspected was lemonade. It wasn't lemonade, though; it was citrus and sweet and woke her palate.

"Oh my goodness," she said, delight rushing through her. "What is this?"

Colette beamed. "Calamansi juice."

Margo stared at the magic drink. "I need to find a way to grow calamansi. Anyway, no, I don't want to miss Manang Flora when she wakes. I can walk around the grounds or read a magazine, anything, really. I'm not the kind of woman who gets bored." Although, a tingle of guilt ran up her spine from her ignored work and communications with her friends that she should be responding to.

"Hm." Colette gnawed on her lip, looking deep in thought. Then her face broke into a smile.

"What?" A smile burst from Margo's lips, too. Colette was a

joy, and Margo couldn't help but be enamored by her. Was her half sister, Marilou, Colette's mother, just as charming?

The thought brought tears to her eyes. A sister. She'd cherished her friend-sisters. How much more would she have loved Marilou? She took a drink of the calamansi juice to steer her thoughts away, and thank goodness that Colette had turned to the refrigerator.

Colette dug into the fridge with both hands. "Remember when I mentioned that you should show us your version of arroz caldo? Would you mind doing it now? I have chicken, ginger . . ."

"Oh, I don't know." Margo hedged. This woman was a restaurateur. Surely, in comparison, Margo's food would taste like it came out of an Easy-Bake Oven.

"I know it's going to be delicious!" Colette turned around with ingredients in her arms. "Thank God for my belly. It's like a little perch!"

Margo giggled and helped her unload ingredients onto the wooden kitchen island: bone-in chicken, ginger, fish sauce, onions, and garlic.

"Oh, and of course we have rice." She gestured to a waist-high receptacle with buttons labeled *1*, *2*, and *3*.

"What is that?"

"A rice dispenser. So will you do it? Not only is this Lola's favorite dish, but the baby is hungry." She splayed her hands against her tummy.

Margo acquiesced, never one to say no to a pregnant mama. "Fine. C'mon, let's do this before I lose my nerve."

It wasn't that she was a horrible cook; Margo was a great cook, in fact. But Margo had never questioned if what she was making was authentic. She'd trusted her mother's taste buds and then her own, and gradually morphed her recipes. For example, she used teriyaki and oyster sauce to liven up her chicken adobo, and she used sweet potatoes instead of regular potatoes in her picadillo. She didn't want to insult Colette.

But when she began to cook, and the scent of ginger and garlic frying in the oil hit her nostrils, Margo relaxed. She was back in her mother's kitchen. She worked with ease, adding the chicken to brown on both sides, and then taking it out, then pouring in the rice to be coated in the seasoned oil.

"Interesting, so you don't cook the chicken in fish sauce first?" Colette asked.

"I don't. Honey, when you get old, you have to watch things like sodium," Margo admitted. "But I have it available at the table, along with lemon."

"We add hard-boiled eggs and green onions to garnish."

"What a great idea. I'll do that next time," Margo said. Finally, she added water to the brim of the stockpot and covered it to boil.

When she turned, Colette's smile was gone, though her hands were still on her belly.

"Are you okay, Colette?"

"Yes and no." Hesitation lined the sides of her eyes. "This is so . . . so wonderful. I love spending time with you, but in doing so, it highlights the precarious situation we're in. Lola isn't doing well, and our lives feel so upended with you here. The briefcase—Joshua said you were able to open it, and you found letters—goodness, it's like everything I thought was . . . really isn't." She shook her head. "I'm sorry, I just totally upchucked my emotions right there, didn't I?"

"It's okay; it is," Margo reassured. "I'm a mess, too. Diana is feeling all kinds of emotions, too, though she is not quite as expressive. And those letters: they give us more of what happened, but not everything."

There was a big question that had yet to be answered, though Margo kept that to herself. Margo didn't reiterate that Colette's grandmother was the reason Antonio steered away from Leora, and she would not blame Colette for that.

"Can I say something else? Something that I hope doesn't offend you?"

"Colette, I don't think there's anything you could say that could offend me. I think we're past it."

She smiled briefly. "I'm not sure how I feel about Joshua and Ate Diana. Not only because of the whole 'he's my adopted brother' thing, but because I've never seen him so riled up and excited about anyone in such a long time. I'm a bit sad for him that she'll be leaving soon." She sipped on her juice. "But, Tita, I'm sad that you have to go, too. I guess I'm realizing this all might not end well."

"This trip doesn't have to be my last," Margo said. She was decades older than Colette and felt like she should say something wise, but at the moment, the tables could have been turned.

Colette's eyes glistened. "I want you to come back. You remind me so much of . . . my mom. It's just the little things; you might find it silly."

"Tell me more," Margo said, intrigued now. "What was Marilou like?"

"She was smart, funny, and beautiful of course." Colette smiled. "I only remember all the good things. Her laugh, the way she hugged—she used to wrap me in her arms so tightly and rub my back. She also loved chocolate." Her smile faded, and she heaved a breath.

"I'm so sorry, Colette. I know you must miss her."

"Thank you—God, it was so long ago. The car accident was just that, an accident. But seeing you is a little like having her here." She sniffed. "Lola feels it, too; it's in the way she looks at you. Since she's gotten worse, she hasn't wanted to speak to anyone. In fact, I don't know the last time we had a meal together in her wing. We were all quite excited yesterday that she invited us for an after-party. You have given her energy. We don't like to say the *d* word, but she *is* dying. And I think—I think she was waiting for something to give her some peace. Peace that might be you."

Tears bubbled just below the surface of her eyelids, but Margo kept them at bay.

"If . . ." Colette's thumb ran along the lip of her cup. "If you decide you'd like to stay longer, you are absolutely welcome. Even if no one else says it, I would like to invite you to stay, for me."

That was it, Margo let the tears go. For what came with Colette's invitation was something she hadn't planned on when she arrived in Manila. She'd hesitantly signed up to learn her family history, and what she'd received was so much more. She'd found a connection. A tangible connection by DNA and an emotional connection to this woman.

"Sorry, I'm just . . . overwhelmed," Margo said.

"I hope in a good way?"

"Yes." Margo laughed, just as the pot bubbled. She turned the burner to low, and now she had a raging appetite. "A very good way."

Chapter Twenty-Four

*O*n the boat trip to Corregidor Island, Diana shifted her focus from the quiet man next to her to the whirr of the engines and the rock-and-roll motion of the boat. With the wind blowing and the choppy water sending drops of water overtop, it was a relief from the heat.

She had not been completely honest with her mother: she was thrilled to find out that they would be going their separate ways this morning. In truth, Diana had missed Joshua as soon as she left his arms just shy of 5:00 a.m. Their night of glorious intimacy, as perfect as it had been, was not enough, and she clamored to be with him, one-on-one. To chat, to be.

But at the moment, something didn't feel right. Sure, Joshua greeted her appropriately, was kind in the car; he joked as they boarded the boat, but he was holding back. Something was wrong. She wasn't a woman who subscribed to public displays of affection, but he wasn't showing any signs of any difference in their relationship.

She ran the night over in her head. His hands, his kisses, his

caress, his teasing words—it all felt organic. Natural. Comfortable. Had she been too cold? Too clingy? Was he not satisfied?

He sure had acted like he was.

Joshua turned to her then. He'd taken off his sunglasses, now
hooked onto his V-neck tee—Diana decided that the V-neck
shirt was the sexiest style, ever—with an arm resting behind
Diana, his right leg crossed over his left knee. "Look if you're not
going to ask me what's up, then I suppose I should just tell you."

"I knew you were upset." She barked a laugh, then realized
how insensitive that sounded. "What I meant was, I've been sitting here trying to figure out what I missed."

He sighed. "I didn't . . ." But his words became indecipher-
able, and Diana didn't catch the rest of his sentence.

"What's that?"

He repeated his sentence, and still, she didn't understand.

She leaned in closer, gesturing for him to repeat it once
more.

"I didn't appreciate you leaving me in bed while I was
asleep!" he declared, promptly shushing the rows of tourists
packed around them. He slumped lower into the bench.

"You're mad at me for leaving your room?" she asked. She
took in his hurt expression.

"*Mad* isn't the right word. I . . . wished that you woke me.
There should be some etiquette about it, about waking the person after a night of s-s-s—" He looked around and lowered his
voice. "Sex."

She stifled a giggle, though her heart squeezed at his sincer-
ity. God, he was so . . . sweet that she couldn't help but tease to
cover up how she was melting into a puddle. "Doing the deed?
The horizontal hokeypokey? The nail in the—"

"Must you?"

"Oh, must I? How are you suddenly so proper?" She crossed her arms. "I am a doctor, by the way, in obstetrics and gynecology. Sex is biological."

"But it's also private, so if you would please, I don't want half this boat in this majority-Catholic country to burn us at the stake because you and I frolicked last night."

"Frolicked?"

"What?" He was laughing now.

Diana could have done another round of banter and teasing, but his message seeped through. This man cared about her, and he was asking her to consider his feelings. Whatever this was between them was beside the point. He wanted respect, so she would make sure he received it. "I'm sorry I left without saying goodbye. I just didn't want an awkward moment with Colette or anyone else, like we had with my mom. And I knew we were seeing each other this morning. I guess I didn't think twice about it."

He took her hand in his, brought it to his lips to kiss it. "I'm sorry, too. I just don't like to be surprised, not when it's about the coming and goings of people."

"Point taken." She nodded. "And I'm the same, in many respects."

"I know. You've gone over your travel itinerary several times in the few days I've known you, remember? Although, it surely wasn't that way last night. You were quite . . . open to the possibilities."

Heat blazed through her at the change of subject. Jumping into the water might be a good thing to cool her suddenly naughty thoughts. "Shhh."

"What happened to 'sex is biological'?"

"Shut up." She looked over her right shoulder. Surely everyone could see how she had turned McIntosh-apple red.

"What would our family say," she joked, though when she said it, she bit her lip.

He frowned, sensing her concern. "And here we are again, to the awkward conversation of family . . ."

The scattered voices of tourists flittered around them. From the left, someone yelled, "*Ticket ko!*" and a singular rectangular ticket fluttered between them in a curlicue trajectory over the hull of the boat.

"I'll get it!" Diana jumped to her feet just as the ticket fell within arm's reach, but as she got there, it took flight, going the opposite direction. She followed it and lunged at the ticket in the air, promptly collided into Joshua's chest, smashing it between them.

"Oh, thank God! I needed that for my album." The woman plucked the ticket between them. "But *napaka cute naman kayo.*" She winked, waving the ticket flirtatiously.

Joshua laughed, while Diana sorted out the syllables. *Napaka*, meaning "so much." *Cute?*

Cute? Them?

She jumped back at the realization that his arms were locked around her waist, and that the woman thought that they were a couple. Because sex was one thing, but couplehood? Them? He was stubborn. She, possibly more so. They were oil and water—it was evident even in the few days of them knowing each other. And while they threw off sparks in the sheets, reality put them on opposite sides of the world, and in the same family tree.

Which put their relationship, or whatever this was between them, in trouble.

"It's unforgivable our history hasn't been told enough."

Diana turned her head to the dissenter during the Corregidor Island tour. She had been distracted most of the tour despite her best effort to keep up with the history of World War II in the Pacific. Her mind jostled between Joshua, who listened with rapt attention, and her mother, who had yet to respond to her text for an update. But this was the second time this visitor had spoken up.

"Filipinos thought the Holy Grail was to leave their own country, only to work as migrant farmworkers being paid pennies on the dollar, to fight in the war, and then to be discriminated against, ostracized, and ignored in the history books." The man, dressed in a T-shirt and basketball shorts, pointed to an elderly gentleman in a wheelchair, graying and frail. Whiskers white, hands clasped within themselves, he was unperturbed by the man speaking for him. "My lolo was an Alamo Scout, but it took decades for him to receive recognition."

As the tour moved on, Diana hung back until there was some distance between her and Joshua and the group.

"What's an Alamo Scout?" Diana asked.

"Special Forces." Joshua stuck his hands in his pockets. "US Special Forces, though it wasn't just manned by White American soldiers. Filipinos, Native Americans, and Latinos staffed them, too. But their stories are rarely told. Many times, they weren't awarded the accolades they deserved." He glanced at her. "When I was in college, I didn't hear of how Filipinos took an active position during the migrant farmworker riots. Did you know?"

Diana looked down, ashamed. "No, I didn't, not until I read Antonio's letters."

"Not enough of our history is out there to be taught and celebrated. And it's so important to know it. It's our identity, our pride in being both Filipino and American. When I lived in the

US, it felt so . . . so confusing, to be me, to defend my heritage, though not really know enough about it. I'm a US citizen because of Lolo Tony, but I returned here to Manila to grapple with what I'm made out of, and who I want to be. Do you know what I mean?"

"I . . . I think I do." Diana croaked out an answer. "I think that's why I'm here, too. To learn." Because now that she thought of it, she really didn't know a damn thing. She'd lived her life in the status quo: a good job, a steady relationship with Carlo, a simple if sparse family tree. These things comprised her identity.

What was she now? Now that she risked being unemployed, was single, and suddenly part of a family on the opposite of the world? What had she ignored altogether?

"Lolo Tony was proud to be both Filipino and American, though at times he felt like he was living a contradiction—he told me that, once. I understood what he meant by it, because sometimes one must choose. Where to live, what language to speak, who's history to believe."

Diana took half steps to hang back from the tour group as it moved. He did the same.

"And Antonio chose the Philippines," Diana said. "The question is, why?"

Why did he choose Flora over Leora?

Why did he choose Manila over California?

"I don't know why he did it. But I chose the Philippines because of him."

"Is this why you're so protective of his stuff, even with the rest of the family?"

"I'm protective of his stuff because I loved the man. He was getting old, and he knew Colette would need my help whenever it was time for him to retire. Colette is a talented chef, but she didn't want to manage the hotel. She and Philip always talked about having a family. But, yes, I take personal responsibility for his things because that is our specific family history. When you first arrived, I thought that you were here for his wealth, even though now I realize that it's Lolo and Lola who have, or had, a lot of explaining to do." For a moment, he looked stricken. "I hope I didn't offend you."

"Surprisingly, I took no offense at that. It's fair." Diana stopped, and he turned back to look at her. "I understand protectiveness because I feel the same way toward my mother. She's all I have in the world. We don't always see eye to eye, but she has been through a lot. No offense to your family—even though I'm related to them, and you've been so gracious—but my mother is trusting, emotional, and I'm scared that all of this is just another fairy tale to her."

"That's fair, too."

The island was silent except for the occasional sound of a bird chirping. Yards down, someone laughed. Light burst through the trees, and in the sun's filter, Diana's respect for this man grew. It blossomed in her chest.

"Look, Joshua."

At the same time, Joshua said, "Diana—"

"Go ahead," she said.

He settled his hands on her hips, tugged her gently toward him. They were so close, she saw the specks of black in his brown eyes. It was a tiny public display of affection, but it felt as intimate as the night they spent in bed. His lips were inches away, and she watched him bite his lower lip before he said, "I like you, Diana. I suppose that's why I was a little bent out of shape that you left without even a note. I don't want to get this wrong. We can't get it wrong."

"I agree . . . with all of what you said. I mean, the feeling is mutual." Her face burned. She envied people who just said what they felt, while she mulled over every word. "What do you propose?"

"I'd like to hear what you think first, because I'm pretty sure I will go with whatever you choose." He grinned.

It was sweet, this back-and-forth nature of his, from grumpy, to unsure, to complete honesty. It was also utter bad luck that Joshua was who he was. "I . . . I don't want to stop what's happening between us."

"Well, I don't want to stop, either."

"But I'm only here a few more days. Can we make this work, without . . ."

"Without getting serious?"

Without getting hurt. She nodded. "Can we try?"

"I would like that."

The rumble of his voice made her knees go weak. He stared at her intensely, as if he was undressing her. Or maybe that was her wishful thinking. His lips grazed hers in an almost kiss, a seduction Diana knew she would fall for time and again.

She swallowed her desire and said, "Good. Me too."

"What do we tell your mother, my sister?"

"Why do we have to say anything at all?"

He laughed. "Because I'm sure they'll ask."

"Hello. Yoo-hoo!" the tour guide called. She waved at them from several yards away. "We're moving to the next stop."

"Let's think about it, then," Diana said.

"Okay."

But as they raced to catch up to the rest of the group, hand in hand, now with one question answered, Diana was left wondering if her mother's had been, too.

Marysville, California
April 24, 1944

Dearest Antonio,

   *Receiving a letter from you is like Christmastime. Even
my father, who is usually too cross to notice my presence,
commented the other day that I was smiling. Yes, it was a
day I received two of your letters at once.*

   *It gives me much relief that you have found
friendship there, that you have people to speak to and
are not alone. As for me, it has been quite busy here at
Mrs. Lawley's. I'm now staying at her place past supper
so I may read to her. She says she is loneliest right before
bedtime, and since she will pay extra for my time, my
father has agreed.*

   *At first, I wasn't keen on the idea of spending more
time with the woman. You remember her hard exterior
and her cutting insults. However, these days, she has
fewer harsh things to say, but more advice. In all honesty,
I don't mind her company, either. On the days I don't get
a letter from you and the loneliness is heavy in my heart,
a chat with her brings up my mood.*

   *Her family came to visit from Washington, DC: her
daughter, son-in-law, and two grandchildren. They took*

the train across the country! While here, I overheard
them trying to convince her to move, saying she should
retire now that she's a widow, but Mrs. Lawley says
it is too cold out east, that she prefers the climate of
Marysville. Then her family suggested that I move with
her and be a permanent caregiver.

No, sweetheart, you don't have to worry about me
running off. I will be right here when you return. My
father would never agree. While he acts angry, he needs
me, needs my contribution to help with our own home. I
know I have spoken ill of him on more than one occasion,
but he is still my father, and my place is with him. That
is, until you return.

I haven't been feeling well as of late. My usual weak
stomach is upset most of the day. Joy, another girl that
works at the shop, thinks I might have developed a
sensitivity to cow's milk, which would be such a great
disappointment. But that doesn't seem likely, all of a
sudden.

As for your father, I have seen him time and again,
sometimes taking a break behind the restaurant. While
he and I haven't spoken, I can tell he misses you in the
slump of his shoulders, like the energy has been drained
out of him. The restaurant itself is busy, as the asparagus

harvest has begun, and there are more workers in town. Since so many boys have left for the war and the farms continue to bloom, more workers have come from up north to fill the need.

The tension has increased here. Farmworkers want more pay and better living conditions. They want water and rightly so! When Joy and I are in town, we hear things. Yes, we eavesdrop! No one seems to notice us in the background, us girls. She and I hear about violence and, at times, we see it, too.

Sweetheart, I don't want you to worry. I am sleeping on a bed, under a roof, whereas you are . . . you are in a land I cannot fathom. Your description of the ship was foreign enough, and now in New Guinea, I feel very far from you. Yesterday, I found a map in one of Mrs. Lawley's books and drew a line with my finger from the United States to New Guinea, imagining what it's been like for you to take that trip across the world to a brand-new country.

It's only now, as I write that sentence, that I realize your trip to New Guinea was not your first such journey. You did the same coming from the Philippines. How brave you have been. How brave your father was. I declare now that if you can cross the ocean, my dearest, I

can do it, too. I can very well survive being lonely without
you.

As for me, it is more of the same. I wake, I work, and
I go home and think of you.

I love you,
Leora

Chapter Twenty-Five

"Ah, you stayed." Flora's hoarse voice lured Margo into the dark expanse of her bedroom. Behind Flora stood Edna, who assisted her to a sitting position. "I hope you weren't waiting too long."

"No. I busied myself," Margo smiled, tentative. Flora looked markedly more tired this afternoon, despite having slept most of the day.

"You should smell the kitchen, Manang." Edna nodded at Margo, eyes gleaming. "Manang Margo made arroz caldo."

"For me?" Flora's voice was a squeak, and she cleared her throat.

"Um . . . sort of . . . though, don't judge if it's not what you expect." Margo shied at the idea of serving Flora her arroz caldo. While Colette said it was delicious, she was surely just being nice. "Here, let me help you, Edna." She picked up her step, took Flora's other side, and slid her hand under her armpit, to help position her the rest of the way. Once she was propped by pillows, Edna fixed the oxygen tube running from Flora's nose to the tank below.

"Fix me a bowl, Edna, please. I'd love to try it," Flora said, then added, "Margo, come and sit with me."

Margo did as she was told, pulling the closest chair bedside so it faced Flora. As Edna passed, she patted Margo on the shoulder, which felt like an encouragement of sorts. "I'll be right outside the door. Is Colette here?"

"She's in the guest room taking a nap."

"I'll let her be." She turned back to Flora. "Want something else with your food?"

"A shot of bourbon."

"Sure, with a cigarette, too?"

"The good stuff. Hand-rolled. No filter," Flora croaked.

Edna threw her head back with a laugh.

Margo waited for the door to close. Watched the elderly woman for a beat. Today, large pearl earrings dotted Flora's earlobes, and a hefty gold bracelet graced her left wrist. Her hair was loose, thin and wispy, grazing her shoulders. "Thank you for seeing me."

"No Diana today?"

"She's on an excursion, with Joshua."

"Ah." Flora's sharp cheekbones raised into a mischievous smile. "I can only imagine their conversations. Joshua has very strong opinions about many things, though he is a very kind soul. As I'm sure your daughter is, too."

"Yes, but she is a handful sometimes."

"But that is a blessing, to have such a loving child who is also headstrong. We all need people like that around us, especially during hard times." The last of her voice scratched, and she pointed at her nightstand, at a cup of water with a straw. Margo handed her the cup and took it back after she sipped. "You're lucky to still have your children with you. I always prayed for health, for a long life, but no one tells you that it's at the expense of having to see people move on. No mother should have to bury her child."

"I'm sorry," Margo said, and winced. The statement was so empty, so generic. "You're right, and I pray I'll never know the pain you've experienced."

"So." She swallowed a breath. "You opened the briefcase?"

Margo nodded.

"And."

"There were more letters. But there are still . . . holes in the story." Diana flashed in Margo's head, chanting, "Out with it!," so Margo strived to do just that. "I'm here because I need to know the truth, and you are the only one who can supply that. You wrote a letter to my mother. You said that he was choosing not to return to the United States, but after reading all of my mother's letters to my father, I still don't understand. Why would he choose not to return?"

"Anak, how would it help? Would it change your life if I told you what I knew? Would it matter?"

Margo paused, truly reckoning with the questions. Margo had seen seventy-five birthdays come and go, all without the truth about her father. Despite that, she'd lived a life full of both triumph and challenges. "Yes, it would."

"What if I said that in telling you everything, about who you are, there's a responsibility in accepting who you are?"

"What kind of responsibility?"

"The kind that binds you not just to me, but to this estate. Las Cruces, and this country."

Margo didn't know what all these leading questions meant. "I . . . I don't think I'm worried about that."

The woman took another sip, and she shut her eyes, inhaling

the oxygen through her tube as if to fill herself with courage, but as she opened her mouth to speak, Margo understood that it was she who would need the fortification.

I was only a young woman, but I knew enough of the dangers of the world. The Japanese had occupied Tacloban. I lived in fear of danger to our lives. But before the war, the situation was already dire. My brother had left for America. He worked the fields in California, although I didn't know that at the time. He sent money home and that was the only way we survived. My younger sisters wanted to be just like him, wanted to leave because America promised a better life. But as the oldest daughter, I couldn't leave my family, my parents. I couldn't leave my home, even as my father began to sell away parcels of our land, and even if we were running out of food.

Our family needed help, and our neighbors became our family, and we all did what we could to survive under the Japanese occupation. Then the American invasion that would save our country destroyed everything first. When we looked out onto the waters, into Leyte Gulf, it was no longer beautiful or serene, but a horizon of boats, the outlines of soldiers coming onto shore. The nights were no longer a quiet peace. We no longer enjoyed the expansive inky sky or the stars dotting us from above. Everything changed, and we had changed, too.

But we were still hopeful. Our brother, Ignacio, had sent a letter early in the war that he was coming home. He was enlisting in the Army and he was an American. He said that no matter where he landed ashore, he would find his way back home.

That was why we stayed where we were. We were waiting for him.

He never came home. Instead, Antonio Cruz appeared at our doorstep. At first, when I opened the door to his uniform and muddied face, I thought it was my brother. I almost leaped into his arms. He looked a lot like him, you see. Over time, I found out that all the soldiers had that same look—gaunt, haunted.

My mother came to the door, curious, and at seeing Antonio, she wailed. Up to that point, I didn't understand. You see, I was still hopeful. Hope is, essentially, what makes us Filipino. I thought that this Antonio Cruz was simply a messenger, like another one of Ignacio's letters.

When Antonio fell to his knees, I knew. I knew that my brother was dead. We would never see him again. My heart broke into a million pieces. I thought it had already been broken with the war, with all we'd lost, but this was different. Ignacio was my big brother. I knew him the moment I was born. He was like the sun to me.

While on his knees, this Antonio said a lot of words, many through tears. I couldn't understand them, but later on, over the course of years, he would tell me what had happened upon landing in Leyte. Their unit was told that they would be "mopping up operations" from the invasion, as if people were like water to be soaked and then squeezed for discard. As if there wouldn't be fighting, defending, or dying. My brother had saved Antonio's life, had thrown his body over Antonio's, to shield him from harm during a rain of gunfire. My God, Ignacio almost made it home.

Antonio promised his devotion to our family. He had made the pact to my brother as he died, and he made the pact to God.

I hated Antonio and didn't speak to him for his short stay at Tacloban. The Army continued on to Luzon for the rest of the war and then returned months later, and I still hated him. He lived by himself, worked around town. He helped my parents rebuild our home. He gave my family money and kept largely out of the way. Soon, my parents forgave him, but I didn't, not for a long, long time.

One day, I accepted his presence. Something happened that year: I realized that he was a good man. We became friends, and in that time I learned about the nightmares, about his fears, and about his love for a woman whose father would never approve of him. The guilt of my brother's death ate him up inside. But late in 1945, he received a letter, which he wanted me to respond to. He didn't show me the letter, but he begged for help, said that it would be the last of his past. I was eager to move on, to build a life with him because he was a good man. So, like everyone did in wartime, I did my part to survive. I wrote the letter for him.

Flora coughed and wheezed, and it became interminable. Margo rose from her chair and rubbed the woman's back, still in a daze from what had sounded like a fairy tale coming from her lips. Through Flora's shirt, Margo felt her vertebrae, saw the thin gold chain necklace that held a delicate crucifix. This reminder of her age punctuated her story with even more sadness and regret.

"Your brother was Ignacio?" Margo's voice shook. She had wanted to be angry. She had wanted to lash out in frustration, but she felt no animosity. Instead, empathy arose. She half laughed at the convoluted way the truth showed itself. "I didn't expect for you to say that."

"Your mother didn't deserve the letter I sent her, Margo. And I am sorry."

Margo's hand stilled on the woman's back. She came around and sat on the edge of the bed. Flora gripped Margo's hand.

"Antonio kept secrets. I did, too. And we accepted that we wouldn't talk about the past, that we wouldn't force each other to do anything we didn't want to do. It was our unsaid agreement."

"What did that letter say? The one that came for him?"

"I don't know. It was from America, forwarded by the Army." She shook her head. "At first, I refused to help him, but he begged. I couldn't bear to see that; he'd suffered too much already. So I did it. I wrote what he dictated."

"So it wasn't you?"

"It was me, Margo, but it was Antonio who dictated those words. I didn't know your mother was pregnant with you."

Pain pierced through her as Roberta's words from just a few days ago came flooding back: *Prepare yourself for the worst-case scenario.*

This was the worst-case scenario. "So my father didn't want me?"

Flora tore her eyes away from Margo's face, and that was the confirmation.

It was her father who hadn't wanted her, not this woman. There was no one to blame but him, and he was dead.

Margo was speechless.

What could one say to that?

"But there's more, anak. Your father, my husband, had a stipulation in his will. That stipulation is what binds you." Flora laughed. It was the oddest thing, but she looked up at the ceiling and said, "And now I know why you insisted on writing it so, Tony."

Margo frowned, jostled back into speech. "What's that?"

Her eyes gleamed with mischief. "Joshua even questioned it, fought it, because he felt it was too vague and muddled. But I understand now. That stubborn, infuriating husband of mine."

"Joshua?" Margo whispered.

"That boy is precious to me; his mother was a part of this family from the moment she arrived to the day she died, gone too soon, so young. And Antonio—Antonio trusted him. Antonio saw him squarely as a grandson, and it makes more sense now." A smile graced her face, her eyes staring just above Margo's head, as if she were getting answers from another plane.

While Margo had witnessed Flora's clear devotion to her Catholic faith, Margo was far from religious. She considered herself pragmatic and didn't believe in ghosts. But even she could feel that, right then, the two of them weren't alone in that room.

"*The eldest descendant will inherit the Cruz Estate.*" Flora blinked, the glaze in her eyes falling back to clarity. "That was the line in the will, Margo. And that descendant is me. Then I'd assumed my daughter, but she is no longer with us. But, Margo, it's you. It's you, then Diana."

"Who would have come after you, had me or Diana not shown up?"

"Joshua."

Chapter Twenty-Six

The complete tour took only four hours, but to Diana, an entire lifetime had passed. She felt heavy from all the words she'd read in the brochures, from the history explained by the tour guide. It was like trying to digest a dense piece of medical literature all at once, with names and dates and consequences crammed into one page of minuscule writing.

In that half day's span, the divide between her and Joshua had fallen away. Her small bit of vulnerability had been reciprocated in spades. They walked a little closer, shoulders rubbing every so often, sometimes standing so close that she felt the barrier she'd erected so long ago give a little. Perhaps it was their near-familial bond, now undeniable. Perhaps it was Joshua's ability to take her breath away when he committed to the moment, as he was now, in his car, with his lips on hers.

They were in the back seat, still parked next to the dock. His hands were entangled in her hair. She gripped the front of his shirt. The air around them had spiked several degrees, despite the blasting AC.

Diana worked the buttons of his shirt, inching it down so she could run her fingers across his chest, and he had started to slip his hands under the hem of her shirt when a knock threw them apart.

Diana watched as a gaggle of kids passed them, laughing, making smooching noises in the air. Her heart beat in her throat. Oh my God, they were just making out in the back seat of his car. When was the last time she'd gone parking with a man?

She couldn't even remember.

He eyed her devilishly. "Damn, Diana."

She giggled, shocked and impressed with herself. *Damn right.* "We should go, right?"

"Yeah." He was still breathing hard. "Home?"

"Yes, home." Then Diana's brain woke. "No, not home. My mom is at Sunset Corner." There was nothing like the thought of her mother to bring her libido back into check, that was for sure. "I'm sorry. But later?"

"It's a promise." He took a breath. "I think the only thing that will cure this feeling is a cold shower or some good food. Are you up to eat before we see everyone?"

"Sounds like a great idea." She already had her phone out, and with one click was in her notes app. "What about this restaurant on my list? I think it's nearby." She tilted the phone toward him.

He gave it a cursory glance. "That place isn't good."

"But it has five stars."

"It's overrated, caters to tourists. Do you want to try something new? Something that might be out of your comfort zone?"

It was a silly challenge, but who did he think he was talking to? When it came to food, there was no such thing as a comfort zone. "I'm down. Take me there. But will there be choices because—"

He touched her wrist, to halt the beginnings of a litany of demands, and it had the desired effect. The gesture was kind, gentle, and in another measure of letting go, she adjusted her hand, opening it so his entwined with hers. For a moment, he just took a breath, and with a quick upturn of his lips, said, "There will be so many choices, your head's going to spin."

"Okay."

They both climbed out of the back seat and into the front. After he started the car, he took Diana's hand in his. She settled into the leather seat, suddenly aware of how stiff she was, and how clammy her hand was in his. Could he tell she was giddy, that she loved this small bit of affection? That the cold AC blasting from the vents did nothing for the fact that her entire body was steaming hot?

"Tell me about your work." He tugged on her fingers.

She could feel herself beaming with pride. "What do you want to know?"

"Anything. Everything." He navigated the car with one hand, as if unaware of the traffic and the assertive drivers around him. The landscape had changed once again, and Diana didn't recognize where they were headed.

Her cheeks warmed. "I love mamas. I mean, I love babies, too, but I'm in awe of the mother's part in childbirth. Hence becoming an OB versus a pediatrician. For them, not only is it biologic effort for their bodies to become mothers, but there's also that emotional effort, too. When I say I've seen a pregnant woman go mama bear, I mean it. It happens in labor, when they are literally trusting nature by enduring pain. It happens after the baby is born, when they put aside their own discomfort to care for a little one. Women are amazing, you know?"

"I know," he said, his voice teasing. "I'm surrounded by women."

"Consider yourself lucky." She tugged at his hand. "With that said, being a doctor is a privilege, but I haven't been happy for a while. I'm tired from the hours I pull, though admittedly that's somewhat self-inflicted. But the profession is money-driven, not the selfless ideal I had going in, and the hospital I work for caters to the upper crust, so I'm not sure it's where I belong."

"Can you do something else?"

"I can, of course, but it's not that easy. I can't just leave my job. I've got student loans, responsibilities to my patients." She shrugged, not wanting to say too much, aware that her thoughts were jumbled and all over the place. Hence the reason why it was always easier for her to just do rather than speak, to act rather than explain. Having to illustrate her intentions just made her sound superficial. "I was raised by a single mom, who was raised by a single mom. My entire family is comprised of women. Women helping women to raise children. Aunts and best friends, neighbors. Ultimately, I'm compelled by a desire to be a contributing member of the village who raised me and feel obliged to it. And have you heard teachers say they feel like their students are like their kids?" she asked him. When he nodded, she said, "That's how I feel about being a doctor. I feel like I'm the sister, that I'm the aunt who knows what to do in the most vulnerable times in a woman's life. This is me giving back in the best way I can. I can't imagine *not* working with mothers."

She hadn't realized that she'd pulled his hand onto her lap

until he took it from hers when they reached a red light. He tucked a fallen strand of hair behind her ear, then padded a thumb lightly along her cheek. He held her gaze, and Diana's heart escalated as she held her breath.

"I totally just spewed my life story right there, didn't I?"

"Yes, and I loved it."

Behind them came a cacophony of honking cars. The light had turned green, and the cars next to them had lurched to life, already speeding down the highway. Good thing he looked away from her and to the road; Diana needed a second to catch her breath. This feeling was better than her runner's high or her doctor's high. It was the feeling of . . . belonging.

He cleared his throat, pressed on the gas. "I think it's admirable, your profession. I certainly couldn't do it. The screaming women. All the . . . fluids."

She laughed. "Well, there is definitely that."

"And screaming."

"Yes, that, too. But I call it a battle cry. Sometimes it comes in the form of tears, but it's pure determination."

"I've got major respect for it. Child-rearing, too. My ex aside, the girls are a wonder. I don't know how this screwup got so lucky to have become a part of their lives."

She rubbed his knuckles with a thumb. "You're not really a screwup, are you? Antonio wouldn't have called you back here to Manila if you were anything but capable."

"I guess." He sighed. "Truth be told, my resumé is actually pretty kick-ass. And yet . . ."

"What?" Diana waited at his pause, not knowing if she should pry further. "Do you want to talk about it?"

"I guess since you shared, I should, too, right?"

Diana shook her head. "No, you don't have to."

"No, I want to tell you. It's just hard to talk about." His lips pressed into a line. His gaze darted left, then right. "I said I came to Manila because Lolo Tony called me back, but I was ready. I graduated from UCLA, in business, but I didn't feel at ease enough in California to live there permanently. I missed Manila. So I came back, started grad school here. I also went through a wild streak—I was a spoiled little shit, you see. That's what money sometimes does to you. Anyway, I was finishing up my last semester in school, and I cheated, on an exam. And was caught."

Diana winced. "Oh no."

"Yep." He tore his eyes away from her and fixed them on the road in front of them. "Bad move. I regret it every day, even if Lolo saved me from all the consequences. I got kicked out of school, but I still worked for him. I still had a place to live, food to eat. He could have thrown me out into the street. He was so shamed. I was ashamed." He half laughed. "The man worked me hard. He never brought it up, but I felt the gratitude every day. He taught me everything about loyalty and family, and hard work. And I swore to be better."

The car swerved into a space where around them a mass of pedestrians walked in every direction. In front of them was an entrance marked with an archway. The entrance itself was as wide as a one-lane road. Vendors with aquariums and tubs of clams and other shellfish lined the sidewalk.

"Do you still want to hang out with me even after knowing this?" he asked.

Diana didn't hesitate. "I do. Very much so. One decision shouldn't determine your fate."

"I'm glad you feel that way." He glanced askance at her, lips turning up into a smile. "You've just made me a happy man. So, are you ready for a mind-bender?" He gestured at the windshield. "Because that is an outdoor dry and wet market. Welcome to the Philippines in the way I know and love," he said, getting out of the car, then opening the door for Diana. "Open mind, okay?"

When she stepped out onto the noisy street, she leaned forward and kissed Joshua, and said, "Open mind." But inside, two other words sprung to mind: *open heart*.

At the *palenke*, vendors sat almost atop one another, and the squawk of conversation invaded the air. Conversation volleyed across narrow pathways, flanked by contrasting colored goods. Deeper into the market, as Joshua led her through with a firm grip on her hand, the smell of fish, chicken, beef, and pork hanging from hooks assaulted the senses. The space seemed unending. One corridor only led to another, the changing landscape of the food like the switch of a neighborhood mid-jog in DC.

It was the most magnificent thing Diana had experienced. It was loud and overwhelming, true, but it was alive. Laughter rang out among the exchange of goods, and storytelling mixed with negotiation.

They spilled out into a square, where the smell of fried foods filled the air. They passed a cart grilling meat on a stick, another vendor pan-frying nuts. A woman poured water in a clear dispenser for juice. Another dipped quail eggs into batter before tossing them into a vat of oil. All of it tempted Diana, whose salivary glands were on overload.

"What do you feel like having?" Joshua asked.

"Anything." Diana's tummy growled. "One of everything?"

"That's what I like to hear." He let go of her hand and spoke to one vendor after another, then gestured. "Lunch is almost served. Let's go find someplace to sit."

"So, what do you think?" Joshua asked later, after a quick negotiation with a vegetable vendor for two plastic chairs. "Honestly."

She took a second to think about it. "Honestly? Freaking chaotic. But fun. I could get lost in here. And my mother would have a field day with all of this. We'll need to bring her."

He bit into the fried calamari on the stick. "Would you give me five stars?" Seeing her confusion, he said. "On your restaurant app, would you give me five stars?"

She narrowed her eyes at him before dipping dried fish into vinegar sauce and shrugged.

"Seriously? I even finagled chairs." He turned to the vendor, behind his vegetables. "Manong—five stars, *po*?"

The older man nodded, smiling in cahoots. "Five stars."

She laughed. "Fine. Four and a half stars."

He leaned into her ear and whispered, "I think I know exactly what I can do to round up that last star. The question is: How much time will you give me?"

She shivered at the suggestion, until—with the sudden clarity—the answer to his question descended upon her. "Forty-eight hours."

"Two days." His voice lost its gravelly tone.

"Yeah." Her emotions had been a vast spectrum since her arrival, but for the first time since arriving, she wanted to stay longer. She hadn't seen enough; she hadn't learned enough. There was more to explore with Joshua. But this wasn't real life. "I have a house that's being renovated. I have a job."

She thought of her mother, who didn't have the same obligations. Margo, who always seemed to have a choice. And not for the first time, she wished she had the same freedom.

Joshua handed her a bottled water, thank goodness, in time to clear the lump that had formed in her throat. "Can you extend your trip?"

"Not really." She halted, then dove into it headlong: what happened that night in the emergency room, her decision, and the aftermath.

He listened to her patiently, nodding, then asked. "Would you ever return here? To the Philippines. To visit," he quickly added. "There's so much family you haven't met yet. We have a whole contingent in Leyte, my lola's family."

"Yes, of course, when time permits," she reassured, and yet, something tugged at her between the lines of his question. But if he wasn't ready to talk about it—them—then she wouldn't, either. Their situation was early. It was casual, right? "How about you? Do you come to the US ever?"

"I usually visit once a year. These days, someone is always getting married, having kids that need a godfather. But the hotel—and Colette will need my help with the restaurant after this baby comes. And, of course, there's Lola. When she passes, it's me and Colette left to run the business. If I visited, I wouldn't be able to stay for too long. This is my home."

Diana understood; she empathized. In fact, she sympathized. And from the resigned expression on Joshua's face, she knew he was thinking the same thing, too—it could never be, no matter how she wished for it.

Marysville, California
July 15, 1944

Dear Antonio,

I'm still not feeling well. Everything smells bad, and my stomach is suffering for it. One minute I'm so hungry I can eat everything on the table, and then the next minute, I recoil at the idea of food. I have also been oversleeping. I was late to Mrs. Lawley's three times this week because my body feels so heavy it's like I've been weighed down by bricks. Even my father, who cares for no one but himself, has shown concern.

I believe I am pregnant, my love. Three months pregnant. No, I haven't seen a doctor yet, and I can't, not until I have a plan. But I have all the signs. And I can't imagine what else could make my body feel this way, like it is not my own. It's like I'm asleep and awake all at once.

I have told Joy. I had to tell someone. Joy's sister, who has had two babies, says that I will be showing in about two months, that I won't be able to hide it even if I tried.

I write this letter through tears because I'm not sure what I should do. I don't know if I'm supposed to be happy or upset. I'm not sure if I should scream with fear or with joy. This baby is half you and half me. It's as if,

*finally, the world is acknowledging that we do exist, that
you aren't a figment of my imagination. That our love
means something.*

*Joy is worried. She has brought up many scenarios
where I have imagined the worst. No one will want us.
Marysville is against this—us, this baby. Not to mention
the law.*

*Please don't be angry with me, or regret what we did.
I can't bear it if you had any doubts or thought that you
and I and this baby were mistakes. Joy thinks I am naive,
and maybe I am, but what I know is this: I love you, and
I love this baby despite how scared I am. I'm going to
sit here, and I'm going to make a plan, and I'm going to
write you and tell you about it, all right?*

*Please take care of yourself. Please keep yourself safe.
At every sunset, I will pray to the heavens above for the
end of this war and for you to come back to me.*

I love you,
Leora

Chapter Twenty-Seven

*F*lora's directions in mind, Margo entered the house hidden behind the trees in the backyard. It was just as Diana had described it, but Margo didn't slow down to appreciate the details. She had one thing to retrieve and her focus was solely on that. With Edna taking the lead, opening the home with a key on a key ring Flora had retrieved from her bedside table drawer, Margo followed her through the tiny home, to a closet in the home office.

"No one has been in this closet for a long time." Edna flipped to another key and stuck it in the doorknob. The lock clacked, and the door popped open. "There's a light up above. I have to go back to the house. Will you be okay?"

"Yes. Thank you," Margo said, already moving past her and pulling the chain. When the light flickered on, she inhaled a slow, shallow breath.

This room was a pack rat's dream. Books upon books burgeoned from the built-in cabinets, with trinkets poised on stacks of paper and newspaper clippings. Rocks, big and little, from—

Margo could only assume—places Antonio found interesting, were piled in the corners.

"So this is where I get it from," she mused. All at once, she felt at home in this space. Her fingers skimmed a dusty shelf; she fingered the beads of a plastic army-green rosary hanging from a nail on the wall.

The sight of all of it put a smile on her face for the first time since Flora revealed that Antonio had dictated the letter. She had been ready to blame Flora; she had also been ready to forgive her, but how could she forgive someone who was already dead?

But Margo pushed all that aside for now. There would be days, weeks, and months to process. Right now, more pressing issues remained.

When Flora had informed Margo of her father's will, Margo had wanted proof. The idea of taking on the family's properties was outrageous and far-fetched. And if the man had known there was a possibility she existed, why hadn't he tried to find her?

According to Flora, her father had two copies of his will: one kept by his lawyers in a separate safe, another in a brown leather-bound folder in this closet.

Margo's phone buzzed in her pocket. When she looked, more text notifications flashed on the screen. But she didn't want anything to distract her. If this had been last week, she would have taken a picture of this closet and then slumped into a chair and spent too much time composing a message to accompany it.

Now, she had neither the time nor the emotional bandwidth to do it. As she looked for the folder through the stacks of papers and books packed in the shelves and corners, the gravity of what she was doing caught up to her. She was in her dead father's office closet. Her hands shook; to ground herself, she whispered her instructions. "Leather-bound portfolio. Leather-bound portfolio."

Then she caught sight of something brown and shiny. She touched the smooth spine.

"This is it," she whispered.

She stepped out of the closet and sat in the office chair that looked out to the backyard, where the sun had begun to descend, casting an orange hue in the sky. It dawned on her then—the home's name now made perfect sense. *Sunset Corner*. This seat Margo had taken, this view, *was* Sunset Corner.

She untied the straps of the portfolio, fanned it open, and lifted a stapled document.

The legalese was relentless. Margo was an artist and not a scientist or a lawyer for a reason—her eyes glossed over technical terms like skates on ice. She scanned down, turned pages, until she found the words *Las Cruces* and then backtracked to the beginning of the section. She read aloud: "'I hereby bequeath the ownership and management of the Cruz Estate to Flora Cruz until her death or until she determines she is unable. Thereafter, the eldest descendant will inherit the Cruz Estate. The Cruz Estate consists of Las Cruces Hotel, Sunset Corner, and all its assets. Forthcoming owners will have authoritative control and input in the hotel's board of directors.'"

Her chest tightened with the start of tears as emotions slammed against her. Anger at her father, then wonder as to how this development would play out. How would this new truth fit into her current life? What part of herself would she have to give up for this legacy? Would Diana miss her if she moved?

The thought came so suddenly that she dropped the stapled

papers in her hand. Not once had she contemplated leaving her daughter's side permanently, and vice versa. Home base had always been with or near one another, in Old Town Alexandria. But this will might change that.

Margo buried herself in words for the next few hours: in the will, in newspaper clippings her father saved that marked the passage of time, in the titles of the books he kept, in the annotated margins. She cataloged the way he grouped his memorabilia. Rocks in one place, marked by a black marker for the date, receipts in a wooden box. Photos, sepia with time, interspersed throughout. Soon, night truly fell.

But aside from the will, there were no other hints of her mother, of their love and relationship. Margo searched for clues in all the ways readers search for Easter eggs in their favorite authors' books. But it was to no avail. After sorting through another receipt, she slumped against the desk chair.

It was as if, for her father, Margo's life had been written in chalk, then wiped away with one fell swoop.

"Tita Margo?" Colette's voice echoed through the house. While it had been only a few hours, it felt like days had passed. Margo sat up in her chair and took stock of the state of the office, now littered with items she'd examined.

"In the office!" she called back.

Several sets of footsteps followed, and Colette appeared at the doorway. Her hair was slightly askew, but she bore a sad smile, probably in response to Margo's state of being. "Hi."

"How are you? How was your nap?"

"Okay." Her eyes bounced around the room. "You haven't been answering your texts."

"Sorry, I put it on silent. I was looking for . . ." But Margo couldn't pin down the right word. Instead, she shrugged.

"I have people here to see you."

Margo shook her head, not understanding. "Oh?"

Colette stepped aside, and two figures came into the room. At first, they were so out of place that Margo didn't recognize the man and woman. Her mind was so mired in the past, in simply catching up on decades of denial and days of shock. But here were her dearest friends. Cameron and Roberta. Handsome, steady Cameron in his polo and shorts, and travel-weary but perfectly made-up Roberta. Her two bookends. She stood, and they rushed toward her.

"Oh my God, what?" was all Margo could say, tears streaming down her cheeks. "How did you know?"

"I gave you twenty-four hours after I knew your flight landed to contact us, but you didn't make contact. You didn't text us. And we weren't going to let you get away with it," Roberta said, and slapped at her gently. "You're lucky I love you or else I would disown you. Did you expect us to sit there in LA and go on with our normal lives when you didn't text or post or anything?" She frowned. "I'm mad at you still, so this is not over." She hugged Margo again. When she pulled back, her eyes were as wide as saucers. "What is all this stuff?"

"I have a lot to catch you up on." Margo patted her face free of tears as Roberta rifled through the papers. She looked up at Cameron, who was a sight for sore eyes. Seeing him soothed some of her ache, and in her relief she felt no awkwardness between them.

He wrapped his arms around her, and she sank into his hold. She'd needed someone to hug her, to hold her, and for a moment she felt protected and secure.

"I'm just so glad you're okay," he said.

"How did you guys even find me?"

"C'mon now, you're talking to me. I can work the Google." His lips crooked up into a half smile. "And, my memory is still on point."

"But your plans . . ."

"*Our* plans."

"That's right, old lady, where you go, we go. Besides, I couldn't stand being around Cam with his sad face," Roberta yelled from the closet. "Just kiss her again already. I'm not looking this time!"

"Oh, Bert." Cameron shut his eyes slowly and shook his head.

From the desk chair, Colette giggled, her fingers on her lips.

When he opened his eyes again, he stared intently into Margo's eyes, all trace of his usual whimsy gone. He took both of her hands in his, squeezed them gently. "I don't want to have to admit when Bert's right, but when we kissed at the airport, and then you left? It tore me apart, Margo. It dawned on me that we've known each other all of our lives, and that was only our first kiss. You and I know that time can be a jerk, and I don't want to waste any more of it."

"What are you saying?"

"That I'm here. That if you don't mind, can I hang out wherever you are?"

"Cameron, spell it out," Roberta interrupted, voice muffled.

Cameron cleared his throat. "I love you, Margaret. Can we— can we have a go at this?"

And somehow in the middle of Margo's deep sorrow, gratitude sprouted for what she did have. She had these two out-of-this-world friends. And, with one of them, love. *Love.* Love in a way that wasn't instant or earth-shattering, but the kind that bloomed slowly like an agave flower, and in their case took almost eight decades to see its potential.

"I love you, too." She stepped forward and kissed him on the lips. From beneath her fingers she felt the smooth fabric of his shirt, and leaned in. He tasted of caramel, of comfort, of home.

"Ma?" a woman's voice piped from behind her. "Cameron?"

"Who are these people? What is this?" boomed a second voice. Joshua. "His things, they're everywhere . . . everyone, out. Out!"

part six

Dawn

Every sunset brings the promise of a new dawn.

—Ralph Waldo Emerson

Marysville, California
September 8, 1944

Dear Antonio,

My heart is broken as I write this letter. Onofre told
me that you have already been informed about your
father's death. I am so sorry, my sweetheart.

The church has provided a plot with donations from
neighbors and friends. I spoke with Onofre, and he
will use the money you send to make sure it is properly
marked. I promise to visit him as often as possible, as
often as Mrs. Lawley will allow.

Speaking of Mrs. Lawley: She had decided to move
to Washington, DC. Her family will return within the
year so she may travel with them back. She misses her
grandchildren. I'm not sure where I will go after she
moves on. It's my hope that you will have returned by
then.

It is increasingly hard to hide the evidence of the baby.
My father is sure to turn me away. Joy says I should run
away with her instead, but two women cannot make it on
their own, not when one is with child. I've got no choice
but to tell him.

I pray for you, Antonio, that you find peace now that

your father is gone. But please pray for me, too. I will have to tell my father soon, and I will need your strength to do so.

I love you, with every sunset.
Leora

Chapter Twenty-Eight

They'd had a glorious day, she and Joshua. With a plastic sack of fresh mangoes from the palenke, they strode up to Sunset Corner, discussing their plans for the next day: a visit to the Ayala Museum. It would be the last tourist visit for Diana; the rest of the day would be dedicated to whatever else her mother wished, before she had to face the reality of home.

"They're in the house," Edna said, when Joshua inquired about Colette and Margo. They'd caught her coming from the laundry area, carrying an armful of towels.

"Where in the house?" he asked.

"Over there." She gestured with her lips.

Joshua laughed. "Can you be more specific?"

"The little house." She led them to the nearest window that looked out over the top of the backyard. The light in the house was on, and the front door was open. "All of them are there."

"All? Who is all?" Diana asked aloud.

But when she turned to Joshua, he was already striding past her. She chased after him, remembering his penchant for over-protectiveness, especially about the little house. As they traipsed through the backyard, she noted the varying octaves of voices. Meanwhile, Joshua's concern was palpable, his body tense and rigid.

Diana reached the door first, the voices clearer. They were familiar. Her mom, Colette. And was that Roberta? On the threshold were four sets of shoes. It couldn't be—that seemed impossible for her mother's best friends to . . .

No, not friends. Because when she walked into the door, her mother was kissing Cameron. Cameron, the man Diana had grown up with, an uncle by nickname, who'd gifted her with a twenty-dollar bill at every birthday, and who could man a grill like no other. For all of her mother's adventures, she'd never once showed interest in dating. What was going on? "Ma? Cameron?"

But before she could say more, before Margo had a chance to respond, Joshua pushed through, his face in a panic. "Who are these people? What is this? His things, they're everywhere . . . everyone, out. Out!"

Diana realized that what he was perceiving as chaos was just a typical scene with her mother: standing in a room of clutter. He was stern, on the verge of hysteria, arms out, as if he had been summoned to save these things. As if Margo was a thief.

Bodies halted at Joshua's intrusion, and to Diana's surprise, Roberta emerged from the closet. Colette stood next to the desk, frowning.

"Joshua?" Diana said.

"You all . . . you all just need to go. This isn't your stuff." He turned to Margo. "How did you even get in here?"

"Joshua," Diana warned. She was sympathetic to his shock, but his insinuation, that they didn't belong, raised her hackles.

Instead of answering, he turned to his sister. "Colette, how could you let this happen?"

"Josh," she snapped at him. "Tita Margo is rightly going through her father's things."

"Who says she has the right? Just because of the DNA test? These things are my responsibility. Mine."

"I say she has the right," a raspy voice said.

Diana spun to Flora, in a wheelchair, with Dr. Sison behind her, sweat blooming on his forehead.

"Lola. I—"

"Hush, Joshua." Then she spoke upward. "Push me closer."

Dr. Sison did as instructed and pushed her to the middle of the room. She nodded at everyone. "It's time for a family meeting. Tonight. All of you."

Roberta raised her hand. "Um, excuse me, but I'm not really—"

"Everyone at Sunset Corner, in thirty minutes."

Twenty minutes later, Diana was pacing the driveway of Sunset Corner, eyes toward the curve in the road. Everywhere around her was an inky black, and as she took each step, she willed her phone to light up with a notification, a reply from Joshua to her last text.

The guy had simply taken off. He'd followed Flora into the home after her announcement—Diana had given them space—and later on she found out from Colette that he'd gone on a drive. A drive, during what Diana thought was a crisis. She might've not known Joshua well, but this seemed unlike him. His family was his priority, and now—she checked her watch—with eight minutes left before the family meeting, he should've already been back.

Colette, too, seemed off. She had been irritated by Diana's questions, her ear against the phone, eyes glassy. An extrovert taking solace in the corner of the room was not a comforting sight.

And her mother had been distracted, which wasn't new, but it was with a seriousness that was disconcerting.

Something was going to happen. Her instincts were screaming at her.

Diana's phone buzzed in her pocket. Her heart leaped. *Joshua.* Except when she checked the caller ID, it wasn't Joshua, but Aziza.

Disappointment filled her. "Hi, Aziza."

"Diana. How are you? How is the Philippines?"

"Good, good." And yet, nothing about the conversation felt good. Phone calls with Aziza were synonymous with bad news. "What's up?"

"I had a meeting that was . . . interesting. Diana, would it be possible for you and I to speak face-to-face somehow? I know you don't come back for another few days, but maybe we could Skype or FaceTime?"

Diana frowned. "I mean, sure, that would be fine, but I don't see what the difference is from just telling me now?"

She heaved a breath. "Well, the media has died down quite a bit since you left town, and while it was touch-and-go there for a bit, the questioning had begun to slow."

"That's great, exactly like you wanted." Diana pressed her lips together to keep her nerves in check.

"But it's sparked some turmoil within the hospital staff itself, among the board of directors, many of whom now question the mission of a VIP service. Some, apparently, had kept their thoughts to themselves, until the situation with you opened up the conversation. Some are actually against it, and two of our most generous donors have asked to have the service reconsidered. The optics are unsettling for many of our donors who didn't realize the major disparity—they don't want to be associated with it. While they don't get a say as to how we manage their donations, they aren't sure that they will commit their future support.

"Diana, basically, the situation has caused a bit of stir, and our CEO was very clear in that . . ."

Diana shut her eyes. She thought back to her last nightmare, her fear of being stark naked and exposed—it was exactly like this moment. She'd given herself entirely to this job. Not merely in the amount of work hours, but in her commitment to her patients. They were her mothers, her babies, their shared experience.

"I'm sorry, Diana, but in my opinion, they are going to ask you to resign. The board thinks that in addition to breaking protocol, your actions have led directly to the donors' malcontent."

She dropped her chin to her chest.

"I'm sorry. This is why I wanted to tell you face-to-face. On the day after you return, there will be a meeting with you and me and the entire board. I'm on your side, and I scheduled this meeting for you to have a say, to justify your break with policy."

Her breath left her. *Resign.* She thought of her patients. It was easy enough for them to transfer physicians, but it was at the cost of their connection, their trust. The nursing staff came to mind, their friendships soldered over days and nights of trust in the most joyous and tragic events. They were her family, too.

Not to mention, without a job, she wouldn't have income. Now with her reputation, her name in the public sphere, who would hire her?

"Manang Diana?" Edna said, from the front door; Diana hadn't heard her.

"Diana?" Aziza echoed in her ear.

"I hear you. I heard you," she answered into the phone, and nodded at Edna, who turned and disappeared back inside. "I—I don't know what to say."

"Well, it's not over yet. Come back from the Philippines refreshed and strong, and you can fight for your job. I did the best I could in that room, but now it's your turn."

"I know you did, and thank you." She looked back at the house, where another meeting loomed. "Can I, can I call you back? I need to process this a little. There's a bit of a situation here."

"Of course. I'll be here."

Diana hung up, but before going inside, she looked back to the empty driveway. Now if only Joshua was here, too.

Chapter Twenty-Nine

Margo, sitting on one of the couches in the living room, raised her face as Diana entered the room, and from her downtrodden expression, Diana deduced that Joshua hadn't returned. She patted the space next to her, and Diana sat, exhaling.

"Are you okay?" she asked her daughter.

"Are you?" Diana shook her head. "I'm sorry he got so angry, Ma. He didn't have the right and—"

"Honey, stop. I'm fine. I'm not angry or hurt about that. Joshua was in shock."

"And when I walked in, you were kissing Cameron." Diana cradled her forehead with her fingers. "I'm so confused."

"The day has been . . . interesting." Margo recounted the afternoon, from cooking with Colette to her talk with Flora, which brought on some tears. She stopped short of telling her about the will since it was unclear what it might mean for Diana, if anything at all. She wiped her eyes. "And then, of course, Roberta and Cameron showed up, and yes, I kissed Cameron, and I love him." She laughed.

"Oh, Ma." Diana hugged her.

Hugged her.

So Margo took advantage. She leaned tight into her daughter's formidable, strong body. She reminded herself that this, this was now. Her daughter's love was tangible. Her daughter's love was unquestionable. "But there's more. My father didn't choose me, Diana. He didn't choose my mother. And I'm mad, and upset, but things turned out right, didn't they?"

"Yes, they did," she said firmly, then leaned back. "Things turned out right because it was you and me and Granny. And we are still okay without Granny."

Margo breathed out her nervous energy. She nodded.

"The question is, what are we doing here? What is this meeting about?"

"I'm here," Flora announced as she was being wheeled into the living room, except it wasn't by Dr. Sison or Edna. It was a different man, dressed casually in a T-shirt and jeans. On Flora's lap was a black briefcase, wiry hands draped over, clutching it.

Colette walked into the room. "Mr. Hidalgo?"

"Good evening," he answered as he parked Flora's wheelchair and took the seat next to her, relieving her of his briefcase. Edna, Roberta, and Cameron entered and took their seats, Cameron on the other side of Margo. He squeezed her hand; she melted in this show of support, although Diana's jaw slackened at the gesture. An empty chair remained for Joshua.

"It's nice to finally meet you, Mrs. Gallagher-Cary," Mr. Hidalgo nodded at Margo, and then to Diana, "Dr. Gallagher-Cary."

"What do you mean, finally?" Diana interjected. "And please, call me Diana."

"I told him all about the two of you," Flora said, eyes gleaming.

Mr. Hidalgo rested his briefcase on his lap and flipped up the cover with a flourish. He dug into what seemed like a Mary Poppins bag as he took out a bottled water, his phone, his wallet, a book, and his glasses, setting them on the floor next to him, and finally retrieved a stapled set of papers.

"Thank you, Mrs. Cruz, for inviting me here today. As you all know, I am here to go over the stipulations of Mr. Cruz's will."

"His will? I didn't know we were doing this. Philip's not back from Hong Kong until next week. And Joshua's late—he hasn't returned any of my calls, but I'm sure he'll want to be here." Colette sat up taller in her seat.

"Not everyone has to be present for this reading, Mrs. Macaraeg. It is a courtesy I am providing for Mrs. Cruz, though it will be followed up via legal channels for notification."

"But why? Why now?" Colette's voice was shrill.

"Because I'm dying, anak," Flora said, exasperated.

"Lola," Colette whispered. She clutched her belly. "Not in front of the baby."

Flora shot Margo a look. "See what I am up against? I'm a hundred years old, and these children think I'm going to live forever."

"I am emotional, pregnant, and my legs are so swollen I can't see my ankles. We are not going to talk about death. I'm supposed to be a cute pregnant lady." Her eyes glassed with tears. "Instead, I feel like sh— I mean, crap, and I'm not even close to delivering."

Roberta reached out for Colette's hand and squeezed it.

Flora lifted a hand to cue Mr. Hidalgo to move on.

"Oh, okay. Allow me to amend. Mrs. Cruz invited me here to read the stipulation of Antonio Cruz's will, because there have been two changes. One, we have two descendants who were previously unaccounted for and are now present, and second, because Mrs. Cruz has expressed her desire to execute the will early."

"Early?" Margo gasped.

"I'm tired. I no longer want to make any decisions. I trust all of you," Flora croaked.

"All?" Diana said. "I don't get it."

Mr. Hidalgo continued, "Before Mr. Cruz passed, he discussed his legacy at length. That in the event Mrs. Cruz was no longer able, Joshua Cruz would inherit Las Cruces Hotel and Sunset Corner."

"This is about me?" a voice said from the hall. Joshua entered the room. "Because if you all remember, my return to Manila was because Lolo Tony needed me. I learned everything inside and out about Las Cruces in the last decade; I got up every day without fail to make this place better. Just an FYI." He stopped at his grandmother's side and kissed her on the cheek. "I'm sorry I'm late. I needed some air."

Mr. Hidalgo dropped his gaze to the paperwork, discomfort evident in his tight expression. Flipping to the third page, he adjusted his glasses so they were sitting on the tip of his nose. "'I hereby bequeath the ownership and management of Cruz Estate to Flora Cruz until her death or until she determines she is unable. Thereafter, the eldest descendant will inherit the Cruz Estate. The Cruz Estate consists of Las Cruces Hotel, Sunset Corner, and all its assets. Forthcoming owners will have authoritative control and input in the hotel's board of directors.'" His eyes peered above his glasses. "After Mrs. Cruz, it would have naturally gone to Joshua as the oldest grandchild. But now that Mrs. Margaret Gallagher-Cary is here, she is first in the line of beneficiaries. And because Dr. Diana Gallagher-Cary is six years older than Joshua Cruz, then she would be next in line. I was also instructed to provide this to the next descendant after Mrs. Cruz." He held up a manila envelope, then handed it over to Margo.

"Wait a minute. Wait." Diana brought her shaking fingers to her forehead, then looked at Margo. "We're in line to inherit this place?"

"Sooner rather than later," Flora confirmed.

"And now that Mrs. Cruz has decided to execute the stipulation of the will," Mr. Hidalgo said, "all that needs to be decided is if you will accept it, Mrs. Gallagher-Cary. Should you not accept, then the will stipulates that it will be offered to the next person in line."

Margo's eyes darted across the room, to Diana, who looked out into space; to Colette, who'd begun to cry; to her friends, mouths agape; and finally to the smooth envelope in her hand. Another letter.

"If you accept," Cameron said, "then that means you'd have to live here."

"Yes, it does," answered Flora. "She would make Manila home."

"No more Old Town," Roberta supplied.

Margo opened the envelope. The room was silent as she read the document. As she took in each word, she felt her stomach give way, much like how it felt when an image came through as she made a print in the darkroom.

The letter made this all a little clearer.

"Ma, you're not objecting. Are you considering this? It'd mean we'll be living in different countries," Diana asked, face stricken.

Did she want to stay? The answer was yes, but not for this. It wasn't to take over a business she had no idea how to run. But a niggle of a call tingled in her periphery, like a whistle that beckoned her to turn. "But if I don't accept, what will that mean for you? What would you do? Refuse it, too? We are part of this family."

"As of a week ago! Our lives are in the United States, Ma. That is our home."

Joshua's eyes darted from Margo to Diana and back, as if letting the words settle in. Then he shook his head, and laughed. Arms out, he pleaded, "They're Americans, Lola. Please tell me that this is just red tape. You heard Diana. This isn't their home. She doesn't want to stay."

Diana stumbled in the beginnings of her response, eyes widening. "It sounds like it's you who doesn't want me to stay. So what was that last night, or at lunch, or in the car?"

Margo reached for her daughter's hand, held on tight. She wanted to jump into the exchange, to settle this fight. She didn't want to see Diana this way: troubled and hurt. But she herself did not know the right answer.

"Diana, *you* just said that your life was in the United States. Why am I the bad guy now?"

Diana snatched her hand from Margo and stood. "You're right. I . . . excuse me." Her eyes glassed over with tears. Then she walked out of the room.

Tears.

"Will you look at that," Roberta said.

Flora's mouth dropped open. "*Ay, nako.*"

"Oh my goodness," Margo echoed.

Her Diana.

Her sweet child finally let go.

Margo couldn't let her daughter run, not now, so she speed-walked through the house, with every intention of chasing her down, but when she threw the front door open, she found Diana just over the threshold.

"I'm . . . I'm just so frustrated," Diana said, piercing her with a pointed look. "I can't believe you're considering this. Your life, your real life is back in the States. That man didn't come back for you, Ma."

"It's called forgiveness, Diana."

"No, it's about taking responsibility. *He* should have taken responsibility. Which is what you should be doing now. But as usual, you're shirking it."

"What are you saying?" She was taken aback.

"Oh, come on. You followed your passions, and you still do. Except for the time you took care of Granny, you do whatever you please."

"And that's supposed to be a bad thing?" Margo shook her head, confused. She didn't understand where this anger was coming from. She thought Diana was upset because of Joshua, not because of her. "I have followed and still do follow my passions, but I did so with my mother's support. And I've done the same for you, in all of your endeavors, haven't I? Wouldn't I be taking responsibility by staying here?"

"No, you wouldn't. It's about you thinking of you first, and then of everyone. And not thinking about me."

Margo took a step forward and lowered her voice. "Is that what you think? That I don't think of you? It's you I think of first, each and every day. You are who I'm thinking about now. But deciding to stay would be me taking responsibility for my life by figuring out who I am and following through on what's needed of me. That's all I ever wanted: to find my truth so I can be my best, for you. I'm sorry if my intention didn't come out that way." The worn-out seams of Margo's heart were starting to give. She'd known she'd made mistakes in her life. She certainly was not like her mother or her daughter—these intimidating, tough women who people placed on pedestals. She had always been a little bit of a mess. But never once had she doubted her intentions. Had she really only thought of herself? "But, Diana, it's not just me who has a choice to make. You do, too.

"You say that, but I don't have a choice. C'mon, I'm even being punished for making a choice, a damn good one, at work. And I can't just take off. I can't stop my life for others, nor can I afford to. Others certainly haven't done it for me." Diana's shoulders slumped, and a growl escaped her lips. Then she shut her eyes and spoke. "Everyone leaves me, Ma. First Granny, then Carlo, and then Josh . . ." Her mouth slammed shut, and she looked away. "And then you. I am alone."

"You're not."

"Yes. Yes, I am. I will be, if you stay here. Ma, I intend to get on that plane in two days, and I'm asking you to please come with me."

Marysville, CA
October 10, 1944

To Mr. Antonio Cruz,

My name is Irene Lawley. I employ Ms. Leora Gallagher, the young woman whom you know very well. She has been in my service for years now, and I have seen her grow to a hardworking young lady.

I recently found out that she is with child, with your child. She came to me one morning, distraught. Her father had intercepted her letters to you. Since then, he has turned her out. She has nowhere to go. She is staying with me for the time being.

I plan to leave for Washington, DC, very soon to live with my family. I offered her a chance to come with me, but she refuses. She is waiting for your return, you see. Her only desire is to be with you.

I don't want to leave her here, in Marysville, with no one to care for her. She is vulnerable here, alone. I'm asking you to help me help her. My family has graciously agreed to care for her, to care for your baby because I am fond of Leora, but they will not accept your relationship while under their roof. I am in no position to refuse, as I am also at their mercy. I hope you understand.

I'm asking for you to let her go. I'm asking you to give Leora and your baby a fighting chance for a life that, although it might not have you, can be filled with opportunity.

Sincerely,
Irene Lawley

Chapter Thirty

*W*hat was home?

    Was it where one was born?

Was it where someone lived the majority of their lives?

Was there a residency time limit?

Was there a minimum stay requirement?

Diana pumped her arms, grunting effort into the last leg of her run, as she mulled over these questions and her future, possibly without her mother. She was on the baywalk, adjacent to Roxas Boulevard on the way back to Las Cruces. The city had just begun to wake, the road starting to fill with pedestrians and commuter traffic.

Yet, despite her five miles, she hadn't been able to tamp down her uncertainty and anxiety. That soon, she would be returning to an empty town house, to a job that she would likely be fired from. That the truth she'd sought might separate her and her mother, and the man she cared for.

After her outburst last night, she'd refused to go back into that living room to those people, unable to face their judgment.

Shortly afterward, they had all gone their separate ways. Flora offered her home for the night and to Diana's surprise her mother took it—was it a foreshadowing?—which left Diana to return to Las Cruces on her own.

Diana reached the end of her run, slowed, and linked her fingers behind her head. Manila Bay was on her right, and across the street, to her left was towering Las Cruces. The family hotel. Home to Colette and Philip and Joshua. Home, potentially, to her mother. All at once, pain sliced through her, and she coughed, bent over, hands on her knees, because this was a no-win situation, not for her.

The phone rang through her wireless earbuds. She twisted her arm to view the phone strapped around it. Sam's face appeared on the screen, so Diana answered it. "Hey."

"You don't sound happy to hear from me."

"I just finished up a run. I guess I'm a little exhausted." She swiped away sweat that had begun to trickle down her face.

"Um, I'm your running partner, Diana. You are extra happy after a run. It's called endorphins. What's up? You texted me back one-word answers last night."

So, after a deep breath, Diana caught her up. She gave up walking in circles and plopped down on a cement bench to look out over the bay. The sky had a haze today, a thin gray over blue.

"I'm so sorry, D. I am," Sam said after Diana finished. "It sounds like you have a lot of decisions to make."

"It's not me who needs to make a decision. It's my mother."

"You have to make a decision about work, right? If you're going to fight for it?"

"What do you mean *if I fight*? Of course I will. It's my job."

"That you have fallen out of love with." Sam lowered her

voice. "I mean, you can always come and work for me. I'm just saying."

"You wouldn't want me to work for you. I'd boss you around."

"You might be right." She paused. "And I shouldn't speak too soon, since you might really *not* want to quit your job. I've got some news."

A sense of dread came down upon her. "Oh, God."

"You'll get a phone call soon, but while they were inspecting your house in prep for your deck, your contractor found some issues with your house's foundation."

Diana's eyes shut in dread. "The foundation."

"It's stuff I don't understand except that they completely stopped work. And while he didn't say what needed to be done and how much it would cost, I have a feeling that it's going to be a lot."

"Damn it."

"I'm sorry to be the bearer of bad news. I wanted you to be prepared before you got on the plane tomorrow."

She heaved a breath. "Thank you."

"Okay, now I have a tougher thing to discuss with you."

"Shit. Out with it."

"What are you going to do about Joshua?"

Diana slumped into herself. "Nothing? I don't know. What can I do?"

"You can tell him how you feel."

"He knows how I feel."

"But does he? Or did you assume? I hear emotion in your voice, Diana. Real emotion. You like him, so tell him. Don't come back here until you do." A car horn sounded in the background.

"I'm headed onto the beltway and it's a mess. I have to run, but text me your flight info later."

"Okay. Love you."

After hanging up, Diana checked her notifications. No texts or calls from Joshua, but one from Carlo, who'd sent a photo of Flossy snuggled into his blanket, with her shiny nose sticking out.

> I think I should create an Instagram for Flossy. Do I have your permission?

Diana balked. Pets had actual accounts? Her curiosity was piqued, or perhaps it was another method of distraction, but Diana clicked on her Instagram app, something she hadn't done in weeks.

Her feed loaded, the first a gram from Ms. Margo. It was a mouthwatering picture of beignets. From New Orleans. It was liked by thousands.

Diana clicked onto her mother's profile, and square tiles of photos loaded onto the screen. She thumbed and swiped from one to another, captivated, lured, and enamored by the emotion in the photographs of the tiny details of Granny's house, of the things Granny owned. The pride in her mother's eyes, and in one photo, the devastation after Granny died.

God, Diana was wrong. So wrong. Her mother didn't shirk responsibility. She was living life as honestly as she could, saw beauty at every turn, and tried to show it in her art.

Diana was just too stubborn to see that she could have learned from it.

Diana decided not to veer from her plan and went to the Ayala Museum after her run, mostly to pass the time. A formidable corner edifice on Makati Avenue, it blended in among the taller high-rise buildings of downtown.

But as she approached the front door, she heard her name called from behind her.

She turned. "Joshua," she whispered, heart leaping from her chest, and yet, she kept her voice still. "Hi."

"Hi." As he approached, Diana noted his unshaven face and the dark circles under his eyes. He looked like she felt. Just exhausted.

"What are you doing here?"

"I took a chance that you wouldn't veer from your schedule. Do you have time . . . or would you consider taking a walk with me?"

"Um, sure." She took his side as they walked down the street, not intimate by any means, but Diana was relieved to have the distraction of the noise and the traffic.

"I'm sorry, Diana. My actions last night were disrespectful, and exactly the opposite of what Lolo Tony would have wanted. Look, here in Manila, at Las Cruces and Sunset Corner, I know who I am. Even if I'm not related to the Cruz family by blood, they are my family and there are no pretenses with them. I don't know who I am without Las Cruces. My anger stemmed from this fear, and I put you in the middle of it. I didn't mean to hurt you."

But that was the thing. Here, in the Philippines, Diana was starting to feel. The more she learned about even just the little things, the more out of step she felt. She stopped and moved aside, and he followed suit. "I believe you. I know you didn't mean to hurt me, but I am hurt. And I'm also scared about the future, and I'm also so happy to see you, here." She shook her head. "What more can I say? I'm overwhelmed.

"This visit has changed me. You have changed me, too, for the better. But now I don't know where I fall, with this family, with my mother, with you. I don't . . . I don't know what to do with all of this, with all this information, at Corregidor, the letters between my grandparents, the will. Am I supposed to leap for joy? Cry? What of me is Filipino, is American, of my mom or Antonio? Was I supposed to be more than what I am now? I thought I knew who Diana was before coming here, down to what brand of socks she likes, but it all doesn't seem to make sense now. Who am I supposed to be?"

Was this what her mother wanted her to feel? This pain in her chest? This need to cry once again?

Because it sucked.

Especially out in public, with Joshua. This wasn't the time, with all of these faces passing by, staring at her, like a scene out of one of her stress dreams. She took a deep breath as she would on a steep incline, and turned away from Joshua's eyes.

"Diana, look at me, please," Joshua pleaded, voice soft.

She dared the look despite her glassy eyes, ashamed.

"You are not supposed to be anything." He shook his head. "Because no one is one thing. No one is the standard. You, me, your mom, Colette, Lolo, and Lola, we are enough. I only wish that we . . ."

He didn't even have to complete the sentence, for Diana wished for the same thing. "If only we were enough for each other," she said.

He nodded.

Because they both knew that their lives took them to opposite sides of the world, and she would, without fail, get on the plane the next morning.

At Ninoy Aquino International Airport the next morning, Diana waited at the terminal with her bags. She hadn't spoken to her mother in more than a day, and this would be the moment of truth: Would Margo show up for their return flight? Sitting on an airport bench, she fiddled with the grosgrain ribbon on her luggage.

A pair of shoes halted in front of her—her mother's cheetah-print ballet flats. She looked up, at her wild zebra capris and hot pink shirt, and it made her smile. She scooted to the left, leaving room on the bench, and her mother sat.

"I don't see bags," Diana said, though without malice. She had had a feeling in her bones that her mother would not be boarding this flight.

"I'm staying, sweetheart." Her smile was apologetic, but her eyes were bright. "Are you mad?"

Diana shook her head. "No, I'm proud of you. I'm sorry, for giving you that guilt trip and insinuating that you were selfish. You're not. I'm just . . . scared, I guess."

"I'm scared, too. It would be easier to go back to my life, with Roberta and Cameron, wouldn't it? To continue with Ms. Margo? But I realize that all that time I was taking pictures, I was searching for something. And I believe part of that something is here. My biological connection. I need to see this through. This, I cannot ignore, nor can I pretend it didn't happen."

"How about Roberta?"

"Staying, just until the end of the week."

"Cameron?"

"Also yes, but indefinitely."

"That is . . . Wow, Mom. But I approve. He is the nicest man."

"He is. Diana . . . thank you, for telling me how you feel, even if we did fight. I—I need to know what you're thinking. I think we'll do better apart if we can speak to each other, you know?"

Diana nodded, her sadness giving way to hope. "We'll talk every day."

"Yes, we will," Margo said. "I'll update you on everything. And *everyone*."

"There's no need, Ma." Her face tingled with tears of disappointment at her mother's insinuation. Why did she let herself even think that they were a possibility? How could she have fallen so quickly?

"You might change your mind. I asked Joshua to be my partner. In running the hotel, that is."

Diana raised her eyebrows. "You did?"

"Yes. I certainly can't run the place on my own. And what kind of person would I be to take it all from him?"

Diana was awash with relief. Joshua would still have the hotel, if at least in part.

"Don't forget me," Colette said, feet away as she waddled toward them. Diana stood, hands out to take hers. "Please promise me you'll come back. You're going to be the ninang of this baby, you know."

"I'd better be a ninang," Diana said, letting the rest of her worry slip away. "This will be my first godmother position, and I intend to be the very best in the world."

Colette threw her arms around Diana, smashing her belly between them, then stepped back.

"It's time for me to go," Diana said, warmth coursing through her. Her eyes misted with the start of tears. Everything would be okay in the end, romantic happily-ever-after be damned.

And as she recalled her and Joshua's conversation about happily-ever-afters, her heart squeezed in bittersweet pain.

"I'll walk you a little ways down," her mother said.

Colette gestured to a bench and grinned. "I'm parking my butt right here."

Diana and her mother walked silently to the start of the security line, where they turned to each other.

"I know he's not here, but don't hold it against him, sweetheart," Margo said. "This transition can't be easy, and he's only been gracious toward me. I believe in him."

"I don't know how you do that, Ma. How do you let the small good things outshine all the stupid stuff?"

"It was something your Granny said." A pensive smile graced her face. "A penlight is enough to shine through a dark tunnel. For me, the penlight was you: your birth, challenges you've outgrown, how you've been one of the strongest people I know. Did you know that? It was you who brought me to the end of the tunnel, which is here. Which is right now."

"And what's that?"

"Doing something we're most scared of doing. Taking a big leap. Learning a little more about ourselves."

Diana thought of what was waiting for her now. An empty, broken home, an equally broken heart, and a meeting that she would have to face in forty-eight hours that could possibly end in a broken career. "And what if I mess up? What if things go downhill anyway?"

"Then we mess up. Then things go downhill. But next to

your grandmother you are the most capable woman I know. The kindest. Most loyal. You are and have always been someone I admire. And, I am here and so is your granny in spirit. Sam, Roberta, and Cameron. And now, now you know after this trip that you have more behind you: Colette and Flora. Joshua. We are your family, and we're not going anywhere."

Diana leaned in to her mother for one final hug. She relished her strength.

"And oh, Diana?" her mother said into her hair.

"Yes, Ma?"

"Thank you for liking all of my pictures on Instagram. I love you."

Chapter Thirty-One

I want to start," Diana said as she sat down at the head of the table in Alexandria Specialty's admin conference room. Five male faces stared blankly at her, so she drove on before nerves got the best of her. "Thank you for being willing to see me today. Dr. Sarris was kind enough to ensure that I was given a fair chance to speak my mind."

She glanced at her boss, seated against the wall. Aziza emitted a hopeful smile, though they both knew that it would take a miracle for the board to keep her on staff.

"Go on," said the person sitting opposite her, the CEO, Dr. James Meyer.

She nodded. "I had quite the speech planned on my plane trip back. I just returned from Manila, Philippines, where I was visiting family, and it was an upheaval. I discovered a lot of things about my family and about myself in the last couple of weeks during my hiatus. But the bottom line is this: I would like to offer my resignation. Not because I don't believe that what I did was right, because it was one of the most right things I've done throughout my life, but because I realize now that I've always had a choice, and I'm taking it. Without getting too personal, I am . . . was . . . the kind of person who needed to know the answer right then and there, and I'm choosing now not to know it all. I'm choosing to discover.

"I'm going to be what my mother and grandmother were: a woman who takes risks. I'm choosing to continue to be that woman who took the risk that night to admit that patient into the VIP suite. Thank you, Dr. Sarris, Dr. Meyer, and to all of you for allowing me to work for Alexandria Specialty. It's been an honor, a privilege."

And with that, Diana stood and shook each of the men's hands, hugged Aziza, and walked out the conference room door without, for the first time, a concrete plan for what the next step would be.

An hour later, Diana took a seat in a less brightly lit location— the Whistling Pig, an Old Town bar locals frequented. The place was still deserted, as it was only 11:00 a.m. But it was five o'clock somewhere, and in Manila it was 11:00 p.m, and a good enough excuse. She stuck her purse on the barstool next to her to save for Sam, who was just about to take a lunch break, but mostly because she wanted space. She ordered a white wine.

At the moment, her body was spent, tired from her flight and from a restless night. And she was freezing, still not acclimated to the change in weather. But her skin tingled with excitement. She was free. Unemployed, true, but she tamped down the negativity of that phrase. She would hit the job boards later, but right now, she was celebrating.

She was scanning the menu when giggling from across the

bar captured her attention. It was a couple who'd just toasted with their beers. They looked like they had not a care in the world, eyes only for each other, faces animated in their storytelling. She imagined the banter they must be having, the fun and the tenderness between them, and not for the first time since she left Manila, she thought of Joshua.

"Get a room, am I right?" a man said, two stools away.

Mid-sip of her wine, Diana coughed, swallowing tentatively, eyes glued to the couple in front of her, who had since looked up at the commotion.

It can't be.

No, she was delirious. It was someone who only sounded like Joshua, because there was no way the man could be in the United States because . . . because that would be simply ridiculous.

She dared herself and snuck a peek. Turned her head just until she caught the man's profile at her periphery. Dark hair, tan complexion. She twisted an extra centimeter, and then she caught it. His sardonic smile, mischievous expression. Though it had been only three days, he was a cold drink on a hot summer day. He was the antidote to the heaviness she'd carried since she boarded the plane from Manila.

"Joshua?"

"May I?" He gestured to the seat next to her. When she nodded, he placed her purse on the bar.

"How did you . . ."

"Well, I have this thing called a US Passport. And you're not the only one who can do research." He turned his body so it faced outward as hers faced inward, déjà vu sparking. "Actually, your mom put me in touch with Sam. I left on the flight after yours and Sam put me up for the night."

"She did?" Diana said, impressed.

"I'm here to deliver a letter." He slipped it out of his pocket.

The thought of another letter, from anyone, turned her stomach. The high she had felt upon seeing him crashed down. "In person? You couldn't just have mailed it?"

He shook the envelope, a sign for her to take it. "You and your questions. Read it, please."

So she accepted the letter, but this time, read it aloud.

Pacific Ocean

Dear Diana,

I'm writing you from somewhere over the Pacific Ocean. It is only now—midair—that I've gotten the courage to put words to paper. I'm in awe of how Lolo Tony and your grandmother did this during a time of duress, when nothing—not even the basic comforts of life—was guaranteed for either one of them. Your grandmother, in her letters, was so hopeful. Yes, I read them. Your mother was kind enough to share their correspondence with me so I could understand.

Their letters inspired me to write to you. My first plan was to write this letter and simply send it over snail mail as they did so long ago. You wouldn't have had to wait long. Maybe a few days for it to cross the ocean on a plane, then be sorted by machine to reach your door. But I didn't think it was good enough for what I wanted to tell you. Which is something I regret not saying in person the last time we spoke.

I didn't want you to go, Diana. I wanted to see where this—you and I—could take our few days of bickering and intimacy. I don't think I've ever wanted anything more in my entire life. In one week you completely upended my world. From the moment we met, I haven't gotten you out of my mind, and especially our discussion about happily-ever-after. You had said that the happily-ever-after was just a snapshot.

But to me, it's more than that, because there is this thing called hope. The hope of the happily-ever-after keeps it so the snapshot is always of the high.

That snapshot, for me, is the two of us. While I don't have the answers of where we both need to be in the future, I have a passport, and I am here, now.

Will that be enough? I hope it is, because you are enough for me.

Yours,
Joshua

Diana looked down at their intertwined hands, at how he gripped hers with fervor, begging for a response. For the life of her, she didn't have a single rebuttal. Instead of words, what emerged was a goofy smile that split her face.

Yes, this was enough. This, having him here, was enough to go on while she figured out the way forward, to face what she wanted with her brand-new life.

"Is this a 'I want to work it out with you' smile or 'I'm about plan your destruction' smile?" he asked.

Diana leaned in, her lips within an inch of his and said, "It's a let's 'kiss and make up already' smile."

To her relief, he crossed the way and planted his lips on hers.

Epilogue

Three Months Later

*W*henever Diana entered a delivery room, she became the person in charge. It was an automatic assumption; this was her calling.

But here, in Makati Medical Center, she was a nobody.

"Her BP's climbing," she nagged at Colette's nurse for the second time.

The nurse glanced at the machine and then at her chart. "Just a little."

Colette stifled the conversation with a gasp—the beginning of her contraction. She gripped her husband's hand; Philip screwed his face into pain, though he didn't say a word. She'd had an epidural, but the doctor had stopped the infusion an hour ago. Diana looked at the clock—Colette had been pushing for the last half hour.

With the next push, Diana coached Colette on her breathing and instructed Philip how to properly support her legs. But this time, the baby's heart rate dipped after the contraction.

"Looks like the baby isn't tolerating the contractions," Diana said. "Let's lay her on her side."

The nurse eyed Diana with disdain, even as she assisted Colette to her side to help bring the baby's heart rate up. The nurse turned to pick up the room phone. "I'll call Dr. Campano."

Objectively, yes, Diana knew she was meddling. Too many cooks spoil the broth, but she was a doctor, damn it.

And even more than that, Colette was her cousin.

Her cousin.

Her heart squeezed at the thought. No, she couldn't let herself fall apart, not now—she was a professional! She blinked her tears away and focused: Colette gripping her hand, the too bright overhead lights, and the beeping of the machines. She bent down so she was level to Colette's face. "What do you want to do right now?"

"I want to get off my back."

"Okay, we can get you off your back, maybe sit you up." Diana pushed the hair out of her eyes. "You've got to give it all you've got, okay?"

"Okay." She took two breaths. Panic flashed in her eyes. "Maybe the baby doesn't want to come out? Maybe it knows that I'm completely irresponsible and I don't even make a good adult. I can barely take care of myself . . ."

Philip bent down and whispered something in his wife's ear.

"Don't tell me everything is going to be okay!" she yelled. "Must be easy when you're just standing there!"

Philip's eyes rounded into large discs.

This was normal, the lead-up to the final finish, but Diana wanted Colette to have the perfect experience.

Every woman deserved the best treatment in labor. Every. Single. Woman.

It had become her mission ever since she quit her job. Now, she worked with Sam at the center, mostly as a community liaison, where she networked with businesses to fund-raise. It was also something she could do remotely, to manage her house renovation and sale, and to allow her to spend time in Manila for big occasions such as these. She and Joshua had just taken a small vacation to Bohol as he had suggested months ago, complete with the unencumbered view of the sunset, when they were summoned to Manila for Colette's labor.

Even Carlo didn't mind. The more she traveled, the more time Carlo had with Flossy, who had helped him snag a date or two, especially thanks to Flossy's new Instagram profile.

Dr. Campano returned, donned a gown, slipped on goggles, and ensconced his hands in sterile gloves—the uniform for battle. "Are you ready, Colette?"

"Can I, can I sit up?" Colette breathed out. "I don't want the stirrups."

"Well . . ." The doctor glanced at the nurse, a scowl forming on his pursed lips. He glanced up above their heads—to the clock, Diana presumed. She thought of how she would have acted in his place, at how she'd acted toward her patients in the past. Had she expressed impatience or a lack of flexibility? At her worst, did she insist on her way?

Diana opened her mouth.

"Let me speak for myself, Ate Diana. Damn it. You are not in charge," Colette said.

Diana stilled.

"I want to sit up," she demanded.

The doctor backed away from Colette's opened legs, the sign. The nurse all but bounded from bedside, lowered the bottom half of the bed, and attached the squatting bar. The nurse took the other side of the bed from Diana, and both women assisted Colette to her feet.

"Are you okay? Can you do it?" Diana asked.

Colette leaned on the bar, squatting. "Yes. I already feel so much better." With the next contraction, she pushed, grunting. From her side, Diana watched her cousin's face, lined with determination and strength. Something sparked in Diana. A longing, the joy in the moment, the hope in the possibility that life was soon to follow.

It was almost time.

"I can do this," Colette gasped, gripping the life out of Diana's hand.

"Yes, you can," Diana whispered.

"Another contraction," Colette warned, panic in her voice, her breathing erratic. She inhaled deeply, and she bore down.

And she birthed the most beautiful baby Diana had ever seen.

"It's a girl!" Dr. Campano announced, lifting the baby to Colette, now on her back, who accepted her with open arms. The baby wailed, protesting the light and the fuss around her, from the blanket draped over her, the nurse toweling her face dry, and Philip showering her with kisses.

And from Diana, who had burst into tears.

"Leora," Colette said, gazing at her child, then up at Philip. "Her name is Leora Marilou Cruz Macaraeg."

"She's perfect. And the name . . ." Diana pressed a tissue against her eyes and backed away from the bed. Her cousins needed their time alone with their daughter—her niece, oh, and goddaughter, too!—without the emotional godmother hovering around. Taking out her phone, she texted the Cruz family group chat with one line: *It's a girl!* In a separate text to Joshua, she wrote: *Iniibig kita.*

Then she went to the west-facing windows, where she discovered that the sun now hovered just above the horizon.

Sunset, as if Granny had planned it.

Author's Note

Once Upon a Sunset is a story close to my heart. It has churned inside me ever since I was fifteen years old, when I visited the Philippines. It was a solo trip from the United States, at a time when I was searching for my identity. During that summer, I reconnected with relatives and met new ones. Notably, I spent many an afternoon with my Lolo Naldo while he sat in his rocking chair, and in the ebb and flow of his memory he told me stories. At times he simply had someone bring each of us a banana cue and we'd sit there in silent companionship.

He was an immigrant, a lawyer, a US Army soldier, a community builder, a father, and a grandfather. He was also a writer and my pen pal; he inspired my patriotism.

Once Upon a Sunset came from the question of *what if* as it pertains to my personal family history, and some details were inspired by my grandfather's stories and records, but the work is fiction. However, if you are interested in learning more about Filipino-American history, I suggest these books:

Little Manila Is in the Heart: The Making of the Filipina/o American Community in Stockton, California by Dawn Bohulano Mabalon

Strike!: The Farm Workers' Fight for Their Rights by Larry Dane Brimner

America Is in the Heart: A Personal History by Carlos Bulosan

Shadows in the Jungle: The Alamo Scouts Behind Japanese Lines in World War II by Larry Alexander

And the following links:

"An Untold Triumph—The Story of the 1st & 2nd Filipino Infantry Regiments U.S. Army," www.youtube.com /watch?v=pU-kSnAXu7s

Alamo Scouts Historical Foundation, Inc., website, www .alamoscouts.org

"The Alamo Scouts," armyhistory.org/the-alamo-scouts/

"New Film Depicts Filipino regiments' exploits," the.honolulu advertiser.com/article/2001/Nov/30/ln/ln03a.html

"California in World War II: The First Filipino Infantry Regiment and San Luis Obispo County," www.militarymuseum .org/1FIR-SLO.html

"Callout to all 1st Filipino Infantry Regiment Families,"
www.hawaiipublicradio.org/post/callout-all-1st-filipino
-infantry-regiment-families#stream/0

"Congressional Gold Medal for Filipino World War II Vets
Is an Honor '75 Years in the Making,'" www.nbcnews.com
/news/asian-america/congressional-gold-medal-filipino
-world-war-ii-vets-honor-75-n814436

"U.S. Army 1st & 2nd Filipino Infantry Regiments training in California during World War II," www.criticalpast
.com/video/65675053496_Filipino-Infantry_recreational
-activities_bolo-knives_Colonel-Robert-Offley

"Little Manila: Filipinos in California's Heartland," www
.youtube.com/watch?v=FNCZ8sGJs8I

"Filipino Migrant Workers in California," opmanong.ssc
.hawaii.edu/filipino/cali.html

Acknowledgments

This is the hardest acknowledgments I've had to write, purely because I'm not sure where to start. *Once Upon a Sunset* has left me vulnerable, perhaps because it touched on history, both told and untold, identity, and home. What I am sure of, however, is that the support given to me in the writing of this book has been immeasurable.

To my fierce and kind agent, Rachel Brooks, who champions my dreams, and my brilliant editor, Kate Dresser, who just gets *it* and gets *me*. I have been so lucky—no, blessed—to have you both by my side for five books. With *Once Upon a Sunset* especially, which I consider thus far a legacy above all. You both did this for me, for my family. I am so grateful.

Molly Gregory, Mackenzie Hickey, Jen Long, Jean Anne Rose, Abby Ziddle, Tara Schlesinger, Christine Masters, Erica Ferguson, and the entire Gallery team—thanks for being amazing! Michelle Podberezniak, thank you for fielding every email and question with such patience. To Kristin Dwyer of LEO PR: you are a beacon of optimism and professionalism. Ella Laytham, thank you for my truly stunning cover; it is only matched with such gorgeous interior design by Davina Mock-Maniscalco.

My squad: April, Annie, Rachel, Stephanie, and Sidney. #Thermostat/#Batsignal. #5amwritersclub. #TeamBrooks. Tall Poppy Writers. You have made this writer's journey so damn fun. Special thanks to Jasmine Guillory, Susan Mallery, Jennifer Probst, Nina Bocci, Kristy Woodson Harvey, Amy E. Reichert, and Kate Meader for lifting up this baby author.

Tito Bonjoy and Daddy, who shared so much of Lolo with me. Ate Hazel and Maida Malby for your generous time. Karen and Mindy, who shared their family history with me. Jez from the Ayala Museum for my one frantic email. I am indebted to you all.

My brothers, JR and Racky; my sisters, Connie, Aimee, and Liz; and my mom-in-law, Cheri—I love you! To my parents, who allowed me to get on that plane solo to the Philippines so long ago, and then trusted me when I handed them Army enlistment papers to sign before I even turned eighteen: thank you for letting me fly.

I am so absolutely thankful to readers, bloggers, librarians, and reviewers who have boosted and supported my work. You are who I write for.

My children, my Fab Four—always know, especially from this book, that you are not alone, and You. Are. Enough. Finally, to Greg, who completely supports the idea that the entire main floor of our home is my writing office, who is my partner and my best friend: iniibig kita.